AFTER THE SNOW FALLS

Carey Jane Clark

ISBN: 0991688600
ISBN-13: 978-0-9916886-0-9

Quote taken from *Harry Potter and the Philosopher's Stone*, p. 102
by J.K. Rowling, copyright 1997, Bloomsbury.

For Brian, who has walked
through the hard places with me.

CHAPTER ONE

Celia

The morning betrayed her. No evil portent, no cool northern wind, no ominous cloud hinted at what the day would bring--only the cool scent of leaves and pine needles and river-smell.

Celia had been working toward this morning for more than a month. She stepped out of the house, anxious to get to the schoolyard and check on preparations for the soccer fundraiser, when the phone rang. She ran back in and grabbed it. Melissa Foster on the other end, her voice low and scratchy, said, "I'm sorry, Celia. I don't think I can come today. I'm real sick. Do you think you can get someone else to run the doughnut booth?"

The cancellation was the second disappointment of the morning. Multiple tries to Sarah's cell phone were fruitless. Sarah had all the pumpkin and apple pies, the raffle tickets, and the last of the donated items for the silent auction. And she was supposed to be running the haunted house.

Celia stepped back outside and down the steps and took a breath of autumn while she waited for Caleb. Hershey, their chocolate Lab, ran up and shoved his muzzle into her hand. She gave him a scratch behind the ears and looked out over the property. The lawn needed mowing and the garden hadn't been weeded, but still the sight of the yard made her smile.

When they built this house in Point-du-Fleuve on the edge of the Renous, one of the smaller rivers on the Quebec side of the Ottawa River, they'd overlooked few details. The home fit perfectly into its surroundings as though native to them. Large windows faced every direction but north, where tall spruce trees lined the drive and would have obscured the view. On certain autumn mornings, the announcement of daybreak broke forth from flocks of ravens inhabiting the stand of trees behind the house. This morning, though, the only sounds were the first of the fallen leaves skittering across the gravel drive and the ever-present whisper of water moving.

The screen door slammed and Caleb bounded down the steps from the deck. He shrugged one strap from his backpack onto his shoulder and leaned against its weight.

"You ready?"

"Yup."

"Nervous about the shoot-out?"

"Naw. Justin and I are the best scorers on the team." He smiled, eight-year-old mischief emanating from him like sunlight.

Jeff had loaded up the van before he left this morning on a last-minute errand. Celia made a quick survey of the boxes and bags stacked in the back, shut the hatch and climbed in the van.

She turned the ignition. "Okay, Mr. Confidence, let's go have a soccer fundraiser."

* * *

At Caleb's school, she scanned the yard for Sarah as she lined up cups and poured cider.

"Not here yet," Jeff said. He managed to keep the I-told-you-so out of his voice.

"Put out an all-points bulletin on her, okay?" Just like Sarah. What would it be this time? Justin took too long getting dressed, the car wouldn't start, she'd had to run back for something forgotten at the house. She tried not to let Jeff see her frustration. After all, she had no choice but to forgive her best friend.

"She's not answering her cell?"

"No. I've given up trying." Celia pushed a box of cups under one of the tables. "That should be enough for now, don't you think?"

Jeff stepped to her side of the table and surveyed her work: eight perfectly aligned rows of plastic cups, evenly filled. "I believe your work here is done." He laughed and planted a kiss on her head as she stood.

Coach Lassiter strode up with Aidan McCall, Caleb's friend and a midfielder for the team. "He's bleeding," Coach said.

Aidan's face glowed red. His chest puffed out, as if he held his breath to keep from crying. He maintained a steady focus on his knee. Grass stains and dirt covered it, and underneath, blood oozed out.

Celia leaned down to take a better look. "We've got bandages and antiseptic. Don't worry. You'll be okay, honey." She put her arm around Aidan and led him to a chair behind the cider table, dug out her first aid kit, and set to work. "Would you hand me that water bottle, Jeff?"

"I'll leave him in your capable hands," Coach said. He jogged back to his station near the goal posts where he and the team prepared for the shoot-out between the boys' team and the Rideau Raiders from across the river in Ontario.

"Hey babe." Jeff touched her on her shoulder as she crouched in the grass in front of Aidan. "You have any of that acetaminophen for kids?"

"Another headache?" She cut through the gauze, tucked the scissors back inside the first aid kit, and peered over the table. Caleb stood on the other side drinking a cup of cider. Something gripped her in the pit of her stomach, but she pushed it aside.

"Yeah. He says it's not too bad."

"They're in my purse." She pointed under the table. "In the box right here."

She ripped off a piece of tape, put it in place over the gauze and smoothed it over the wound. Aidan winced.

"Sorry." She smiled up at her patient. "You're all set now."

The red was fading from his face, his chest deflating. "Thanks, Mrs. Bennett."

"You're welcome." She stood up and smiled at Caleb. "You okay, baby?"

He made a sideways glance at Aidan and glared at her. She tried again. "How's that headache?"

"Fine." He made a face at the bottle in Jeff's hands. "I'm okay, Dad. I don't need those."

"All right, Champ. If you say so." Jeff tossed the bottle back in the purse, and smiled at her. "Sorry. False alarm, I guess."

She ignored him and studied Caleb, her eyes dark under a furrowed brow. "Are you sure, sweetie?"

Jeff waved his hand in the air. "Go on. You have things to do. I'll hold down the fort."

3

She glanced again at Caleb, but he was already heading across the field to catch up with Aidan. She gathered the few things needed for the auction and crossed the field, still wet and glistening from the rainfall the night before. Father Lafontaine had agreed to run Melissa Foster's doughnut stand when she suggested he was also free to give out some of the church's literature. It was hard to tell which was doing stiffer business--the doughnuts or the diocese.

Spry for his age, the Father clung to tradition--he still held mass in Latin, a practice regularly protested by younger members of the parish. He was nevertheless surprisingly evangelistic, which often offended the sensibilities of the older congregants. Celia had heard stories of barely clad girls showing up on a Sunday morning and causing one dear old parishioner to lose consciousness. She couldn't be sure if they were true, since she wasn't in attendance. St. Francis had mostly francophone members, and she had no interest in religion. But in Point-du-Fleuve, a tale like that hit the streets before three o'clock on a Sunday afternoon.

During the last hour, the field had filled with families and all the stations, including the doughnut booth, were busy. She squeezed through the cluster of people and joined the priest on the business side of the booth.

"*Bonjour, Madame* Bennett. How are you today? it's a beautiful day for your event, *n'est pas?*" He smiled, took a customer's money, dropped it into a glass jar on his table, and handed her a flyer photocopied on pink paper. A picture of hands folded in prayer adorned the cover.

"It is. Do I have you to thank for that?"

He chuckled. "Me? No, I'm afraid not, but perhaps our Wednesday morning prayer ladies. You must be on their list."

"How are the sales going?" She peeked into the jar.

"*Ah, bon.* Such a lovely day, everyone is ready to support your cause."

She smiled. The pile of literature had shrunk by half. "Yours too."

He flushed and smiled. "*Ah, oui*, I suppose so." He nodded toward the pile. "Take one."

"Oh no, thank you, Father."

He leaned in and pressed one of the leaflets into her hand. "*J'insiste.* Take one," he said. "You should read it."

She laughed. "Well, thank you. I need to check and make sure everything's ready for the auction. Will you be able to stay the rest of the

4

day?"

"*Ah oui, pas de problem.*"

"I appreciate this. Keep up the good work." She turned toward the school building and shoved the leaflet into her jacket pocket. Next to the building she found a trash can and reached for the brochure to throw it away, but the bottom of the can was already lined with them. Poor old man. She'd dispose of it at home.

Before walking into the building, she scanned the schoolyard and checked her watch. The auction was an hour-and-a-half away. The soccer shoot-out would be starting soon, and she didn't want to miss Caleb's turn. The field crawled with people. Long lines snaked their way toward the face painting booth and the haunted house. She'd conscripted a teenaged brother of one of the boys on Caleb's soccer team to run the haunted house until Sarah arrived. He fumbled with tickets and ignored the person talking to him from the front of the line. He peered out dubiously from under bangs that hung too long over his eyes, as though he hoped they would shield him from being recognized by anyone he knew.

Where on earth could Sarah be?

She stepped inside the school building and took the first right into the kindergarten classroom. It had been the best room to use, since no desks needed to be moved out of the way. All the auction items had been set up on tables around the perimeter of the room.

Something rustled in one of the closets at the back where Mrs. Davies, the kindergarten teacher, kept the art and craft supplies.

"Hello?" she called.

Sarah emerged from the closet and closed the door behind her. She wore a long skirt, a knit cap, and her sunglasses. "Couldn't find the darn tape." She held up a roll of masking tape. "Figured Mrs. Davies would have some in there."

"Sarah! You're here."

"Hey, do you have any more clipboards? I set up all the auction items, but two don't have a clipboard." From behind the sunglasses, her eyebrows raised in expectation. "You know, so people can write their bids?"

Celia stared in disbelief. She'd been waiting for well over an hour, called Sarah's cell phone innumerable times. She expected an apology, at

5

least.

Sarah shrugged. "I guess I'll just use some Scotch tape or something and stick the paper to the tabletop." She pulled out the tape, bit off a piece with her teeth and ran it down the side of the paper. "Yeah, Sarah, that's a great idea. You do that." She changed the inflection of her voice, supplying Celia's side of the conversation.

"This tape sticks to everything. it's ridiculous. Look. Now it's stuck to itself." She wadded up the piece of tape, searched for a trash can and finally shoved the sticky ball in her pocket.

"Pens. Where did I put the pens? I mean, the bidding lists are here, but no pens now. Think I'd be able to find any in Mrs. Davies' desk?" She opened drawers and slammed them shut. "Oh look. Here. On the desk. There's a whole pencil holder thingy with pens."

"I'm not sure you should--"

"I'll put them back later, silly."

"Did you bring the raffle tickets?"

"Oh yeah. Right here." She pulled them out of a cardboard box and handed them to Celia.

Celia glanced at her watch again. "Okay, well, I guess I'd better run these over to the sales table. You going to the soccer field to watch Caleb and Justin in the shoot-out?"

"Wouldn't miss it." She flashed her broadest smile. "I'll come over after I finish taping these."

"Okay," Celia said, lost in her flurry. She walked away without mentioning how important today was, how she had been counting on Sarah, how disappointed she was.

Sarah wasn't easily ruffled--something Celia envied her for--but this morning went beyond good composure. She wanted to forgive, but Sarah hadn't even asked. Shouldn't she at least acknowledge being late?

As she crossed the field, raffle tickets in hand, Celia tried to talk herself out of holding a grudge, but succeeded only in making herself angrier. After all, Sarah had been her principle sounding board while she coped with the frustrations of gathering donations, recruiting volunteers, and soliciting school and board cooperation. It wasn't as though she had begged her to be involved. Sarah had volunteered to take on everything she was supposed to do this morning. Celia tried to call up Jeff's voice of reason, but the thought only made her more irritated. Sometimes Jeff could be too reasonable. She dropped the raffle tickets at the booth without a word to the volunteers, and marched back to the soccer field for the shoot-out.

She couldn't come up with a reason not to stand with Sarah. The shoot-out was the day's main event. Everyone had gathered at the field. She walked past the unmanned food sales table. Only five full cider cups remained and a dozen or so tipped-over empties. Where was Jeff? Sarah's long slender arm appeared above a group of heads. She smiled and indicated the spot she'd saved beside her.

Celia cringed. She wouldn't be able to pretend nothing had happened.

Coach held a clipboard and the boys circled around him, peering over its edge. He flipped through a stack of papers and blew his whistle sharply. "Okay, Justin MacKenzie, you're up next."

Sarah erupted in loud cheering, raised her fingers to her mouth and whistled long and hard. Justin put his toes on the painted line.

"You must have had quite the morning," Celia said.

She scowled and nodded toward the field. "Hang on. it's Justin's turn."

Justin was attacking, the Rideau Riders on defense. Justin dodged in front of the goal, took his chance, and sent the ball past the goalie. Sarah held her fingers to her lips and whistled. She called the kids in from the playground blocks away with that whistle. Justin usually blushed when his mom made her ruckus, but as he jogged across the field to take his defensive position, he didn't hide the smirk of pride over his accomplishment.

Sarah let out another whoop, and another of the boys' teammates squared up to take his turn, focus on the goal, tongue tucked into the corner of his mouth in concentration.

"So, your morning?"

"What about it?"

Celia studied her face. Was she really so immune to the frustration she'd caused? "Must have been eventful."

"You could certainly say that." She let out another loud cheer. "Did Jeff ever get back?"

"Get back?"

"Yeah. From the errands he was running. He stopped at the store this morning."

Sarah's husband owned the hardware store in town. But what did that

7

have to do with anything? Why was she being evasive? "Jeff came back a long time ago."

"Some kind of bucket emergency?" she said.

Celia touched Sarah's arm. "Listen, you really messed me up this morning. I was counting on you."

Sarah glanced around at the people standing nearby. Her face first registered agitation, then sadness. She turned back to the field. One of the boys took a run at the goal, dodged around an opposing player and ran smack into another defenseman. A few seconds of silence followed until he stood to his feet and brushed himself off. More loud cheering erupted. Coach Lassiter boomed from the sidelines. "Great work, son. You'll get 'em next time."

"If you'd just apologize--" Celia said, bothered that her tone sounded like Caleb's when he wasn't getting what he wanted.

Sarah ignored the words and pointed across the field, her voice distant. "Caleb's up next. You don't want to miss that."

Celia took a deep breath and focused on her son as he lined up against the opposition. He ran up the field dribbling the ball, the other boys in pursuit. He tackled, dodged. The other boys were sharper now, having adjusted their strategy, and warm from their last victory. Caleb dodged again, went for the goal. He had a clear shot.

Celia tensed, ready to cheer. Then in an awful, awkward moment, Caleb landed on his face and chest in the grass. All the air left her lungs, as though she felt the thud in her own body.

He didn't move.

Justin screamed, and the clear morning air shattered with the sound of perfect terror in his small, shrill voice.

CHAPTER TWO

Alfie

Alfie rubbed his fingers together and felt for the cigarette that no longer dangled between them. He tapped the ends of his fingers on the rig's steering wheel, picked up the box of Nicorette from the cubby hole under the stereo and shook it. Empty. He'd pick some up at the next stop.

He glanced at Adele. She shifted in her seat and waited patiently for somewhere to "freshen up." How long had it been since she asked him where the next stop would be? Twenty miles? Thirty? More? She wasn't like other women. He couldn't just hand her the toilet roll and send her to find a bit of brush while he waited by the truck. Even the way she sat beside him made her different--stretched out, drinking in the sun's rays through the window, smooth and graceful as a cat.

He scanned the barren highway ahead to find his bearings. Years had gone by since he'd traveled this stretch. He couldn't recall the next stop. Looking for landmarks was useless. The only sight for miles was brush and tumbleweed, the occasional fallen-down billboard. Jagged mountains in the distance all looked the same to him. She didn't flinch when they'd sailed past the last reasonable place to stop, and didn't ask why. He sure wasn't about to offer the information. Bette. That was the name of the girl who worked behind the counter at the last diner they'd passed--at least he thought so. If he could, he'd blame her for Adele's current discomfort.

He didn't want to keep secrets from her. Time had passed for secret-keeping. He meant it when he told her he was going straight, that she meant more to him than any of the women he'd known all those years

9

since they'd been together. But no point in bringing her face to face with one of his regrets.

He was new at guilt. It hadn't entered the equation before. When he thought it through logically, he convinced himself he didn't regret much. It's not as if he could have prevented the leaving. That had been as inevitable as dawn. Maybe, in fact, the best thing would have been to leave earlier--not that it hadn't crossed his mind every day of the eleven years he stayed. In the end, Adele didn't say much when the suitcase packed with his things appeared at the door. He guessed she knew too, that it was unavoidable. Even still, sometimes the guilt threatened to swallow him, like one of those mirages on the highway ahead when the heat made black holes in the road, ready to devour the truck.

He wasn't supposed to have guilt now. Forget what is behind. Strain forward to what is ahead. Press toward the goal. He repeated the words to himself under his breath like a mantra.

"Did you say something?" she said.

"No, nothin'," he said. He straightened in the seat, stretched out the muscles, sore from inactivity. He loved the truck, and the seats were more comfortable than he'd found in any car he'd ever driven, but the trucking life meant more hours sitting down than he had ever spent in his life. "Roy's should be comin' up soon, I think. At Amboy, if you wanna check on the map."

"I can wait," she said.

More miles of sizzling terrain passed in silence, and she spoke again. "Are we still in California?"

He hoped she wasn't tiring of the trip already. She had sounded excited when he asked her to come. She impressed him as ready and willing when he picked her up at the airport yesterday, carrying just a backpack crammed with her things for the trip. The only woman he knew who packed that light.

"Yeah, another ten or fifteen miles to go, I'm guessing."

She pulled her legs off the dash and reached for the guidebook sitting between them. "I never realized just how much of this kind of landscape California had." She smiled the smile that made his chest constrict, "I guess the whole state can't be beach, can it?"

Guilt grabbed him, tightening the grip on his chest. It was his fault she'd never traveled farther from her home, while he'd traveled this road several times, and countless others in the same stretch of years behind them. But getting her out on the road was part of the reason he'd asked her on this trip. It was his way of inviting her back into his life, of making them part of the same thing again. They'd see these things together, share these memories, hold these things in common. As the miles grew shorter between here and the place he once called home, maybe the distance between them, too, would shorten.

He'd wondered if this would be her kind of thing. Her easel had always been full of wildlife and the harsh, stunning landscapes near her home--of the Canadian Shield jutting skyward amid rushing waters--paintings that virtually leapt from their canvases. He'd wondered if she'd see these sights as kitsch, this landscape as too well-worn to suit her tastes. But the first thing she'd pulled from her backpack was her camera, "to capture things to paint later." She'd murmured her admiration of everything they'd seen at the California Route 66 Museum--old gas pumps, neon signs, black-and-white photographs of the way things had once been.

"So sad," she said.

"What's that?"

"All these lives, dried up, just like the landscape. Here yesterday, and now they're gone."

She bought a brown-and-white, metal historic Route 66 sign on their way out, as a souvenir. Said she had a place already picked out for it in the little cottage on the lake.

Ahead, blue against the horizon, rose what looked like a mountain that had lost its top. "Look." He touched her arm, and she pulled her glasses off and looked up from the book. "It's the Amboy crater. Town's not far away."

Within a few minutes, a tall sign for Amboy loomed in the air, a life-sized metal traffic cop attached, holding up a warning, "Slow School Zone." Alfie pulled the truck off the side of the road into Roy's Motel & Café and knew immediately. It was closed.

He jumped down out of the cab onto the dusty pavement and walked to the front door. "Notice says the whole town's been sold," he yelled back over his shoulder. He didn't hide his disappointment. He wasn't the type to want perfection, or worry about small details, but she was right. Here more lives had dried up like the landscape. The sun blazed from high in the sky now, mercilessly hot.

"You're kidding. How do you sell a whole town?" She hopped down from the cab to stand beside him and stared at the desolation. "Too bad."

"Yeah. They used to sell the best milkshakes here. Burgers too." He scuffed the edge of his boot on a rock and it skittered off with a lonely echo under the carport.

"Maybe whoever bought it will open it again."

"Maybe." He wiped the back of his hand along his forehead, swiped at sweat.

"Give me a minute?" She held up the roll of toilet paper he stashed in the sleeper, and walked behind the building.

A slow smile tugged at the corner of his mouth.

* * *

Long after he'd said goodnight to Adele, Alfie stayed awake and stared up into the night sky. They'd driven far from the lights of any city, and all the stars were visible. How could city folk deprive themselves of this spectacle? Forced to stare at gray concrete and bright lights all day, didn't their eyes crave this beauty? As he lay listening to the crickets and the mosquitoes, the distance vanished, and he could dive into them, swim around in the Milky Way. For a while, he played childhood games and sought out the falling ones, imagined wishing on them. But he had more serious star-gazing to do tonight. He needed to penetrate beyond them to the heavens. He had decisions to make.

The desert cold began to take hold and he rolled out his sleeping bag and the pop-up tent. Adele slept in the cab, where she'd have the heater and the soft mattress of the sleeper. He wanted the fresh air and the cold to keep him thinking clearly. Before he cocooned himself in the bag he was sure. He would ask her in the morning if they could take a detour to Las Vegas, and he would ask her to marry him. They'd been down this road before, but this time was different. He didn't know how she'd react. That part was up to her. He'd made his decision, and slipped easily into sleep.

The next morning, she woke him, her soft touch across his stubbly cheek. "Wake up," she said. "I think something's wrong."

CHAPTER THREE

Celia

Jeff must have asked a hundred times for her version of the events of the next few minutes. She could never clearly call them to memory. All she remembered were flashing red lights, paramedics, IV bags, and respirators, the smell of dirt, the taste of brine, and a slow, steady panic rising from her chest and washing over her. It clouded her thoughts, made her at once both numb and vulnerable to the chaos swirling without meaning around her.

She had clung to Caleb's unmoving body on the soccer field. She ignored the moisture on the grass that soaked her so thoroughly Sarah later asked if she'd wet herself.

She tried to penetrate the fog. She stared at the faces of the emergency workers, desperate to focus. She followed their instructions on auto-pilot and strained to hear every word they spoke over her son's motionless body. Later, she couldn't recall a single feature of any of those faces.

During the confusion Sarah left. She must have said something about dropping Justin off at her husband's store, but Celia couldn't remember having had that conversation. Sitting on the field, she tried Jeff repeatedly on his cell. The voice mail answered right away. When had he left the school grounds? Where was he? She left no message, afraid she wouldn't be able to keep the terror out of her voice. By the sixth or seventh attempt to reach him, she was already in the ambulance. She finally left a frantic message, the pitch of her voice rising involuntarily higher with each word she spoke.

While the sirens blared, inside the ambulance the IV bag swayed over

Caleb. He was hooked up to a respirator, paler than she imagined he could be. He stared at the ceiling of the ambulance with a dull, sleepy expression. Longing seized her. She needed her mother.

She tried Jeff once more as the ambulance arrived at the hospital. Still nothing. The attendant touched her arm. "You'll have to turn that off, I'm afraid. Hospital policy for the E.R. Check with the information desk. There are zones in the hospital where you can use it." She stared at the phone, afraid to lose her only connection to Jeff. She called again, changed the message from "call me on my cell" to "come to Pontiac County Hospital Emergency Room," slapped the phone shut, and followed the gurney into the hospital. A flurry of pale blue and white descended on Caleb as the emergency workers set to work, and she breathed deeply for the first time since he had fallen on the field.

A doctor approached with the first set of questions. She searched his face for some sign of reassurance, but his lips were pressed into a grim line, his tone flat, grave. "Has your son ever suffered from asthma?"

"No."

"Bronchitis?"

"No."

"Any history of respiratory illness in the family?"

"My husband's father died of emphysema. But he smoked--"

Something floated to the surface of her memory. The coach's voice on the soccer field while they waited for the ambulance. "I think the coach said something about Caleb having some trouble breathing just before the shoot-out. Yes. He said he was wheezing." The information made its first impression on her as the words tumbled out. She puzzled over its meaning as the doctor continued.

"We'd like to run some tests--a chest x-ray, possibly an MRI. Here's a release form."

She took the clipboard he offered, scanned the form, but couldn't focus.

"Just sign at the bottom."

"Okay." The signature didn't look like hers.

They wheeled Caleb away.

She followed, but the blue-clad woman at the foot of the gurney turned and said, "Please wait outside, ma'am," and disappeared beyond a thick metal door.

A teenage boy with crutches sat on one end of a row of seats along the wall. His leg stretched across two seats and his foot dangled over a third. A girl with black and blue hair sat with him. She wore a black T-shirt, innumerable silver rings in her lips, nose, eyebrows and ears. On the other end of the row sat a young woman. A man sat with her, his hand on her back. Their voices rose and fell in French while she rocked and sobbed. Blood stained her flowered blouse, hand and arm.

Celia pulled out her cell phone but remembered what the emergency attendant had said about not using it in the E.R. and stuffed it back into her purse. She couldn't leave the E.R., even for a moment. A payphone hung on the wall across the hall. She picked up the receiver and began searching her purse for change. Only pennies. Caleb had begged for a cafeteria lunch on Friday, and she'd emptied her purse of change before he left for school.

It hadn't been a good morning. She'd resorted to raising her voice when he didn't get up the first three times she went to his room. Later, she'd crabbed at him about the way he'd made his bed and the mess he'd left in his room, and then the lunch money argument. So what if she'd already made a lunch? Why couldn't she just be flexible?

She put the receiver down and a tear splashed on her shoe, although she hadn't realized she'd been crying. She searched her purse for a tissue, gave up and wiped her sleeve across her cheek. Unable to face the sad collection of humanity waiting on the row of seats, she walked down the hall, away from the door where they'd taken her son, looking over her shoulder to make sure it was still in sight. She wanted to be waiting when he came out--when the doctor or nurse emerged to announce it was just a minor thing, nothing to be concerned about.

She reached the main entrance of the emergency room, about to turn around, when she spotted a hand waving behind the frosted pattern on the sliding door of the emergency room. Sarah.

She approached the door and it slid open automatically.

"Thank God!" Sarah said.

"What's wrong?"

"They won't let you in beyond the waiting room unless immediate family gives the okay, but of course they can't go and find you for me." She threw a hand in the air. "I've been peering through that window for fifteen minutes. I saw you, but you weren't looking this direction."

"Thanks for coming." Celia took her hand and squeezed it.

"Where did they take Caleb?"

"X-rays and tests--It sounds like they think it's his respiratory system. They asked me if he's ever had asthma."

"You know, Justin told me something in the car." She said it slowly, as though she were afraid of breaking something with her words. "He said that even before the drill started, Caleb wasn't breathing well."

"The coach told me that too. What do you think is wrong?" She searched Sarah's face for an answer that wasn't there. "Do you just get asthma out of nowhere?"

"I don't know." Sarah linked her arm through hers and huddled close as though they braced against a cold wind.

"Oh, I almost forgot. Jeff called my cell. Is yours off or something? He got your message. He's on his way."

She pictured him driving to the hospital in his car by himself--the thoughts that must be racing through his mind.

Sarah eyed the same seats along the wall Celia had surveyed earlier, apparently drew the same conclusion, and shifted her weight. She pulled her sweater tighter around her.

Celia shivered. "I hate hospitals."

"Everyone hates hospitals."

Maybe so. But she wasn't talking about the sights and smells and sounds. As a child, the person she loved the most in the world besides her mother was her Nana. She was the old-fashioned kind of grandmother who baked cookies and told stories and was ready with hugs when the world of a five-year-old fell apart. When Celia was six, Nana suddenly developed pain and tenderness in her abdomen. She said she felt constipated. Celia's mother insisted she go to the hospital. There Celia leaned against her mother's skirt as they poked Nana and took her temperature, assured her it was "just gas," and eventually sent her home. The nurses talked to Nana the same way they talked to six-year-old Celia--with loud high-pitched voices and small words. They punctuated each sentence with a pat on the hand and "Okay?" as though wonderful wise Nana was an idiot, incapable of understanding them.

A few hours later, Celia stood by her mother and watched Nana as she sat on the toilet in the cramped house on Vine Avenue. Her stomach swelled up like a balloon, right before her eyes. Her mother called her father in a panic--because this happened before he left--and they rushed Nana to the hospital again, but it was too late. Doctors said her bowel had ruptured and infection had spread through her entire body. The infection had too much of a head start on the antibiotics, they said. Had it been caught earlier--

In the end, it was her heart that finally gave up, but not before her body labored to fight the infection for several more hours. Later, doctors came up with a name for the condition: peritonitis--an infection of the peritoneum from the gastrointestinal tract. But its name didn't matter by then. By then, Nana was gone.

Jeff finally arrived. He caught sight of her and ran ahead of a nurse who tried to keep pace with him. She ran into his open arms. He pulled her close and then released her, holding her by her shoulders as though bracing her against falling, and she released the flood of tears she had held in by some force of will she didn't know she possessed.

"What's going on? I don't know anything except Caleb collapsed."

"I don't know any more than that either. Except it seems like they think he's having a breathing problem."

"Breathing?"

"I know, I know. I don't understand."

Before Jeff could say anything more, the nurse spoke up. "I'm sorry, but it's hospital policy. Only two people can stay in the emergency department with a patient." She raised her eyebrows and regarded Sarah.

Celia felt for Sarah's hand and squeezed it again.

"This is ridiculous," Jeff said under his breath. He motioned toward the people seated along the row of chairs. "What about those people? They have only one person with them. She'll be their extra person."

"It doesn't work that way, sir." She was firm, unapologetic, a health care professional, emphasis on the *professional* part.

"That's okay, I'll leave," Sarah said. "I should go rescue Justin, anyway. Dan's probably put him to work at the store." She smiled weakly, hugged Celia, and turned to leave. "Call me when you can and let me know what's going on."

"I will."

Sarah walked down the hall with the satisfied nurse and the doors swallowed her.

"So what happened?" Jeff's impatience was palpable.

"He just fell. During the shoot-out." He needed to know, but the images were too alive in her mind. She didn't want to talk about them. "It was his turn in the shoot-out. He was just about to score. Where were you, anyway? I thought you were at the field."

"I had to run into town to Dan's store. I never did get those buckets, and the guy from the beanbag toss came and said he needed them." He shook his head. "I can't believe this happened and I wasn't there--over a couple of stupid buckets. I just--I knew you were already stressed out over Sarah, so I just took care of it. Sarah said she'd let you know she saw me."

"She did say she saw you. I thought she meant earlier." She eyed the metal door. Where was the doctor? What was going on?

Jeff ran a hand through his hair, "She had a lot on her mind, I guess."

"What? Who?" She forced herself through the fog and focused on his face.

"Sarah. I went to the back room to say 'hello' to Dan at the store," he said. "Walked in on the two of them in a pretty serious fight. She was crying. You must have noticed when she got to the school."

The pieces fell together. Sarah's strange behavior. The sunglasses. Her confusion and hurt. Celia's chest ached. The words she spoke on the soccer field echoed back to her like the selfish whining of a child.

The heavy metal door swung open and the doctor looked up and down the hall. Jeff practically sprinted toward him, Celia right behind him.

"Do you have news about my son?" He thrust out his hand. "I'm Jeff Bennett." The doctor still wore the grim expression, but he shook Jeff's hand. Celia gripped her purse and drove her fingernails into the leather strap.

"We ran the chest x-rays and MRIs, but they were unremarkable, so we went ahead and took MRIs of the brain as well."

"The brain? I don't understand." She moved closer to Jeff. He stared at the doctor.

"Has your son had any headaches? Vomiting? Instability?"

"Instability?" she said.

"Unusual clumsiness."

"He *has* had headaches." Jeff sounded as though he'd made some kind

18

of discovery.

She shook her head, pushed the thoughts away. The headaches couldn't have anything to do with this. "He did have headaches, but the doctor told us they were from stress--change of routine--and they'd go away."

"He had one this morning." Jeff said.

Why was he arguing the doctor's case? "They've become less frequent."

The doctor turned his attention to Jeff. "Any vomiting with those headaches?"

A feeling seized her stomach, something clawing at her insides. Back in the summer, he had vomited a number of times, but because they had an explanation for the headaches, they didn't connect the two--just figured he'd had too much sun. "Actually, yes." She said the words, abruptly aware she was releasing the detonator switch on a bomb.

"He's been clumsy lately, too," Jeff said. We'd written it off as a growth spurt, his body catching up to itself.

The doctor nodded. "The results of the MRI show an area of increased signal in the region of the brainstem. We think a tumor may be pushing against the brainstem, causing a loss of respiratory function."

Jeff pressed his lips together. Finally, he spoke, slowly and deliberately. "Are you telling me that my son has a brain tumor?"

"At this point, that is what we believe." He had a pained expression, as though this announcement strained his training in bedside manner. "We're recommending a transfer to Children's Hospital in Toronto for more testing and treatment."

CHAPTER FOUR

Alfie

Alfie raised himself up on one elbow and blinked. The sun was high in the sky already. He usually woke at dawn--well, at least when he had a load to haul. "What time is it?"

"Almost nine o'clock." Adele had crawled into the small tent and knelt beside him. Her head poked up against the ceiling.

He smelled coffee and bacon. A coffee would be good right now. And a cigarette. He read the concern in her face. This would take some getting used to--thinking of someone else's interests before his own.

"What's wrong? Something with the truck?"

"No, no, nothing like that. I have this feeling."

"A feeling? What kind of feeling? Are you sick?"

"No, that's not it either," she said, her voice hushed, far away.

He sat up and ran a hand through greasy hair. A shower wouldn't hurt either. A dull ache began in his head. What was she talking about? He didn't do well with puzzles early in the morning. He put a hand on her knee. "Mind if I get a cup of coffee?"

"Sure. It's right here," she said. She crawled out of the tent, disappeared from view for a moment, and came back to the triangle entrance with his mug. Steam danced on the top.

He slid out of the tent, stood stiffly to his feet, and took the coffee from her. "Thanks." He wanted to add something like "sweetheart" or "honey," but it wasn't right, like getting behind the wheel of someone else's truck. She'd flown out to meet him, but he still couldn't gauge her.

"A feeling?" He set his sights on the pair of lawn chairs side by side next to the Coleman stove she'd used to make the coffee, the bacon, and toast. She must have been up for a while. He relaxed into the chair, took a long slow sip of the coffee, and set the mug down in the sand. "Tell me what you think is wrong."

"I'm not sure. I was cooking breakfast--daydreaming, I suppose. And I had a thought or an impression--I don't know what else to call it--that something's wrong."

"That what is wrong?"

"I'm not sure. Maybe something at home," she said. "Do you know what I'm talking about? Have you felt like this before?"

He had. The same kind of feeling had urged him to find her again. It wouldn't go away, like something tapping away at his insides, until he gave in. Not that he had to be pressured. He couldn't remember a time he didn't love her. But with so much hurt to go back over, he told himself the timing was wrong. When the urging persisted, something told him all the ancient wrongs could be made right. He knew then the time was right to find her.

"I do know what you mean." He stroked her arm--the first time he'd touched her that way. She put her hand over his and held it.

"I can't figure it out any more clearly," she said. "I guess I'm new at this. Every time I try to pin it down, I get anxious inside."

She held his gaze, but hesitated. "Could we? Here?" she said finally.

They knelt in the desert sand between the Coleman and the tent, in the shadow of the rig. He held her hand and closed his eyes. The most penetrating kind of intimacy, it left him more vulnerable than anything physical he'd ever experienced with a woman. He didn't want it to end, uncomfortable and sweet at the same time. He spoke words into the morning air and aimed them up into the clear California sky.

"God, it's me and Adele."

* * *

Alfie followed the subject of Adele's lens out the window. She'd spent the last two hours scouring the countryside for subjects for her paintings. They'd already stopped five times to capture just the right combination of red-brown earth and blue sky. He didn't mind, though. He enjoyed watching her just be herself. Wasn't this the point of traveling Route 66? Every now and again, her eyes grew cloudy with the worry he'd seen in them this morning, then turn back to reflect the bright sky.

21

He couldn't tell what this morning's events meant to their trip. He'd scrapped the idea of Vegas, though. It seemed irreverent now, after those moments kneeling in the dirt. The weight of her care had built inside of him and left, and an extraordinary calm settled over him. But he didn't know if she felt the same relief. Was she putting on a brave face for his sake? Did she secretly want to hurry home?

If Vegas wouldn't work, he had plan B in place. He'd had the silence of the last couple of hours to work it out. He figured he'd ask her while they stood at the lookout over the Grand Canyon. They would arrive there today, in under an hour and a half. She'd like that--the poetic notion of the void filling both their lives, until they found each other again. He was pretty proud of himself for thinking it up. He couldn't wait to deliver the lines.

Yes, he was sure of the words to say. Why did the timing feel all wrong? How could he ask her to marry him if her thoughts were back home? He wanted to put the care behind them and engage her in other conversation--about the sights flying by, the small ghost towns, the humble businesses, restored but somehow still under the shadow of the years they'd stood in desolation.

Finally, he had to face facts. "Adele, do you want to call home? There'll be a pay phone at a little restaurant in Seligman. We can get a bite to eat. Route 66 disappears for a while after that, and we'll be on the interstate for a piece." He held his breath. This concern of hers was equally as important to him, but even so, he hoped she'd say no. He was glad he didn't have a cell phone. He hated the things, and ditched his as soon as he'd hauled his last commercial load.

Her hazel eyes showed relief. "Yes. I'd like that." She touched his hand and squinted again at the road ahead, camera raised. "Could we stop while I get a photo here? I want you in this one."

* * *

Alfie paid the cashier for dinner and a pack of nicotine gum and eyed Adele as she stood at the payphone. She pressed a finger to one ear, straining to hear. Before she hung up, she said something he couldn't hear.

"Did ya get through okay?"

"No one's home." She tucked the phone card into her wallet and smiled up at him. "Where to now?"

"Thought we'd take a look at a little place down the street, if you'd like."

"Sure." A warm wind blew and tossed her hair. He'd wondered as he'd stood at the airport and watched for her face in the crowd, if she looked as he remembered. A streak of gray ran through her dark hair now, framing her face. She had a few more wrinkles, just as he did, but otherwise, she was the same woman he'd fallen for all those years ago.

He led the way up the street. "Out of all of these little towns along the old Mother Road, this is my favorite."

She smiled up at him. "Why is that?"

"So much history. Kept alive for years by two brothers--the Delgadillos--the first brother died last year. The brother who's still living--he's known as the Guardian Angel of Route 66." He slowed his pace. She listened with such attention it reminded him of the night they met. "Wait 'til you see this place. Used to be an old barber shop."

They stood in front of the door, his hand already on the handle, and he hesitated. He wanted to tell her how glad he was she'd taken the risk and come on this trip, glad she was with him now. Wanted to tell her she was as lovely, her hair whipping wildly in her face, as she had been when he stood beside her at the altar all those years ago.

"What?" she said. "Something wrong?"

He shook his head and gave a sharp tug on the door. A cow bell inside jangled crazily. "They've got a phonograph in here. Can you believe that?"

She searched his face, as though waiting for more.

"Come on. He still gives haircuts. Think I should get mine done?"

She stepped into the store. They walked around, and he pointed out old newspaper clippings featuring the place. She nodded and smiled but touched nothing. She stood by the barber's chair for a moment and stared up at an old photograph of the owner and his brother. When Alfie struck up a conversation with him, she excused herself, went outside and waited.

She said little while they walked back to the rig, declined a stop in the town of Williams, and remained silent on the drive up Highway 180 to the canyon. Though the scenery was easily the most spectacular they'd seen, she didn't touch her camera.

They pulled into the parking lot near the Shrine of the Ages and

23

walked out to the observation station.

With every step, a growing panic threatened to strangle him. All the words he'd stored up tumbled into the great chasm beneath them. His mouth was dry, his hands sweaty. What was he--some kind of teenager? This was ridiculous. He glanced at Adele. He would give anything to read her thoughts.

They stared out over the huge expanse, gazed down at the string of people. Some trudged down on foot, others rode mules. Miniscule as bugs, they wove back and forth along the switchbacks all the way down.

"Incredible," she said. Her camera hung around her neck, but for the moment, she appeared captivated by beauty. Perhaps she thought, as he did, that the camera couldn't capture this magnificence as well as the eye. She smiled. "Thank you for bringing me here."

"Why did you?" she said. "Bring me here, I mean." She gazed up at him, as though measuring him with her eyes.

"Well, honey, I--" he began, his mouth still dry, his voice gravelly. He peered down into the gorge, as if to search its depths for the words he'd lost. He came up empty.

"You know, I agreed to come out here. I didn't tell anyone my intentions, just that I was going on vacation." Adele tucked the gray streak behind her ear. "I was sure they'd all think I was crazy. As things stand, the girls at the shop were shocked I would leave for a month. And Celia--who knows what she thought."

A vulture or a hawk, too far away to tell for sure, circled below them, and spiraled down into the depths of the canyon. Her eyes followed its flight.

"I came because I believed you'd changed. I believed you're a different man." She turned the intensity of her gaze on him.

He searched for the bird. It had vanished.

"I am," he said. His words sounded dull and flat, even to him.

"Then don't hold back on me, Alfie," she said, taking his hand. "I know you. I can still read you as well now as years ago. Back at Seligman, you were going to say something and you didn't."

His gaze followed the trail of people again. How had he messed this up when he wanted so badly to impress her?

"It's like being here," she said. "My guidebook says that you can camp on the canyon floor. They have lodges and cabins. Did you know that?"

24

He nodded.

"We could stay right here at the rim with this lovely view, taking it all in. I'll take some pictures, and we'll get back into your truck and drive away. We wouldn't be lying if we told people we'd been to the Grand Canyon." Her voice sounded as though pulling emotion from some deep well inside her. Her eyes were moist.

"But if we never hiked down to the bottom, never experienced the canyon floor or saw the wildlife and animals that live there, we wouldn't truly know what the Grand Canyon is. Don't you see?"

She took a slow, deep breath that sounded remotely like regret--or hope, he couldn't tell which. "If you and I are just going to scratch the surface, Alfie, I'm not interested. Take me to Flagstaff and put me on the next flight home."

She took both his hands in hers now, looked him square in the face. "If we're really going to go deeper, just say the word, and I'm with you all the way." She tapped a finger on his chest. "But you can't hold back. You have to let me in."

He wanted more. That had never been a question. But she was right.

He drew in a breath. "Okay. Back at Seligman I wanted to tell you how much I love you. I reckon I really never stopped. Back at the door of the store with the sun on your hair--" he reached out to touch her, but his hand fell limp at his side. "You've changed--in good ways. At the same time, in all the good ways I remembered, you've stayed the same."

He looked down and scuffed the corner of his boot in the dirt. "I had some fancy words all ready to say, but you're better at that kind of thing than me. What I really want to say is this: Adele, will you marry me-- again?"

* * *

A breeze teased the curtain beside Alfie's bunk in the lodge. He shifted in the bed, his legs moving reluctantly after the long, hot walk down the canyon. Sleep should come easily. But an energy pulsed within him, an excitement like he hadn't known in years. She said "yes."

CHAPTER FIVE

Celia

Celia and Jeff followed the square of lights on the ambulance during the long drive to Children's Hospital. Few words passed between them. Jeff said he was glad he'd filled the tank with gas earlier that morning. She asked him two or three times to turn up the heater. She couldn't shake the chill that had found its way inside her, as though the dampness of the soccer field still crept into her clothes, her skin.

She kept thinking the doctors at County had to be wrong. They'd drive all the way to Children's Hospital only to have a specialist apologize for their mistake. The doctors would find instead some minor, fixable thing-- something trivial. Or even non-existent. She'd heard stories of illnesses clearing up just as quickly as they'd appeared, no medical explanation ever found. Or tests that were wrong the first time, doctors who blamed malfunctioning machines. But these thoughts weren't as comforting as she wanted them to be. She couldn't bring herself to say them out loud, for fear that like some premature infant, they wouldn't survive without the support of her energy.

The ambulance wound through town after town on the journey south, away from their home. She usually enjoyed this drive, especially at this time of year. They drove this same route half of the way when they visited Celia's mother's cottage. She caught herself wishing for daylight, so she could enjoy the scenery more, when it struck her what they were doing and where they were going. Fresh shock seized her.

At some point, she suspended herself from reality and let herself drift into the usual driving daydreams, but even they turned into nightmares.

She captured vignettes in the rectangles of light from kitchens or living rooms, imagined what kinds of families lived inside the houses. Some sat hypnotized by the blue glow from a television set. Others busily worked in their kitchens. Were some of them families like hers who laughed and told stories over suppers of chili and homemade rolls? Did some of them have little boys who played soccer? Had any of them received bad news recently? Were any of them floundering, haunted by possibilities too unreal to entertain, too real not to?

The country highway emptied onto the freeway, headed west toward Toronto, and she closed her eyes, reclined the seat, and wished for sleep. Surely she would wake and find herself back in her bed in Point-du-Fleuve, Caleb in his room across the hall, all of them where they belonged, warm and secure. She kept her eyes closed for a long time, in part to protect herself in case Jeff felt the need to make conversation, to fill the unfillable silence. She didn't sleep.

She sat up as they turned down the parkway leading into downtown Toronto, the highway still busy at nearly ten o'clock. She let herself be carried away with the flood of memories. She and Jeff had met in Toronto, and lived near downtown for several years after they were married. She graduated from college and began to work at a day care. She made just enough to keep them in pork and beans, macaroni and cheese, and instant noodle soup while he finished his degree and looked for technical writing jobs. He hoped to earn enough money and credibility to start out on his own, and move back to the area where Celia grew up—an area he'd fallen in love with when he fell in love with her. It's exactly what they'd done.

While they lived in Toronto, they had a charming apartment. The rent was exorbitant, given the infestations of cockroaches and mice, windows that leaked cold air during the winter, and perpetual smell of pizza from the restaurant below. But it had a lovely broad balcony where Celia grew flowers and herbs. They could see the CN Tower between the clusters of tall buildings, and they would sit out during the warmer months and dream of the future they now lived.

They exited the expressway and drove between skyscrapers until the ambulance pulled into the emergency entrance of Children's Hospital. Jeff dropped her off at the doors while he searched for somewhere to park the car.

"How is he?" she asked the first paramedic who stepped down from the ambulance.

"He's stable. They'll admit him inside. Someone will stay with him while you take care of the details." He tugged on the gurney. She stood helpless as they unloaded and whisked her son from the cold night air into the hospital and waited on others to care for him.

Midnight came and went before Caleb was admitted and they were settled into his room. Celia pulled out the few items she'd rushed home to pack--pajamas, changes of clothes, Caleb's teddy bear. She'd brought toothpaste and forgotten toothbrushes. Jeff had already fallen asleep in his clothes and jacket on the narrow daybed. She sat on the edge and cried.

* * *

Celia slept little during the night, the strange lights and noises of the hospital and the steady pulse of Caleb's respirator invading moments of slumber. When morning came, she woke with a determination that Caleb was fine, and this was all a mistake. Her determination strengthened when Caleb woke in the morning, confused and puffy-eyed, but aware. She was anxious to have him tested, disprove the doctors at County, and get him back home again. But since it was Sunday, all tests would be deferred until the next day when the doctors assigned to Caleb's case would be on hand to interpret them. An intern came by and ordered the tests and a neurology consult.

They spent the day holed up in Caleb's room. He couldn't go anywhere, hooked up to the respirator. Celia wished she'd brought books to read to him. Jeff ventured out once to get coffee and sandwiches. Celia left most of hers untouched. On another foray from the room he bought a pen and notebook for Caleb. With the respirator in, he couldn't talk.

First thing Monday morning, a nurse came to transfer Caleb to the radiology department. Nurses unhooked him from the respirator and hooked him to a portable one on the gurney. Celia studied Caleb's eyes for signs of fear or panic.

"How will he breathe during the MRI?" Jeff asked.

"We'll hook him up to an MRI-compatible respirator during the test." She smiled at her and Jeff and at Caleb. "Don't worry. He's in good hands."

"Can we come with him?" Celia asked.

"You can come if you like, but you won't be allowed in the room during the MRI because of the radiation." She and another nurse guided the gurney through the door. "You might be more comfortable here."

"I'm coming with him." Celia's gaze remained fixed on Caleb.

Jeff paced the hall outside the MRI room during the test. Celia watched through the small window in the door. Afterwards, in the stuffy heat of Caleb's room, Jeff nodded off while waiting for the doctor. She sat at the foot of Caleb's bed, waited for him to wake up, and mentally packed suitcases for the return trip home.

The doctor finally arrived with a nurse. They came in the room and delivered the report while Caleb slept. He'd sleep a while, the doctor said. They'd administered drugs to help him stay still during the scans, and their effects hadn't worn off yet. Celia waited for the words that would let her know Caleb was okay, but instead the doctor confirmed the diagnosis they'd received at Pontiac County Hospital. And now it had a name: diffuse pontine brainstem glioma.

"We may be able to relieve the pressure that the tumor is placing on the centers controlling the central respiratory system by surgery to debulk the tumor," the doctor said.

Celia didn't look into his eyes as he spoke. She studied the run in the nurse's pantyhose, the small spot of blood where the doctor had cut himself shaving, the paint peeling on the doorframe.

The doctor alternately held up diagrams of a brain and the images from the MRI. "This is the tumor. It's pushing against the areas that control, well--everything." He used a pen and made marks on it. "Reduce the tumor in size, and we may be able to resolve the breathing difficulties."

The corners of the doctor's mouth turned up nervously as he looked at Celia. She tried to focus on his face. Did he expect her to smile in return?

His smile vanished. "These tumors are incredibly infiltrative. They grow between the normal brain cells that are vital for arm and leg movement, eye movement, and even breathing, swallowing, and consciousness. Aggressive surgery is not advisable. We won't be able to get it all."

"So surgery is dangerous?" Jeff said.

"Well, given what we're looking at on the scan, I think we can debulk the tumor in the area controlling breathing without causing damage," he said. "But neurosurgery is always a delicate type of intervention."

"Aren't there other options?"

"We can proceed with chemotherapy and radiation as well, and any clinical trials you want to consider. But to relieve the immediate breathing problems, I would advise the surgery. We can schedule it for tomorrow." He put down the illustrations, closed the folder he'd brought and faced them again. "These tumors have a high rate of progression."

"What does that mean?" Jeff said.

Celia wanted the doctor to stop talking. She wanted Jeff to stop asking questions. She needed time to absorb the rush of words. Everything in her screamed until she convinced herself sound had left her mouth, but both men seemed oblivious.

"With these types of tumors, I'm afraid the prognosis is not good." The doctor said it as though he knew the sound the words made as they dropped with a dull thud to the floor in front of them.

"Not good?" Celia echoed, her voice small and insignificant, a tinkle in a universe clanging with noise.

"I'm sorry," he said.

How was one supposed to react to life-altering news? Pressure weighed on her to be gracious, to hold herself together--to react as she might if her travel plans had been changed. *We're sorry to inform you that your plane will not be arriving in health and happiness, but will be forced to make an emergency landing in cancer. We apologize for the inconvenience.*

"Okay," she said. But it wasn't okay. *Please reach for the mask in front of you. Assume the crash position.*

She sensed the doctor's discomfort, and for reasons she couldn't identify, his comfort was more important to her than her need to grieve this horrible nightmare happening to her baby. Her eyes filled with tears. She looked away.

It was the second of October. An anniversary she would never mark, but she would always remember.

CHAPTER SIX

Alfie

Alfie opened the door of the dormitory and stepped out into the cool morning air. High on every side rose the magnificent, craggy cliffs of the Grand Canyon. Adele had certainly been right. The world on the floor of the canyon couldn't be imagined from above. They'd spied Peregrine Falcons on the way down, and Canyon Wren. Adele snapped photos of the mountain mahogany in bloom. The other events of the day before came rushing back at Alfie, and he took a deep breath. Had he actually asked Adele to marry him again? Fear and hope threatened to overwhelm him. But mostly hope.

He lowered himself to sit on a boulder jutting out from the ground a few yards away from the quaint stone lodge where they'd spent the night.

It was a miracle, the woman who arranged their stay had said, that spaces were available in the dormitories at the lodge the night before. Nothing short of incredible there had been one space in each of the male and female dorms.

"People book months in advance," she said. "This is definitely your lucky day."

"Must be meant to be," Adele said with a smile at Alfie, her eyes shining.

"Check in the morning. Since this is a cancellation, meals may be available too. But normally those also have to be booked months ahead."

They'd made a stop in the village for some food to carry with them in case they couldn't have breakfast, and for lunch and dinner as well. And lots of water. The hike up, they were told, could take as long as eight

---

hours--easily twice as long as the hike down.

His fingers itched again for a cigarette. He popped a piece of nicotine gum in his mouth and set off to search out some coffee. He had no idea how long he would need to wait before Adele emerged from the women's dormitory.

He followed his nose to the aromas of food and coffee and found his way to the canteen, where Adele sat already in a patch of sunlight. Her hands encircled a cup of tea, as though she clung to it for warmth.

"Good morning." He kissed her on the cheek.

"They have extra meals for us," she said.

"That's good. I don't mind those power bar things, but I like me a good breakfast."

"I know." She smiled, patting the chair beside her. He sat down.

This familiarity after such a long time apart was peculiar--knowing someone so well, yet constantly crossing the divide of years that lay between them.

"I know I've said it before, but I'm sorry."

"Sorry?"

"For leaving."

"You have said it before, and this is the last time I want to hear you say it. If we're going to do this--get married again--we have to put the years behind us. Really behind us."

"Forget those things behind, reach forward to what is ahead," Alfie murmured.

"What's that?"

"Something the padre in Tennessee used to say. From the Bible, I guess."

"I like it." She sat back in the chair and basked in the sunlight.

He leaned toward her and took her hand. "You're sure, right?"

"Yes," she said, but she hesitated. "Are you?"

"Yes. How about tomorrow?"

She laughed. "You afraid you'll back down if we wait?"

"No, but I've made up my mind. I wasted a lot of time and I don't want to spend another day of my life not married to you."

"That's terribly romantic, Mr. Hansen." She leaned forward now, her face close to his.

"I'm serious."

"I know you are." She set her cup of tea on the table and stared at it.

"I haven't said anything at all to Celia. I never told her we were corresponding, never expressed to her my feelings for you." She traced the rim of the cup with her slender finger. "She won't understand."

Adele sent pictures, of course, but his memory of Celia had frozen in time as the small sad face watching from the window as he left for the last time. He planned to leave quietly when no one would hear him go. He scheduled no goodbyes. He took a last long look at the house, and saw her tiny suntanned face framed in the small upstairs window. The expression on that face haunted him. Less like grief or even disappointment, more like resignation that the inevitable had finally happened.

He wanted to earn his daughter's love too, but not at the risk of losing what he had right here, right now with this woman, truly the one love of his life. If Adele waited to tell Celia, if Celia never accepted him, would that mean they should deny themselves their own happiness? What if this meant Adele would never marry him?

Others began to filter in, and servers emerged with breakfast. Alfie and Adele ate their meal in silence, the sounds of silverware against dishes and the conversations and laughter of others harsh echoes in the small, crowded room.

* * *

"Adele? Where are you?" Alfie filled the doorway, letting the earthy scent of morning fill the small room.

"Right here." Adele replaced the receiver on the phone and sighed. "Just trying to reach Celia."

"Still no answer?"

She shook her head.

"Maybe they went away on vacation or something."

She scowled and tapped the pen against the nightstand. "That doesn't make sense. School's on."

"Oh, right."

Silence crept between them again.

Alfie straightened and surveyed the room for stray belongings. "I've got the truck loaded up. Ready to go?"

Adele cast a longing look at the phone. "Yes, I guess so." She stood slowly.

"You okay?"

She laughed. "I'm okay. My muscles just aren't cooperating one hundred percent."

The walk up had been long. They'd tagged along with a large busload of tourists from Saskatchewan, made some new friends and enjoyed conversation along the way. Joining the group also gave them a knowledgeable guide who had reminded them to keep hydrated, and made sure everyone took in enough calories to make the long climb. But they were both certainly now aware of muscles that didn't otherwise receive so much attention. They'd used more than one bucket of ice recovering later that night.

This morning, they'd plotted their trip down Highway 180 again, through Flagstaff and winding up somewhere this side of Albuquerque by day's end.

They climbed up in the cab, already warm in the Arizona sun and settled in for the ride. Adele switched lenses on her camera and began fiddling with settings while Alfie pulled away from the little lodge overlooking the canyon.

Several miles down the road, she pulled the camera away from her eye. "The sign says Arizona 64 goes the other way."

"I know. We were going to stay on the 180."

"No we weren't. We were going to take the 64. Check your GPS. It's faster--at least ten miles shorter."

He pulled off to the side of the road and into an abandoned gas station.

"Are we in a hurry?"

"Well no, it just seemed to make sense. And the road is this lovely winding road, less of a highway than this one, which looks like a straight shot, more or less." She pulled out the map and pointed at the route.

He waved it aside. He motioned ahead of them on the road. "If I stay on 180, I'll hook up with the interstate again, but eventually, we'll hit another piece of Route 66. If we go straight to Flagstaff on the other road, we'll miss a piece of 66."

Adele folded the map. She spoke quietly. "I'm sorry. I thought the goal was to enjoy the drive. I didn't realize we needed to cover every inch of Route 66."

Alfie folded his arms over the steering wheel and rested his head. He let the silence fill the space between them.

He sighed. "You're right. The goal is to enjoy the drive. And up until now, I have been. Sorry I got a little caught up."

He gazed ahead at the miles of dusty road. "But I'm not sure this argument is really about what route we take. Maybe it's more about you and me and getting married and what Celia will have to say about things."

She opened her mouth to speak, but he leaned over and put a finger to her lips. "If we let Celia decide this for us now, what does that mean? Are we really starting over again, you and me, or are we going to let our grown-up daughter control this situation, when we both feel this is right?

"I don't need an answer this minute. I don't want to pressure you. But I was serious about what I said yesterday, honey. I've made up my mind, and I know what I want."

He turned the truck around and turned off Highway 180 onto Arizona 64.

She smiled a shy smile and squeezed his arm. "You're a good man, and I love you."

They didn't speak as they drove down the road. Adele focused her lens in the distance. Sometimes she snapped a photo, sometimes she simply took the lens away with a satisfied smile, imagining the scene, probably, in watercolor or acrylic. From time to time she consulted the map or her guidebook.

She sat straight up and pointed. "Stop, Alfie. Stop the truck."

He pulled off to the side of the road and into the driveway she pointed to. Surrounded by a snake fence stood a small, oddly-shaped chapel, small and narrow at the door end, wider and taller facing the San Francisco Peaks. Adele jumped from the cab and walked toward the chapel, as if drawn by a force--a music Alfie neither heard nor felt. Alfie joined her and they walked inside the unlocked door of the building. Inside, the chapel had a dirt floor and several narrow pews all facing the tremendous view from the broad, triangle-shaped window at the end.

"Oh, Alfie," she whispered.

"What an odd little place," he said. His voice echoed in the rafters.

"I like it."

Little papers were tacked everywhere on the walls. "This is like a wall of thanksgiving. Listen to this," she said. "Thanks to the Creator who gave us this glorious creation as our home."

She moved a few feet over. "Here's another one: 'Thank you for saving my marriage.' Listen to this: 'Dear Lord, you are my best friend. I couldn't have gotten through this last year without you,' This one must have been a child: 'Thank you God for bringing my puppy home.' Here's another: 'Thank God for healing my body.'"

"This is interesting." Alfie read a leaflet at the back of the chapel. "The original chapel burned down and had to be rebuilt. This plaque says, 'It is our prayer that all who visit the chapel will experience God's love and power.'"

"Look here," she said. "It's available for weddings. There's a number here to reach ministers with same-day service, if you want to get married right away."

Alfie joined her, reading over her shoulder. "You're kidding."

She turned to face him and took his hands in her own. "You were right back there--right that the argument had nothing to do with the route to take or being in a hurry or who was right or wrong. It was about Celia. We need to make our own choices in this, and I choose you."

She stood on tiptoe, her lips close to his, and whispered, "Let's get married here."

CHAPTER SEVEN

Celia

"Socks, underwear, books for Caleb, and a novel it looked like you were reading, from on top of your dresser." Sarah picked each item from a large paper bag with handles--not the kind available at stores in Point-du-Fleuve, but at the fancy stores in Ottawa. It occurred to Celia to ask when Sarah had been shopping and what she'd bought, as though some part of her mind still sought the normal, mundane details of life. But she realized she didn't care. Sarah piled the contents unceremoniously at the bottom of Caleb's bed.

Celia picked up the novel. "I was supposed to take this back to the library."

"Oh. Okay, we'll put that in the to-go-back-home pile, then." She retrieved the paperback and found an empty spot beside the bag she was still unloading, the start of a new mound. "Here's some mail, and this week's newspaper--I threw out the junk mail. Here are some extra sweaters and a pair of slacks. I grabbed some of Jeff's stuff, too. I had no idea what he'd want."

"Thanks."

"I brought you all the final tallies for the Fall Festival, too. You know--just so you can see them. Linda Foster already took care of the accounting. You don't have to worry about that." Sarah surveyed the piles, and slouched down beside her friend on the edge of the single chair in the room. Her posture conveyed her work here was done.

"Oh yes, and Justin wanted me to make sure I told Caleb 'hello' from Hershey. He whines at the door every day--Hershey, not Justin." She laughed. "I'm sure he's confused being at our house, poor thing, but Justin's loving every minute."

For the last couple of days, Celia had been channeling every ounce of mental energy into a single exercise: wiping her mind clean from the sound of the doctor's voice and the look on his face when he delivered the diagnosis. Despite her effort to call to mind fonder memories, the doctor's white coat, his low voice and his dull expression played over in her mind like a well-worn TV commercial.

She appreciated Sarah. After all, she'd made the five-hour trip here with their things, and she'd have to head back soon. She surprised Celia when she walked through the door--not because such a gesture wasn't typical of Sarah--but because Celia had almost forgotten about her. Her brain was on lock-down, as though no reality existed beyond the last few days, the hospital, Caleb's room.

Sarah's gaze drifted to Caleb. She adjusted positions in the chair, opened her mouth and closed it again. "Will I get to see him? I mean, will he wake up while I'm here?"

"I'm not sure. He's been sleeping a lot."

"How long will he be that way?" Sarah shifted in the chair, one apparently not designed for comfort. Jeff had managed to catch a few hours' sleep there the past two nights. He'd given up trying to fit them both, spoon fashion, on the narrow daybed.

"I don't think they know. They said recovery may take anywhere from one to eight weeks."

"And then?"

Celia looked away. Sarah was sweet to deliver their things. Now she wanted Sarah to go and leave her to her mental exercise. If she stopped for a moment, the commercial queued up again. "Then they'll start treatment."

"Chemo? Radiation? That sort of thing?"

"Yes, so they say."

Sarah shifted in her seat again, still staring at Caleb. A muffled command filtered in from the hallway on the loudspeaker, and she sat up, her gaze boring into Celia. "Have you considered alternative treatment?"

"What do you mean?"

"I mean herbal supplements, teas, meditation, acid/alkaline balance, enzymatic therapy--anything but chemo. That stuff can kill you."

Celia braced herself. She wasn't prepared for a full dose of Sarah today. Jeff had gone out on the pretense of getting coffee. She knew, in part, he wanted to give her time to talk to her friend, but she hoped he came back soon. Sarah wouldn't talk much about what he would call "that new age stuff" with him around. He was her polar opposite--strictly practicalities and realism.

Over the years, Celia had developed a healthy tolerance for Sarah's ideas. She'd even been convinced to join one of the yoga classes at Sarah's gym. But now, she wasn't in the mood.

"I'm serious, Celia. People can get cured of their cancers and then fight the damage from the drugs and radiation for years afterward." She surveyed Caleb's sleeping form. "It'll make him sterile. He'll never have kids."

How many times had Celia imagined what Caleb would be like when he grew up--what he would become, where he would go, what he would look like? Would he be like his dad, tall, slim and muscular without trying to be? Would he be a good husband, a father? But how could she think of any of that now? And yet how could she give up those dreams?

"Sarah, really. I'd rather we didn't--"

"Well, you need to consider these things. Here." Sarah dug around in her purse and pushed a piece of paper into her hand.

"What's this?"

"Some websites I found with alternative therapy information."

"I don't even know if we have internet access--"

"Oh right," she said. "Well, if email doesn't work, I could always mail some things to you."

"I don't know. I guess so, probably. We haven't had time to think about it--"

"Don't worry. We'll figure something out." She smiled, patted Celia's hand, and gently closed her fingers around the piece of paper.

"Oh, I almost forgot," she said. "Your mom left a message on your answering machine. She said she called to see how you were doing."

"Mom?" Celia had longed to turn back the clock to a day, a month, a year before that day on the soccer field. Now she thought of her mother, the tenderness of her touch, the soft smell of her. How much simpler life had been when one of her kisses sufficed to wipe away any pain. "Did she say where she was?"

"Too much background noise. She may have said, but I didn't understand. I could have sworn, though, she said she'd be praying for you. Weird, eh?" She pushed her long hair over her shoulder. "When is she due back home?"

Celia had been longing to talk to her mother ever since Caleb's collapse. "She didn't actually give me a date." She didn't let on to Sarah how little she knew about what her mother was doing. Or how much she ached for her.

*   *   *

Snow fell in October. Celia wanted to believe the freshness, the newness brought hope. Another layer of forgetting. But like the earth, the cold, hard truth lay beneath it still.

She and Jeff stared down at what the early snow was doing to the traffic eight floors below. People had forgotten how to drive in winter conditions since the last snowfall several months ago. Or perhaps they weren't willing to admit to themselves that this much snow actually fell in Toronto on October 13. According to the forecast, temperatures would return to normal and this would all turn to rain overnight. But already during the morning rush hour there had been two pileups on the street below the hospital. Celia watched at the window with Jeff, strangely removed from the storm outside as they battled the one within.

They were waiting to see the doctor. Dr. Nazar--or Dr. Bob, as he'd asked Caleb to call him--was the ICU doctor. He said Caleb shouldn't stay on the respirator beyond two weeks. He'd promised to have the oncologist assess whether he was ready to have the respirator removed. Caleb couldn't talk with it in. Two weeks had passed since Celia had heard her baby's voice.

Buried in his own thoughts, Jeff looked away from the window, surfacing from somewhere deep and far away. "What are you thinking?" he asked. Neither of them had dared ask the question for two weeks, afraid of the answer.

Celia searched his eyes and tried to decide if he genuinely meant to ask.

"Do you think we made the right decision about the surgery?" she asked. Caleb slept remarkably peacefully on the bed. From a distance, the bandage at the base of his skull was almost invisible. She could almost pretend it wasn't there at all.

"Don't do this to yourself, baby. We didn't have a choice. He had to breathe." Jeff stroked her back. She had been grateful for Jeff's presence these past two weeks. He'd put all of his clients on hold. "The only decision I question is our not taking a room somewhere."

She stiffened against his touch. "Not without Caleb."

"I know. I feel the same way, but we need to stay strong for him. You're not getting any real rest staying here."

"I'm resting better here than I would somewhere else." She couldn't imagine not being able to make sure he was okay during the night.

He sighed. This wasn't the first time they'd had this debate. But she wouldn't give in. She needed to be with Caleb.

She smiled and touched his face, as though she might clear away the lines etching themselves into his expression. "When he's well again. Not long now, right?"

He returned her smile, but his eyes were sad and empty.

Fat snowflakes whirled between the tall, gray buildings. Snow used to deliver warmer memories: the season's first snowman, snowball fights in the backyard and afterwards mugs of hot chocolate, warm against cold fingers.

The year Caleb turned five, the autumn had been particularly warm. Christmas Eve arrived without even a hint of snowfall, and the weatherman held out no hope. Toward midnight, Celia wrapped presents and stuffed stockings while Jeff puzzled over the instructions for Caleb's first two-wheeler. Snow began to fall. It fell all night, laying a thick blanket over the world. Like giddy children, they woke Caleb early Christmas morning, threw open the curtains in his room, and unveiled what Mother Nature had done while he slept. As though they'd placed an order especially for him.

She stood and stared at Caleb's peaceful form and wished she could pull off that kind of miracle now--produce something out of nothing to transform his world. Instead, she watched his chest rise and fall to the rhythm of the respirator and wondered whether they would spend this Christmas at home or in the hospital.

She sat down on edge of the bed, next to Caleb. He appeared to be bound by the tentacles of some faceless creature. Tubes and wires ran from him in every direction. Intravenous drip, respirator, heart monitor, blood pressure monitor and pulse oximeter pulsed and beeped and transmitted signals to the nurses supervising the ICU.

She didn't want to know what thoughts hid behind Jeff's mournful eyes. She was certain of something, even if no one else was. She ran her hand over Caleb's sleeping form. Her son was strong. He would fight whatever was attacking his body. She would fight with him. She swallowed against the ache pushing up into her throat and wiped a tear from the corner of her eye.

"Mr. and Mrs. Bennett?"

A woman stood in the doorway. Celia hadn't even heard footsteps approaching the room. The woman held a medical chart and wore a white lab coat. Young and confident, she smiled, stepped into the room and extended her hand.

"Hi there. Sorry I haven't had a chance to come down and meet you yet. I'm Dr. Oster, Caleb's oncologist."

Jeff stood instantly and accepted her hand. Celia stayed on the bed, stroking Caleb's leg. Her heart began to pound.

"Hi, I'm Jeff. This is my wife, Celia."

Dr. Oster was much younger than Celia had expected. Her strawberry-blonde hair was swept up off her neck and tucked neatly in the back. Celia had tried to achieve the same style when her hair was longer, but her unruly brown curls wouldn't cooperate. If not for the white coat and the hint of dark fatigue under her eyes, Celia would have believed the doctor was a model.

Dr. Oster nodded and smiled in Celia's direction, and turned straight to business. "I believe Dr. Nazar discussed with you that we need to remove your son from the respirator."

Celia nodded, shifted on the bed, and felt for the warmth of Caleb's hand.

The doctor's expression strained. "I want to caution you against too much optimism. The breathing issue could return. Since the respirator isn't a permanent solution, we may need to consider other options for assisting your son's breathing in the future."

"Like what?" Jeff asked.

"Most likely an endotracheal tube."

"What's that? What's the difference?" Jeff was too eager with his questions. Celia had the sensation of driving with someone who didn't brake soon enough, her foot pressed hard against the imaginary brake pedal on her side of the vehicle.

"Well, the trach would allow him to talk, for one thing." She opened up the chart and glanced at the empty chair. "May I?"

"Of course," Jeff said.

"I have with me the results of the most recent MRI." She flipped through reports, x-ray films, and computerized readings. Celia wished she could dispense with the doctor, interpret them for herself.

"The MRI does indeed seem to indicate the tumor is no longer placing pressure on the tissues responsible for his breathing." A long pause hung in the air as she continued to study results. Celia held her breath.

"That's good news, right?" Jeff said finally.

"Yes, but tumors like your son's can be very aggressive. The growth that caused the problem in the first place has been debulked, but could easily grow back again to place similar stress on his respiratory function. In that case, as I said, we'd need to pursue other measures."

Celia waged a mental war against her words. She didn't want her to talk about regrowth--to talk about that foreign thing as if it belonged to her son.

Did she expect them to authorize this procedure right there on the spot? Silence grew and ate up all the little sounds in the room they'd come to know--the pulsing machines, the footsteps from the hallway, the air circulation fans. The doctor stared at them and said nothing, as though they were all in some sort of wordless standoff.

Finally, the doctor stood. "I'll tell Dr. Nazar he can remove the respirator. We'll give your son a chance to breathe on his own."

"Thank you, doctor," Jeff said. He shook her hand again.

"Nice to meet you," she said. She gave another nod in Celia's direction and walked out of the room.

Caleb stirred and jerked under the covers, his eyes wild. He looked from Celia to Jeff and back again. He clutched at the tube from the respirator, trying to pull it out. It was a reflex, the doctors had said. Some kids got over it, some did not.

Celia grabbed his hand. "It's okay, sweetheart. I'm here. Mommy's here."

His grip on her hand loosened and his body slowly relaxed, but the uneasiness didn't leave his eyes. He motioned for the small white board

Sarah had brought for him to write on and she handed it to him.

"What's wrong?" he scribbled.

"What do you mean, sweetheart?" Celia held her breath.

More scribbling.

"You're crying," he had scrawled. She touched her cheeks. Sure enough, they were wet with tears. She hadn't even noticed.

She ran her hand over his forehead, smoothed the hair away from his face. His hair was brown, almost black, like hers. But his hair grew warm and rich next to the olive-colored complexion he'd inherited from his dad. His face had lost some of its glow since the surgery, and his bangs were too long, which drove him crazy. They'd been planning to get his hair cut when they ended up in the hospital.

"Nothing's wrong, sweetheart." She smiled. She wasn't sure how convincing a picture she made, tears still wet on her cheeks. "I guess I haven't had enough sleep."

"Hey, Champ, you okay?" Jeff asked. He sat down on the bed and Caleb turned to him and nodded. She wiped the tears from her cheeks with the back of her hand.

"Sounds like the doctor might come by today and check on your respirator," Jeff said.

Feet scuffled at the door. "Actually, the doctor's here." Dr. Bob stepped into the room. He had an apologetic way of walking, ducking under the doorframe, even though he cleared it by nearly a foot. He was followed closely by a nurse pushing a cart with some medical supplies. She had a double chin and waddled slightly when she walked. It struck Celia she'd seem just as appropriate holding a pot of coffee in a diner as she did clutching her son's medical chart.

The doctor smiled at Caleb. "How are we today?"

Caleb picked up the drawing board again. He drew a happy face.

The doctor smiled. "Did your parents talk to you about your respirator?"

He nodded.

"He just woke up," Celia said. "We didn't say much."

"That's okay." He smiled at Caleb. "We need to do something better for you. The respirator can't stay in much longer. It isn't meant to be permanent." He put his hands in the pockets of his white coat. "So we thought we'd try you off it for a little bit, see how you do. If you still need some help breathing, we'll try something else. Something that'll let you talk so you don't have to draw happy faces to let me know how you're feeling."

"Will it hurt?" Caleb wrote.

"We'll be pulling the tube out of your throat. It might have hurt a little when we put it in, is that right?"

Caleb nodded.

"It won't hurt as much coming out, but since it's been in a while, you may find afterwards you'll have some slight irritation or dryness in your throat."

He turned to address the waitress nurse, "Let's make sure Caleb gets a little ice cream for his throat. What do you say?"

She nodded and smiled, and her cheeks made little round plump circles. "You bet." Her voice had a smoker's wheeze behind it.

The doctor turned back to Caleb. "The first thing we're going to do, though, is run a short test and make sure you can breathe on your own. Before we do anything at all, I'm going to listen to your lungs working." He put the stethoscope to Caleb's chest, and Caleb twitched a little and wrinkled his nose. Celia smiled at him, trying to transmit some sort of positive energy in his direction, willing everything to be all right.

"It's cold?" the doctor asked.

Caleb nodded.

"Sorry," the doctor said and moved the stethoscope to Caleb's back, and again to his chest in several different places, each time with the instruction, "Breathe deep."

He stood and let the stethoscope fall to his chest. "Okay," he said, slowly. The tone of his voice made Celia look hard at his face.

The doctor straightened, loomed over the bed. He had a decidedly medical expression--the dull eyes, the lips pressed together. The muscles around Celia's stupid smile twitched and failed.

"I hear a little something in the breathing I'm not sure I like."

The doctor addressed Celia and Jeff. "May I speak with you a moment?" He motioned toward the hallway. Celia didn't look toward the hospital bed.

She was grateful when Jeff said, "Just a minute, Champ. We'll be right back. Why don't you find the page where we left off in the book we were reading."

They stepped into the hallway, and the doctor spoke. His voice was muted. She struggled to hear. Or was it just that the silence in her head was getting louder? She focused on Jeff while the doctor droned on. She'd know by her husband's reaction how she was supposed to react, like when they went to football games together. She didn't trust her own senses.

"I have some concerns--" the doctor was saying. An image flashed—Celia walking on the frozen lake with her father when she was Caleb's age. She remembered having heard the crack a split second before her foot broke through the surface, then icy water chilling every inch of her.

"We need to run some more tests," the doctor was saying. "I'm hearing some pleural thickening in the breathing."

He searched their faces as though for recognition. "I'm suspicious Caleb may have pneumonia."

"Pneumonia? Before--before this--" She waved a hand vaguely in the direction of the room. "He's a healthy little boy, doctor."

The doctor crossed his arms, took a deep breath and faced them squarely. "This can happen for any number of reasons--even as a reaction to the chemotherapy drugs he's been taking to keep the tumor at bay. Or perhaps an infection introduced somehow by the ventilator itself. We may need to investigate a different set of chemo drugs before another treatment is needed."

She wanted a chance to breathe before he said any more, but the doctor kept talking. "I believe we should proceed with the trach tube. As I've said before, the ventilator is not a long-term solution. While his body recovers from the pneumonia, he'll need the breathing support, and perhaps beyond that."

He smiled, but his forehead was still wrinkled. "The good news about the tracheostomy is we can eventually wean him off of it, so during the day, he'll be mobile and able to speak normally."

"A tracheostomy. Isn't that invasive?"

"Well, he'll have to have an incision and stitches, and the trach tube will fit into the incision site, which is in the lower part of the neck, between the larynx and the sternum. The trach stays in. We hook the ventilator up to it.

"I'll make sure a Child Life Specialist comes by to demonstrate to Caleb what his trach will be like, and we'll schedule surgery as soon as possible." He slid Caleb's chart into its place, turned and shuffled down the hall with her hope.

* * *

Celia stood in the surgical waiting room, next to the playroom. Jeff sat with his laptop open, going over outstanding invoices to his clients to check against the pile of mail Sarah was accumulating at her house. Before his surgery started, Caleb had played in the playroom while the doctors briefed them on the procedure. Clusters of kids cooked pretend food in the play kitchen, worked on puzzles and built Lego castles while Celia worked to put the things the doctor told them out of her head. The possible side effects, he said, although unlikely, must be considered: severe bleeding, damage to the larynx, lung collapse. He had referred to the tracheostomy as a "permanent solution." Were those words intended to comfort?

Jeff closed his laptop. "Want to go get a snack?"

She glanced toward the operating room doors. "They said the procedure wouldn't take long."

"He'll still have to come out of the anesthesia."

"I guess so," she said, her appetite for distraction greater than for food.

They rounded a corner in the corridor and she ran square into the broad chest of a man.

She stepped back. "Sorry."

"No, I'm sorry," he said.

"Celia!" Two voices spoke at once--the stranger's and her mother's, several steps behind him.

"Mom?"

Celia looked from her mother's face to the man's. His silver hair set off a complexion that had absorbed the sun of countless summers and refused to allow the effects to fade. His voice was warm and distantly familiar, and something about the corners of his eyes when he smiled made her remember kissing that face. Her father.

As the realization broke, her mother ran up and hugged her. "Celia, I'm so glad we found you."

She shook her head. "What is he doing here? Mom? What is this all about?"

Celia's mother seemed oblivious to the barrage of questions. "We came as soon as we heard from Sarah."

47

"You came. Together?"

Jeff stepped forward and spoke to her father. "Maybe you and I should take a walk. What do you say?"

CHAPTER EIGHT

Alfie

Alfie sat on a bench in the hospital corridor outside the cafeteria. His daughter stood down the hall engaged in animated conversation with Adele. It was wonderful and startling to see her. Of course he knew she had grown up since he'd last seen her, become her own person, a wife and a mother. But the knowledge didn't lessen the strangeness of her breathing the same air as him, several feet away and fully grown. A real flesh and blood woman and not a Kodak image tucked into an envelope with one of Adele's letters. She had her mother's grace and poise, but a lot about her reflected him--the brown eyes, the wide mouth, the dark hair he used to have before it turned grey.

Jeff was inside the cafeteria buying a coffee before they headed out of doors. He'd stood dumb before Celia moments ago, stifling the instincts that threatened to overwhelm him--to hug her and call her Princess.

This wasn't how he'd imagined their reunion. Not that he'd had unrealistic hopes. He wrote her for years and received nothing in return. He figured the hurt had long ago turned to anger and resentment--even hatred. But, God forgive him, he thought that because her son was sick-- his grandson--her heart would be softer toward him. He was ashamed to admit the fact. But there it was.

He had been the one to suggest coming straight here. After the wedding in Arizona, Adele tried calling Celia several times. Each time, the answering machine picked up. She couldn't remember Celia's cell phone number. The concern began to wear at her. She was a good sport, didn't once say she wanted to go home early. But it became obvious she

49

was distracted.

Around Tulsa, she'd finally decided to call Celia's friend Sarah to make sure everything was okay. After the phone call, they'd driven non-stop, straight to the hospital. Another hour and a half and they'd have been at Adele's cottage--their cottage.

He'd seen few pictures of Jeff since the photos of their wedding, striking and formal in his tuxedo. It surprised him, then, how relaxed and easy-going he seemed. He'd grown a goatee he didn't have in the wedding pictures, and he had a disarming crooked smile when he extended his hand to Alfie. "It's good to finally meet you, sir."

"You oughta know you don't need to be calling me 'sir,' if you've heard anything at all about me."

The younger man nodded and laughed. "I take it you've had a long drive."

"Drove 24 hours in that last stretch, give or take."

"Straight?"

Alfie nodded.

Jeff led the way through the revolving doors off the atrium and onto the street. Both men braced against the cold.

"Whew! I haven't been in these kinds of temperatures for years. I think my blood's thinned."

Jeff tugged at his collar. "Came early this year. Supposed to warm up again, though."

"So, Adele's told me a bit about you, Jeff. What is it you do? Technical writing or something? What does that mean, exactly?"

Jeff chuckled. "I make other people look good, I guess. Basically I take something technical and try to explain it so the average person can understand."

"People like me." Alfie grinned.

Jeff returned the smile. "Yeah, that's right."

"And they pay you for that." Alfie winked.

"Pretty well, actually." Jeff grinned again.

They walked along the side streets leading away from the cluster of hospitals and toward Chinatown. A silence fell between them, broken only by the sound of crunching of feet on salt and ice. At an intersection, Alfie stopped. "So where do you stand?"

"Excuse me?"

"About me. Where do you stand?"

Alfie looked the younger man over. He was broad-shouldered and fit--a lot like himself at the same age. Better educated, though.

Jeff leaned back, staring up the side of a tall building. "You know, Mr. Hansen—"

"Alfie. You've gotta call me Alfie."

"Okay--Alfie. I had a pretty abnormally normal family. I have two brothers and two sisters. My parents stayed together, all of us are married--good marriages," he spoke deliberately, as though he'd imagined having this conversation for years, rehearsed for a moment like this. "I can't pretend to understand Celia's feelings about you. I haven't been through what she's been through. But I think forgiveness is important. Not even so much for your sake, if you'll pardon me saying so, but for her sake. It's tough holding onto all that pain."

Alfie grimaced and dropped his head. He liked this kid, though. He didn't pull any punches.

"She never reads any of your letters. But I keep them. Some of them I had to dig out of the trash. They're all in a shoebox on a shelf in our bedroom closet, still in their envelopes."

"Celia know you do that?"

"She must. She does a thorough spring cleaning every year. She must've come across them at some point." He looked around as if he noticed for the first time how far they'd walked from the hospital. "Guess we'd better head back," he said, and the two men turned around and began walking vigorously again. The bitter wind snatched at their breath instead of their backs and necks.

"You didn't really answer my question," Alfie said.

"What question was that?"

"You didn't say where you stood when it comes to me." He shoved his hands deep in his pockets. His breath made small puffs when he spoke.

"Let's just say I have an open mind."

Alfie smiled. "I can work with that." The cold was getting to him more than he liked to admit. His jacket wasn't warm enough for this weather. "When do you suppose I'll be able to see my grandson?"

"I don't know." The tone of Jeff's voice changed and his glance fell to the frozen sidewalk. "I'll see what I can do."

Alfie halted abruptly and faced his son-in-law. "I'm sorry, we've been talking all this time, and I still don't know what's wrong with Caleb. Why is he here?"

"He has a brain tumor," Jeff said, his voice deflated. "They've given him a year at best."

CHAPTER NINE

Celia

"You should sleep for a while." Celia tucked the blankets around Caleb. The tracheostomy tube in place around his neck, he had tossed and turned the night before with the discomfort of this new appendage. Lack of sleep left him agitated, antsy. He was weary from surgery, and whined about the food, the bed, the lack of fresh air, his voice even more pathetic as he adjusted to the trach tube. He refused to lie down, but he didn't want to watch anything on TV.

Celia still felt numb from the day before. Her mom had promised to talk to her over the phone and visit as often as they asked. Celia had no plans to initiate the phone calls, though, and left her cell phone off all day. Jeff hadn't said much about his talk with her dad. Neither Jeff nor Celia was likely to open that conversation.

Jeff stirred, as though her thoughts about him had disturbed him with some psychic signal. He slumped down in the vinyl chair the color of grass stains, across the bed from her. His mouth hung open, and his fingers were slowly losing their grip on the sports section of *The Toronto Star*. He'd fallen victim to the overheated room, the cadence of the ventilator and the hypnotizing snowfall.

Caleb kicked at the covers. "Would you read to me, mom?" His voice squeezed out in a scratchy whisper. A few of the words were barely there.

"Sure." Sarah had gone through Caleb's bookshelves and made a care package of books they were now rotating, for moments like this, when boredom set in. They'd read most of them before twice or even three times, like familiar friends. They needed the comfort.

"What'll it be? *Charlotte's Web, James and the Giant Peach*, or *Harry Potter*?"

He pointed to Harry Potter.

"Do you remember where we were?" She flipped through the pages. "I can't find the bookmark."

"The middle of the chapter where Harry arrived at the school. Just after that part." She fought the temptation to clear her throat as he spoke.

"With Harry in Professor Snape's class?"

He nodded, sat up a little and touched the trach, as if he was afraid it might fall out.

"I think you're right. Here we are. Does this sound familiar?" She opened the book wide, bent back on the spine and read in her best Severus Snape voice:

As there is little foolish wand-waving here, many of you will hardly believe this is magic. I don't expect you will really understand the beauty of the soft simmering cauldron with its shimmering fumes, the delicate power of liquids that creep through human veins, bewitching the mind, ensnaring the senses....I can teach you how to bottle fame, brew glory, even put a stopper on death - if you aren't as big a bunch of dunderheads as I usually have to teach...

As they followed Harry's adventures through the rest of the chapter, Celia kept checking Caleb for signs of tiredness. Wrapped in wonder and lost in his own world, his eyes remained wide open. When she came to the end, she rested the book on her lap, her finger in the place they stopped. Caleb had a distant expression, still caught up in the world of story.

She smiled. "What are you thinking about, honey?"

He shrugged.

"You must be thinking something. I can always tell when that imagination of yours is busy."

"You'll think it's silly."

"Nothing is silly in your imagination." She fussed with his covers.

He shook his head and squirmed impatiently under the covers. "This is real."

"What's real?"

"Harry is lucky."

"Why do you say that?" She found a slip of paper to tuck into the book and laid it down on the tray table.

"He can do magic. He can change things and make them better. It said something about stopping death, right?"

She nodded and held her breath, afraid of his next words.

His gaze locked on her. "Harry wouldn't be scared of dying."

She didn't know what to say. She couldn't think of words. A feeling crept over her--like darkness swallowing her whole--and the sound of blood rushed in her ears. She tucked him in, told him to get some sleep, and rushed into the hallway. She fought for air, fought to surface. In an empty waiting area, she sank down on the cold tile floor and let the tears and the grief consume her.

She cried until there was nothing left in her. She stared at the sterile surroundings--the sickly green walls, gray blinds, gray floors. A nurse and a doctor conferred at a nurse's station somewhere nearby.

"What about Kaitlin in room 854?"

"Is that Kaitlin Sorrento or Kaitlin Reichart?"

The flipping of papers. "Reichart. There don't seem to be any chemo drugs on her chart."

"You didn't get the note from yesterday?"

"What note?" She sounded exasperated, or overworked, perhaps.

"I consulted with Dr. Crawford yesterday. She's palliative."

"Really?" There was something genuine in her voice--surprise or compassion, perhaps.

"Yeah. Just make her comfortable. Nothing else we can do."

Celia couldn't distinguish the rest of the conversation, murmured in low tones. Finally, the clicking of shoes echoed down the hallway as the doctor walked away.

She wanted to scream. These people meant well, but they were guessing. They had no real answers. No cures. None of them had promised to make her baby better. And none of them would.

She refused to wait around to hear someone say "nothing else we can do" about Caleb. She had to find an answer for her son, and she knew she wasn't going to find it in this hospital. Caleb wanted magic. She would have to find it for him.

CHAPTER TEN
Alfie

Alfie sat on the sofa and stared into the last embers of the fire he'd built earlier in the evening. Walking back into the cottage after their return from Children's Hospital was like sliding his feet into comfortable old slippers. He smiled as he walked through the house and took in the homey stone fireplace, the smooth wooden floorboards, the built-in bunks in Celia's old room. Everything was as he'd carefully crafted it years ago when they built this place as a summer retreat, when the dream to retire in this spot was just that--a dream. More than a homecoming, it was coming back to a part of himself he hadn't remembered losing.

They'd come home around dinnertime, but neither of them felt like eating. Adele had kissed him goodnight and headed to bed an hour, maybe two hours ago already. Still he sat staring into the dying fire. He struggled to take stock of the day. He'd known the road back to Celia's heart would not be easy. He'd expected--even counted on--her rejection. But knowing she hated him and seeing the hatred in her eyes were two different things.

And of course nothing could have prepared him for the news about Caleb. He'd thought he had a handle on regret until now. How could he forgive himself for putting off meeting his grandson, now that he might lose him altogether? The place in his heart that ached for this child he'd never even met was so real a doctor could cut him open and identify it.

Coming home was more than he'd bargained for. This kind of circumstance, just a few years or even months ago, would have made him bolt. But more reasons held him now than made him want to leave. He longed to take away this burden his daughter carried--to hold her and tell her everything would be all right. But he was an outsider and unwanted, and he'd made his bed himself.

Adele's feet swished against the hardwood as she walked from the bedroom slipper-clad, her housecoat wrapped around her. She stood behind him.

"I'll be right in," he said.

"So you said an hour and a half ago." She rubbed his back. "Don't worry. I can't sleep either." She came around to his side of the couch and flopped down beside him. She lifted his arm around her and snuggled next to him.

"I'm sorry," he said. The trouble he'd created at the hospital, the wedge driven even further between Celia and him, and the grief he caused Adele deserved more than just "sorry." Yet he struggled for what else to say.

"For what?"

He smiled at her painfully.

She chuckled. "These have been my choices. No one put a gun to my head." She turned and kissed him on the cheek.

They sat for several moments in silence, the only sound the occasional farewell crackle from the hottest of the embers.

Finally Adele spoke up. "I'll give her some time, but I think I should go back to Toronto to be with Celia. Those two haven't had a break since this started. If I know Celia, she hasn't left that room much. I didn't ask what Jeff's doing about work."

"What about the shop?" He didn't want to create obstacles for her. He'd miss her, though, and feel even more useless. There'd be nothing to do but knock around in the four walls of the cottage and a town he hadn't lived in for almost thirty years.

"This is more important."

"How do you think Celia will react?"

She rubbed his chest. "I just think it would be good for me to go and spend a little time with her."

He knew what she meant. Good for Celia, but good for Adele too. They'd have a chance to talk about him without him around. And he couldn't fault her for wanting to spend more time with Caleb.

He suddenly had an idea. "You said Celia made a scrapbook for you with pictures of Caleb."

"*A* scrapbook? Try eight. One for every year of his life." She sat up on the edge of the couch. "You want to look at them?"

He nodded.

"Where do you want to start?"

"Get them all."

She came back with a huge stack of cloth-bound albums, each a different color. Opening them opened a new world--the world of the little girl who had grown up without him.

Alfie insisted they take their time. He drank up the images like a thirsty man in an Arizona summer. Celia had covered the first page with photos of each month of her pregnancy.

"This says month five. Where are the ones from before?" He flipped the page back to make sure he hadn't missed something.

"That's the first month. She didn't take any pictures before then. By the time she got pregnant with Caleb, she'd had too many miscarriages to count. She didn't dare hope. But she'd never made it this far before." She smiled at the image of Celia's tummy poking out and the proud smile looking back at her. Her dark hair was long, her brown eyes shone.

"I think she regrets that--not having those pictures. She's so thorough, you know, in everything she does."

"I remember." Alfie smiled.

Adele still gazed at the pictures, lost in memories. "She's a good mom." Her voice muddied with tears. One dripped on the page and she swept it away.

"Are you okay with this?" he asked.

She nodded. "It's good, to do this."

On the next page a tiny, black-haired baby in a diaper stared up from an incubator, tubes and wires swirling around him in every direction. Alfie looked at Adele. "Yeah. He wasn't in there long. He was born premature, and doctors were concerned about his lungs early on, but he was strong--a little fighter--and they took him out almost right away."

They moved through page after page, story after story of each milestone in his life--big and small: the first steps, first teeth, first day of kindergarten, the requisite school photos, Christmases, soccer tryouts, soccer games, soccer championships. It was wonderful and sweet and painfully sad. He envied her presence for most of these moments, her memories unsullied with regret. How could he have stayed away so long? How could he have missed all of this--a life in miniature, now almost gone?

By the time the sun shot its first rays over the lake and into the cottage windows, Adele had parked a box of tissues beside her on the sofa. They were halfway through Caleb's sixth year.

She touched her fingers to her cheeks. "I must look a wreck about now," she said.

He shook his head and smiled.

"I'll put the coffee on. We can leave these here so we can pick up later where we left off." She laid the open album carefully on the table and stood. "I suppose I should get busy. There's laundry to do, and I need to check in at the shop. And there's nothing in the house. We need groceries."

Alfie stood. "I can help."

Adele turned to face him. "The new you, eh?"

Alfie took her hand. "Come here."

He led her to the back door of the cottage. The sky had brightened, and the first rays of sun peeked out over the lake. He had forgotten how breathtaking sunrises here could be. He opened the door that led to the lake. The spring hinge complained loudly.

"I'm in my slippers," Adele said.

Alfie shrugged. "Let's watch the sunrise together."

They sat and watched as the colors burst over the lake, but as the sky grew bright, something else grew visible.

He had poured the patio slab behind the house the summer Celia was born--in a time when they'd dreamed big and thought of filling this place with kids. They had talked of one day adding a sunroom to the back of the little cottage, to make the place complete. As the light of dawn poured over it, his neglect was clear. Exposed to the weather for too many years, the slab had heaved. A crack cut from one end to the other and branched out in a 'Y' like a dry narrow river and its tributary. Weeds poked up arrogantly here and there through the concrete. One more reminder of broken promises.

Adele followed his gaze, seemed to read his thoughts. "We could still build it," she said.

He circled his arm around her and pulled her close. "Yes, we could."

59

CHAPTER ELEVEN

Celia

Ayesha Farrukh, the social worker for the oncology department, adjusted her position in the green chair beside the bed. Celia perched beside Jeff on the daybed. On the other side of the room, Caleb sat up to the tray table over the bed and played with a K'Nex building set Ayesha had brought with her.

She smiled a teethy white smile and tucked her thick black hair behind her ear. "I just wanted to check on how you guys are doing, and discuss a few issues with you." The smile again.

Jeff and Celia exchanged a look. He studied her eyes. "We're pretty overwhelmed, I guess," he said.

Ayesha nodded, her head tilted to one side and raised her eyebrows encouragingly toward Celia.

Celia nodded back.

Ayesha straightened the papers in her hand. "Having the trach in can be a big adjustment, sometimes more for the parents than for the child. The child has the benefit of feeling how it's helping him to breathe, and can't really see it all the time. The parents have to look at it every day. It can be difficult."

Despite her resolution not to cry, tears pricked at the corners of Celia's eyes.

"The good news about the trach is it presents more options for Caleb's environment. He doesn't have to stay in the hospital anymore."

"But the ventilator--"

"We can help you arrange the rental of a machine that can be kept in

60

your home. Once he has a portable machine, someone will come, for an hour a day at first, and observe Caleb while he breathes independently. They gradually build up that time period until he can breathe on his own during the day, and use the ventilator only at night."

"Is that safe?"

"To be off the ventilator, you mean?"

Celia nodded.

"In patients with respiratory difficulties, very often it's nighttime we need to worry about the most, since the patient is typically alone, others are sleeping, and when sleep is deepest, the brain sometimes forgets to breathe."

"So, if he were off the ventilator during the day, he could move around a little more?" Celia glanced at Caleb absorbed in the creation of some sort of tower on the tray table.

"Exactly. Which brings me to the other two things I wanted to talk to you about. First, have you heard of Ronald McDonald House?"

"I think so, but I'm not sure what that is," Jeff said.

"It's a place patients can live with their families. It's a charitable organization, and their facilities are located in many cities near hospitals. Toronto has one. With Caleb's condition, and the distance you live away from the hospital, your family would qualify for a space there."

Her words sent panic through Celia. Beyond her usual hatred for hospitals, she had searched for someone to hold responsible for what had happened to Caleb. In the haze of memory from the last few weeks, the doctors, with their cold, impassive delivery of the diagnosis seemed the most likely culprits. After all, how was it possible that her perfect boy, healthy and happy one moment, kicking a soccer ball and joking with his friends, could be the same child lying in this hospital bed?

At the same time, faced with the prospect of leaving, she panicked. The truth was, before Caleb's collapse, she hadn't known anything was wrong. She hadn't seen this coming. The days leading up to the avalanche of events and emotions that started on the soccer field lived in her memory as commonplace and unclouded as the ones before. If her strong, fit eight-year-old broke so easily, how would she be able to trust her own abilities to take care of him? How could she take him from here, not knowing what unseen forces conspired to harm him?

She wanted Caleb more mobile, off the ventilator, of course. But the hospital afforded a degree of separation. The room was private, and they had few places to go--the cafeteria and back if they had the appetite. She didn't want to start making trips in and out of the hospital. It would mean facing people in the real world and admitting this wasn't just some horrible nightmare they'd been living. She closed her eyes against the weight of it all crashing down on her. If she could just rewind time to the instant before her baby collapsed, all of this would go away, and they would have their lives back.

Jeff let out an audible sigh and smiled in her direction. "That's great, isn't it Cel?"

She stared at him. Was it great?

"You want to get him out of here, right? You haven't been sleeping in a chair every night, but this bed isn't all that comfortable either." He punctuated his words with a thump on the hard mattress.

Ayesha looked from Jeff to Celia and back again. She pulled some of the stack of papers from her hand and laid them on the bed beside them. "You can discuss things and fill this out when you're ready. I'll come back in a few days to collect it, and send it to Ronald McDonald House with my reference."

She turned her attention to the stack of papers in front of her again and smiled. "Now, about Caleb's schooling."

Celia's mind clouded over. She stared out the window at the dry leaves flying in circles between the buildings and wished she were somewhere far away.

* * *

Ronald McDonald House looked as though they'd hired Dr. Seuss as decorator. Lime green carpets and furnishings in purple--eggplant, the director said--bright red, blue and yellow. Big, geometric designs dominated. Caleb loved the place from the moment they wheeled him in the door. Celia was terrified.

While they stayed at Ronald McDonald House, Caleb would begin radiation and chemotherapy in earnest. He would also be weaned from his ventilator. It had taken two weeks with their names on the waiting list for a room to open up.

Moving to RMH still didn't feel like a step up. Celia had spent these last weeks longing to see Caleb out of the hospital, and was grateful to be leaving. But she wanted to be home. She felt as though she'd been holding her breath since Caleb collapsed, and until she had him home tucked in his own bed, she couldn't let go.

Worse was the prospect of facing other families. Of course the idea of Ronald McDonald House was to have a place more like home. Which meant a lot of other families would be there--all grappling with the same kinds of things they were. She didn't want to go through the pain of getting to know them. She didn't want her family to *be* one of them.

In the room, she busied herself unpacking their things and putting them away. She hadn't realized how few things they had with them until the few sweaters and pairs of pants sat lonely in the drawers. She'd have to ask Sarah to bring more clothes when she came next, especially when Caleb would be up and around a bit more.

With the effort of the move, Caleb was exhausted, and Celia had no interest in exploring the new surroundings. They ordered Chinese food delivery and sat in the room watching movies on Jeff's laptop when the phone rang.

Her mother's voice, bright and excessively chipper on the other end said, "I thought I would come to the city for a visit. Give you two a bit of a break."

"Oh? When?"

"How does tomorrow sound?"

* * *

By the next week, Caleb could spend four hours at a time off the ventilator. During those hours, Celia deflated the cuff, releasing the pressure against his vocal chords, and he could talk normally. Her mother arrived on Wednesday afternoon, put her luggage down in the room and looked at Celia and Jeff. "Now what?"

"I don't know." They'd been asking themselves the same thing every day since they'd been there, coming up empty.

"I have an idea." Adele sat down on the bed next to Caleb. "You have to fix your own meals here, right?"

"The kitchen's upstairs. I guess we should probably buy some groceries and stop eating take-out," Jeff said with a hopeful glance in Celia's direction.

"For tonight, why don't we order pizza? Grandma's treat." She rubbed Caleb's leg affectionately. "We'll stay here and wait for the delivery while you two go out and pick up a few groceries, so you'll have what you need for tomorrow. I brought a little care package in my suitcase too with some treats."

"Like what?" Caleb asked.

"A jar of Nutella, for one."

Celia opened her mouth to object. She'd barely let Caleb out of her sight for the last several weeks. She didn't want to leave him, but Jeff jumped at the offer. "Sounds great. We haven't seen the outside of the hospital for a long time."

He scooped up his car keys from the top of the dresser and winked at Caleb. "Don't eat the pizza without us."

* * *

"I'm glad your mom is here," Jeff buckled his seatbelt and adjusted his seat, even though he drove the car last. "It's good to get out. Did she say how long she'd stay?"

"It didn't come up." In truth, as much as Celia had missed her and was relieved to see her, she was afraid of what her mother might say if they had a chance to talk alone. She didn't want to hear a word about her father. She planned to use Jeff and Caleb as buffers against any deep discussion.

Jeff leaned forward over the steering wheel, and craned his neck to peer up through the windshield at the tall buildings. "Didn't there used to be a supermarket around here? Can you punch something in on the GPS and see what you come up with?" He did a U-turn in the middle of the street and sent Celia hard into the side of the car. He gave her a sideways glance. "Sorry. Must be slippery." They both knew that wasn't true. All evidence of the snowstorm that battered Toronto earlier this month had been erased by warmer temperatures. She didn't argue.

"In 300 meters, turn right," the GPS announced. Celia dug in her purse for her lipstick. She hadn't been in public for weeks, and hadn't worn any. She pulled out a piece of paper she didn't recognize and glanced over the handwritten words. It was the list Sarah had given her with links to alternative medicine websites. She stared at it. She'd completely forgotten the conversation, let alone the list Sarah had handed her. But if she planned to find a cure for Caleb, this might be the perfect starting place. Good old Sarah. Celia could kiss her.

Jeff put a hand on her leg and gave her a gentle squeeze. "So, if your mom's going to stay, what would you think if I went back to work?"

64

If she had taken a moment to think, she would have realized his suggestion was practical. She would have understood, perhaps, how agonizing it was for him to watch their son lie in his hospital bed, helpless to do anything about it. That going back to work would give him purpose, something to contribute to the family, to somehow make a difference in the events assaulting his family. But Celia didn't take a moment to think. Her head knew he didn't mean to abandon them, but her heart pricked with the pain of further loss.

They pulled into the supermarket parking lot and Jeff parked the car. He pulled the keys out of the ignition and turned toward her. "Hon? Did you hear me?"

"Back to work?" Her eyes filled with tears and her voice sounded high and thin. She cleared her throat. "Now?"

He searched her eyes. "Celia, I don't *want* to leave Caleb. I don't want to leave you. But I can't just stop working. We need the money. I thought with your mom here--"

"With my mom here, things get even more complicated." She made an effort to lower her tone. She took a deep breath. She didn't look forward to a conversation about her father.

She took his hand. "Having her here is not the same as having you here. Not to me, and not to Caleb. He's supposed to go into radiation a week from Monday. Couldn't you at least wait until then?"

"Okay, okay, I'll stay until he gets into the radiation routine." He squeezed her hand. "I'll stay, okay?"

She nodded. But it wasn't okay. None of this was okay. Maybe radiation wasn't okay. If another way existed to treat Caleb's cancer, she didn't have long to find it.

* * *

They decided to eat the pizza in the kitchen, up one floor. On their tour of the facilities, Celia hadn't taken note of the seating in the kitchen at The House. Everyone sat at one long, communal table. When they arrived, a dozen or so people laughed and talked around the table in the center of the kitchen. The area had the same playful patterns as their room, but instead of yellow and orange, the color scheme featured red, white and blue. Celia blinked at the brightness.

Caleb hesitated when he encountered the crowd of people--or did he simply pick up on Celia's hesitation? Jeff strode past her with the pizza

65

and greeted the people sitting around the table. She had flashbacks from her high school cafeteria. Only here, she had no desire to fit in.

A woman sitting at the table looked up at her and smiled. She stood up and began to clear enough space beside her for the four of them to pull up chairs on her left. On her right, a blonde-headed toddler in a highchair grinned to reveal two teeth. Something orange swished out around them--pureed peaches, perhaps.

"Hi. I was wondering when you folks were going to surface. You must be across the hall from me. Fourth floor, right? We're in room 406. I'm Leigh." She reached across the table to shake Celia's hand. Just in time, she spotted the orange substance on her thumb and the back of her hand, laughed, and swiped it with a napkin. She extended her hand again. "This is Emily." She said, pointing to the toddler. Leigh had pulled her fine light brown hair into a ponytail, but wispy pieces resisted capture and framed her face. Her nose and the corners of her eyes wrinkled when she smiled.

"And this is Michaela." Leigh motioned beyond Emily to a finely featured little girl wearing a faded sweatshirt and overalls. Celia's breath caught. Surely the child's little outfit would look no different hanging on a hanger in her closet than it did on her tiny body. She wore a red kerchief on her head, knotted at the nape of her neck. She shook Celia's hand, her smile as arresting as the dark circles under her eyes.

Celia nodded a greeting. "I'm Celia, and this is Caleb, my husband Jeff, and my mother, Adele."

"Nice to meet you all."

"Michaela," Leigh said, "I think Caleb must be about the same age as you. How old are you, Caleb?"

"Eight, but my birthday's next week."

"Well, congratulations." Leigh put down her fork. "We should have a celebration, huh, Michaela? We're great party-throwers."

Michaela nodded and smiled again. "I'm ten." The skin of her face looked grey, but her perfect lips were rose pink.

Leigh had sat down again. She swallowed hard on a forkful of frozen dinner lasagna. Still, she talked around a mouthful. "Do you know where everything is? Did you have a chance to get any food yet?" She swallowed again.

"Someone gave us the tour already. We bought pizza and bought a few groceries."

"Well, feel free to help yourself to anything I've got if you need to. We've got extra crackers and soup in cans, cereal and milk for breakfast, some eggs and bread and jam. No peanut butter, though, of course. Every family has a shelf, and there's a dry-erase marker so you can write your name on the little tab thingy on the edge of the shelf."

"Thank you." Celia smiled at Leigh and hoped no amateur psychologists were present to analyze her expression and judge her insincere.

"By the way, Celia, and--" She blushed. "Sorry, forgot your husband's name already."

"Jeff," he supplied.

"Let me introduce you to everyone else." She pointed at everyone, in turn. "The Coopers are down on the end--Doug and Michelle, and their son Andrew, and this is Rosa--Rosa, what's your last name?"

"Vieyra." She spoke quietly and her accent was warm and thick like sunshine.

"Right. Rosa has four daughters, Isabel, Anna, Nadia and Nuria--not necessarily in that order," Leigh giggled a little. "Over here is Margaret Powell and her sons Jacob and Nicholas."

Everyone smiled and welcomed them, and Celia excused herself to help Jeff who located napkins and plates and doled out slices. The seating plan trapped her. She longed for space, for distance, their own corner of the table.

Leigh shifted in her seat. "So Celia, where are you folks from?"

"Point-du-Fleuve. About a five hour drive from here, in the Ottawa Valley."

"Wow. It must be convenient to be so close," Leigh said. "We're from Berry Mill, just outside of Moncton."

Celia didn't know what to say. All she could think to ask were obvious questions, surely inappropriate, like what kind of cancer did Michaela have, or why were the rest of them there. And she didn't genuinely want to know the answers to any of those questions.

"How long are you here for?" she said, finally.

"A week and a half so far this time, eh, Michaela? We're going home next week, God willing." She plunged on, "Michaela's got a diffuse pontine brainstem glioma--a brain tumor. She was diagnosed July 18th."

Celia stared at Michaela and the realization struck her. "That's what they say Caleb has." She spoke without a filter. She hadn't wanted to share their story with these people. She shoved a piece of pizza in her mouth, as though she might stop the flow of words.

Leigh stared at her with a mouthful and a wrinkled brow. She glanced at Caleb and back at Celia again. She chewed slowly and said nothing.

Jeff sat down beside Celia, and set down two plates with the rest of the pizza. He slid one in front of himself and Celia, and another in front of Caleb and her mom.

"So are you going to Princess Hospital to make the mold for his radiation?"

"We don't have his schedule yet."

"Do you have plans tomorrow? Michaela's getting her radiation at 9:30. We could do something together afterwards."

Caleb, usually shy with girls his age, had shared a slice of pizza with Michaela, and the two laughed together over something she whispered in his ear. Something flew from his mouth across the table when he laughed.

"Caleb!"

Celia hadn't heard what Michaela said, but Leigh must have. "Michaela, that doesn't sound like table talk."

Michaela and Caleb giggled, and Caleb struggled to keep milk from spraying out of his mouth while he laughed. More laughter.

Leigh's sweetness wouldn't win her over. Celia didn't want to be her friend. Her thoughts flew to Point-du-Fleuve, the quiet comfort of their home, the river, the stand of trees behind their house. And Sarah and Justin, who planned to visit for Caleb's birthday. Celia mentally counted the sleeps until she hugged her friend and told her how much she missed her. She was happily uncomfortable in this world of cancer people and wanted to stay that way. They didn't belong.

Leigh rolled her eyes and chuckled. "Kids, eh? So, what do you say about tomorrow?"

"I'm sorry," she said. "Caleb's just gotten out of the hospital. He still needs to be on a ventilator most of the day. We're probably going to lay low for the day."

She finished the last bite of her pizza and glanced at Caleb's plate. The crusts of two slices sat discarded and shoved to the side. His appetite had improved, but dark circles under his eyes betrayed the façade of health.

Leigh leaned forward and adjusted her position in the seat, as though settling in to tell a long story, but Rosa turned and spoke. "Miss Celia? I think your boy is tired, no? You no worry about clean up. We take care of it. Go. Is right, Leigh?"

Celia opened her mouth to say she'd stay behind to clean up. Surely Rosa's interruption was too convenient an escape. Leigh just laughed.

"Oh you'll get used to me, Celia. I'm just a talkative old fool. You have to shut me up. I long ago forgot where the 'off' button is. Rosa's figured that out already, bless her. She's right. Go. Leave us to take care of these few dishes. Don't worry, we'll be seeing each other again. I'm just across the hall, remember? Room 406."

CHAPTER TWELVE

Alfie

After Adele left for the hospital, Alfie relished the quietness of the place, at first. He used the afternoon to do some odd jobs around the house. He tightened screws, replaced old hinges, fixed leaky faucets. Toward evening, tired of being cooped up inside, he decided to go for a walk. The weather was mild and clear, although snow must have fallen recently. Most of it had melted, but traces remained here and there in the areas the sun didn't reach.

The road leading in to the cottage went one way and ended abruptly ten properties down. Most of these cottages were winterized, but no one lived in them past September. A few families came for Thanksgiving and Christmas. Adele's cottage--their cottage--and one other were the only ones lived in year-round. Alfie headed toward the dead end. He looked for names he recognized on the mailboxes. Only two. And one of those cottages had a For Sale sign. He turned around and walked back to the cottage but wound around to the back. He intended to walk along the shore of the lake, until he saw the patio slab again.

A smile crept over his lips. He'd found the project to keep him busy until Adele came home. Back inside, he dug in his toolbox for his measuring tape, found a notepad and pencil and began preparations. He calculated the dimensions of the pad. He'd need two-by-fours for the frame, some concrete mix. Excitement built inside him. This would be the perfect surprise when she returned.

* * *

At the lumberyard, Alfie wandered the wide aisles and tipped his head back to look up to the tops of the stacks. He'd seen these big box stores going up all over the place, of course, but he'd never gone inside. Most of the time, he hadn't minded being a person of no fixed address, worn his footloose lifestyle like a badge, in fact. No one could pin him down. He was his own man.

Once, in South Carolina, a woman he'd been seeing asked him to fix her leaky faucet. She drove him around town and pulled her car up to a place like this, but he refused to go inside. Poor woman was dumbfounded when he told her.

"What do you mean you've never been inside a store like this? I thought all men liked this sort of thing."

"I didn't say I didn't like it," he said, "but I ain't goin' in."

He finally convinced her she could manage on her own, and she emerged victorious, elated with herself.

"Thank you," she said.

"What for?"

"For showing me I could handle things myself. My ex-husband always took care of those sorts of jobs. Thank you for forcing me to be independent." She squeezed his leg.

Alfie took the compliment. He never acknowledged that wasn't the reason for his refusal--nothing like it. As a matter of fact, he probably wouldn't have been able to put a finger on it then, but he knew now, walking up and down these aisles for the first time. Walking into a store like this would have reminded him he had no home. True, most of the time, he took pride in the fact. But the reason he never settled down anywhere was because he already had a home. Right here with Adele, where he was meant to be all along.

He pulled the small pad out of his back pocket and squinted at the numbers he'd scribbled in pencil this morning. Where on earth would he find these things here? Whatever happened to the corner hardware store? He'd driven down the main street looking for the place he remembered. This end of town hadn't even existed when they used to come out to the cottage on the lake. He didn't even remember the proper name of the store that used to sit on the corner of Main and William, across from the old Regent Theater. No one likely did. Everyone always referred to the place as MacGregor's, after the spry little gray-haired owner. Was he still around? He'd be ancient now.

71

A kid in an orange apron stepped up, "Can I help you with anything, sir?"

"Does Gil MacGregor still live around here, do you know?" he said, "Course he'd be retired--maybe dead." He mumbled the latter part, mostly to himself.

"Sorry sir?"

"Guy who owned the other hardware store. The one in town."

"What other hardware store?"

Alfie looked the kid up and down. "Nevermind." This young guy probably wasn't even born back then.

He stared at Alfie. "What about that list. Need help with anything on it?"

"Right. Yeah. I'm going to need some bags of concrete, some two by fours, two by sixes, some sand, some gravel--"

"What is it you're working on?"

"I'm repairing a patio slab. Eventually, I wanna build an addition on it." Alfie scanned the list. "I'll need some wire mesh, too."

"You know, the store offers a contracting department. They'll do the work for you."

Alfie looked at the name sewn onto the kid's orange apron in embroidered letters: *Shawn.* He eyed Alfie skeptically, probably figuring he was too old for the work. But this was something Alfie wanted to do himself. "That's okay. I can handle it. It's a repair job."

Why had he offered the additional information?

"That can be trickier than laying down a foundation the first time," Shawn said.

"I know," Alfie said. "But foundations are important. I'm going to fix it right."

"All right then, sir. Good enough. You're gonna need a flat cart for all your stuff. I'll go get you one." The kid turned and jogged down the wide aisle.

Alfie watched him and smiled. He would get it right this time.

* * *

"Hey, stranger!"

Alfie was bent over, searching for a tool in his toolbox. He jumped and almost knocked his head on the two by six on the workhorse.

He rose to the sight of a woman, her flowing skirt brushing the grass on the bank as she walked down the slope toward the beach. She was slender, with the body of a dancer and a sharp, angled face to match. Her hair trailed long and straight down her back past where the skirt began.

"Hello?" he reached for a rag and wiped his hands, trying to decide why the face looked familiar.

"Mr. Hanson," the woman pouted. "You don't remember me?"

He'd been alone for days, his only company the ring of his hammer across the smooth surface of the lake, each strike a word in a love letter to Adele. He worked all morning in a private race against the big clouds rolling in. The lake was gray and impatient. Round waves rolled in with great bravado, but lost steam before they washed up on the shore. Maybe the storm would blow over. Maybe not. He wanted to get as far along as possible with the construction of the frame for the roof. At the very least, he could throw a tarp over everything, if the frame were up.

He'd been at it morning 'til evening. First he'd worked on the cement slab. He marked off the area with pegs and string. He'd decided to enlarge the plan from the original--he had more money to work with now than all those years ago. He had to do a little digging to lay down the gravel in the new sections. The temperatures had cooperated, though. It would have been rough going had the ground been harder.

Next he laid the gravel. Later, he had to run into town and rent a mixer. There was no way to drive a truck down to the lake side of the cottage, so he had to mix his own concrete. A bit more work, but the results were satisfying: the slab lay down smooth and unbroken.

Late last night, he'd sat up and sketched out the plan that had been forming in his mind, to the dimensions of the new slab. His little blueprint lay on a table he'd pulled out here from the workshop he used to keep in the basement.

Now here stood this woman--this woman he was sure he should recognize. She was probably about Celia's age. She'd called him "Mister--"

"Mr. Hanson," she said again. "It's--"

"Sarah! Of course." He stretched out open arms.

His embrace went unfulfilled, for streaking toward the water came a chocolate Lab. Behind him, a boy in a baseball cap shouted madly at the dog, oblivious to either adult.

Alfie opened his mouth to speak to the boy, most likely some neighbor's child who'd wandered off the main road, but he smiled as he realized the truth. "Your boy?"

"Yes, that's Justin. And Caleb's dog, Hershey, who's obviously glad to be back here." Laughter bubbled up from her, free and easy.

Caleb's dog. He smiled and watched with appreciation as Hershey romped.

"He needs to do his business, Justin. Did you bring a plastic bag?"

He still had an image, warm and alive, of Celia and her sitting on his lap. She'd seemed to eat up his affection, like some emotional orphan. He figured it was because her father, a colonel in the Canadian army, was often absent, and when he was home--well, things weren't much better. Sadness rolled over him, like the steady waves of the lake. Had Celia become like Sarah in his own absence?

"How did you know I was here?"

"Celia told me. She still tells me everything."

"Do I want to know how she sounded when she told you?"

Sarah smiled. "No, you don't."

"You're all grown up." He laughed. "You can probably call me Alfie now--not Mr. Hanson."

"Didn't I turn out good?" She did a little turn for his inspection. "You look just the same. And, *Mister* Hanson, old habits die hard."

She glanced at the sunroom, as though she noticed all the lumber, concrete and tools scattered on the ground for the first time. "You've been busy. Just look at this. An addition?"

"A sunroom," he said. "Like I always promised Adele."

"Are these all going to be windows?" She peered at the plan and pointed at the openings he'd drawn all around the room. "Wow. What does Adele think?"

"She doesn't know," Alfie smiled. He couldn't hide his pride over this. He knew Adele was going to love his work, but a second opinion didn't hurt.

Sarah stepped beside him, stood back, her hands on her hips. "Now *this* is romantic," she said.

"Thanks," he said. "I'm glad you approve." He gave her that hug now--not quite like hugging his own daughter again after all the years, but a taste of coming home, nonetheless.

"It's been too long," she said.

"You're absolutely right."

Justin stood beside them now, and the dog, wet and panting, sat next to him in the sand.

"Nice to meet you, young man. I'm--" Alfie faltered and cleared his throat.

"Mr. Hanson. He's Caleb's grandfather," Sarah finished.

Justin's eyes widened. "Cool," he said. "I didn't know Caleb had a grandpa."

Alfie smiled despite the pain that shot through his heart. He'd have a lot of that to face, but at least he knew the boy hadn't intended the hurt his words inflicted. He looked the boy over. He was sandy-haired and full of eagerness for life and trouble, just like he ought to be. "You must be about the same age as Caleb."

"I'm five months older."

Alfie suppressed a chuckle.

"The two of them are as inseparable as Celia and I were." Sarah grabbed the bill of his cap and pushed it down over his eyes.

"Mo-om," Justin complained. He shoved the cap back into place, leaned down, picked up a stick and threw it for Hershey to fetch.

"Actually," she said, and turned back from watching Justin to face Alfie, "that's kind of why we came."

Alfie raised an eyebrow.

"We want to go visit Celia and Caleb, but we've been babysitting Hershey here, and with Dan working so many hours at the store, I don't think it's fair to leave him all alone. I was wondering if you'd mind--" Her voice trailed off, and for the first time, her graceful body seemed awkward. "I probably should've called about this before I drove all this way, but I felt weird just picking up the phone and calling you after all this time--"

"And asking if I'll watch Caleb's dog at this house by the lake that he probably knows as well as the one in Point-du-Fleuve?" Alfie smiled. "My pleasure."

He bent down and patted the thighs of his faded jeans, frosted with sawdust, and whistled. Hershey raised his head and started a gallop toward him. "We'll get along just fine, won't we, Hershey?" he said, and scratched the dog behind his ears.

Hershey wagged his tail, and Alfie smiled up at Sarah. "You bring me some food and a bowl?"

"Food, a bowl, a leash, toys and treats in the car."

Justin had been running up and down the beach dragging the stick in the sand. He sprinted up to Sarah now. "Can I take out the canoe?"

"By yourself?" Sarah's nose wrinkled.

"I'll stay close to the shore. I promise."

"The water's probably kind of cold by now, buddy."

"That's okay. I'll be careful. I'll just do little circles close to shore."

"Is that okay with you?" Sarah smiled at Alfie.

He nodded. "Fine with me, as long as you're not in a hurry."

"Actually, there's something I'd like to talk to you about." She leaned close, as though she intended to start into the matter right there and then.

"Tell you what. You go get the dog's stuff. I'll help Justin get the canoe from the boathouse," Alfie said. "If you don't mind my working while you talk, I can get you a lawn chair so you can keep an eye out while Justin putters around in the canoe."

Sarah started up the slope toward the front of the house and her car while Alfie and Justin walked along the beach toward the boathouse. 'Boathouse' was a swanky word for the little shack shared by all the owners of the cottages this side of the main road. They each kept a key, and each owner had one spot to store a canoe or kayak. One family kept a paddleboat as well. The boathouse stood at the end of the row of cottages closest to the main road, three properties down.

Justin kicked at the sand with his shoes. "So how come Caleb never told me about you?"

"Well, Justin, that's a very good question." One he'd rather not answer. It did come down to this, though. He was done skirting responsibility. Time to own up. "Maybe it was because he wasn't very proud of me, or maybe because he didn't know a lot about me. I've been gone a long time. I've never even met Caleb."

"Oh," Justin said, his voice barely above a whisper, and he was silent until they'd passed the first property. "You're back now though, right?"

"I'm back now."

Justin flashed a smile and slipped his hand into Alfie's, and warmth slid over him like a blanket. If he had the chance to get this close to Caleb, he only hoped acceptance would be as freely given.

* * *

"I want to get the patio slab covered over before the rain comes--if it comes." Alfie picked up a two by four, laid it across the sawhorse and attacked with his saw.

"That's okay," Sarah shouted over the noise. Her forehead wrinkled as she glanced at the sky. "Looks to me like the weather might miss you, though." She settled into the lawn chair with one of Adele's old quilts thrown over her lap. As long as a body kept moving, the weather was pleasant enough for a fall day, but a damp chill filled the air. Sarah had rummaged through the chest in the house for some extra insulation besides the light jacket she wore. She sat outside the new sunroom so she could talk to Alfie and keep an eye on Justin at the same time.

"When is Celia expecting you?"

"She's not, really--not now, anyway. We thought we'd surprise her and Caleb. I pulled Justin out of school for a couple of days. He's been lost without his best friend."

"Even with Hershey to keep him company?" Alfie nodded his head at the dog. He had paced up and down along the beach barking at the canoe, and finally plunged in the water and swam alongside it.

"What do you know about cancer treatment?" Sarah leaned forward in the chair and lowered her voice as though Justin, out on the lake, laughing at the dog, might hear her.

Alfie put down his hammer and hung through the frame of a window. "A little. I had a bit of a brush with prostate cancer not too long ago--part of the story of what brought me home."

"What about radiation and chemotherapy?"

"I was fortunate not to need to find out about any of that. Had some great doctors. They caught it early."

Sarah stared out at the lake, her shoulders hunched. "I realize he's not my child. But I don't think radiation and chemo are the answer."

"What else is there?"

"Alternative medicine."

Oh boy. Had Sarah turned into one of those hippie health nuts? He raised an eyebrow. "Alternative medicine?"

Sarah plunged on. "Yes. Special diets, certain kinds of supplements, lots of vegetables. Most of the therapies are actually quite simple."

77

Alfie picked up his hammer again, afraid if he kept looking at Sarah while they talked, he would find it hard not to laugh. "So you're telling me vegetables can cure cancer."

"Well, you've heard they prevent cancer, haven't you?" she said. "Of course, for aggressive cancers, other therapies have to be added to the program, to help the body catch up."

Silence fell between them. Alfie straightened and stared out at Justin still doing circles in the canoe. Caleb should be with his friend. Not in a hospital. But would that ever happen, even if Caleb followed all the doctors' instructions? His grandson was dealing with Goliath here, and he was only a little boy.

"You don't believe me," Sarah said.

Alfie put down the hammer again, and faced Sarah. "You understand how it sounds, right? People have been trying to cure cancer for years. If there was really a cure, we'd all know about it, wouldn't we?"

Sarah sat forward in her chair. The quilt slid to the ground, and Alfie bent down and picked it up, but she folded it up and tucked it beside her. "The point is, all traditional cancer treatments--radiation and chemotherapy--can do is kill cells. Not just cancer cells, *any* cells, indiscriminately. I've been reading up on this. Brain cancer is the hardest for traditional approaches to cure because the blood-brain barrier tries to protect the brain, and won't deliver the medicines where they'll actually do something for the patient."

Sarah lowered her head and when she raised it again, her eyes were misty. "The thing is, he's not my kid. But if he were, this is what I'd do. I love that boy like my own. He's practically Justin's brother."

Alfie took her hand in his. "He's not my child, either, Sarah. You're going to have to talk to Celia about these things."

"I know." She smiled. "I was hoping someone else would be in my corner. And maybe I needed to rehearse a bit, too."

"Me? You want me in your corner? What good would that do? No one's listening to me." Fresh pain rolled over him. Would he ever get close enough to matter to Celia? Or Caleb?

"You can be a pretty persuasive guy, as I remember things. You got me to go white water rafting with your family when I was a kid, remember? You're the one who turned me into an adventure junkie."

He laughed as memories flooded back. "Sarah Sparkle."

Now it was Sarah's turn to laugh. "I haven't heard that nickname since I was a kid. Since--"

"Since I left. I know." Alfie stared out at the lake at Justin, who was bringing the canoe back to shore now. "You're still going to need an answer to that question I asked you."

"What question?"

"Why, if there's really a cure for cancer, no one knows about it."

"Two words," Sarah said, holding up her fingers. "Pharmaceutical companies."

Alfie put his head down and pretended to focus on measuring the length off on another two by four. A real live conspiracy theorist. He smiled up at Sarah again, and took in the woman she'd become--full of opinions and idiosyncrasies. And Justin over her shoulder, who had pulled the canoe up on to the shore and now raced with Hershey in the sand. Celia had good people in her life. Would she make room for him?

CHAPTER THIRTEEN

Celia

When Celia was a little girl, about a year or so after her father left, a recurring dream began to plague her. It always started with her walking down a dimly lit hallway. She felt a sense of urgency, as though hurrying to something, or away from something--she was never sure which. In the dream, the whole thing seemed to be connected to her father. She had the sense that if she performed some task correctly, she would find him. Or perhaps, if she did everything right, he would come back, of his own accord.

The hallway was long, and she could barely see a foot or two in front of her. Objects ahead were gray and blurred. She ran her fingers along the wall as she walked, searching for light switches. Although she found several, none of them worked. She flipped them on and off, always in vain.

Finally, she came to a corner where the hallway turned left. That second corridor stretched long and gloomy ahead of her. She couldn't see the end. Doors lined both sides. Somehow, she knew, she must choose the right one. She started to run, stopping to try each handle in turn, becoming more frantic with each locked door. She never managed to find the right one before she woke.

As she lay in bed the morning of their third day at The House, the memory of that dream floated back to her, although years had gone by since she'd thought of it. Had she dreamt it again the night before?

She had stopped marking days by the calendar. She counted them from events. Thirty-two days since Caleb had collapsed, eighteen since

80

his trach surgery, three since they had moved to Ronald McDonald House. She didn't know how to count forward. How many days until they were home?

Today was patient education day. At ten in the morning, she and Jeff delivered Caleb to his Child Life Specialist--a young woman named Katie, who, as Caleb said later, wore "normal clothes." She was the same Child Life Specialist who had come to Caleb's room to explain the tracheostomy to him. She smiled and welcomed him to a room full of toys and games. Children's drawings and paintings covered the walls.

"You can stay in the hallway and watch through the window for a few minutes, if you want, to make sure he's comfortable," Katie said. "But it's better if you don't come in the room"

Jeff raised an eyebrow.

"Your son's going to be engaging in play therapy. We can build trust more quickly if parents are out of the room." She smiled. "We'll answer any questions he has about his treatment so far, and afterward you're welcome to ask anything you like about his experience here."

Jeff squeezed Celia's hand as they walked down the hall to their appointment with the Clinical Educator. Aside from the time they ran out for groceries and left Caleb with Celia's mom, this was the first time they had left him in someone else's care since their arrival at the hospital. The first time they'd been alone.

"So where do you want to go now?" Jeff tugged playfully as he held her hand. "What do you say to lunch at the Plaza?"

She said nothing.

The Clinical Educator introduced herself as Marnie Helm. They met in her office, a homey room with a corner window and a soft leather sofa and armchair. She offered cups of coffee. Celia refused; Jeff asked for his black. She set a mug down in front of him and then handed them a large binder.

"This is yours to keep," she said, smiling. "There is a lot of information in here. We'll talk about some today, but you'll want to read through this and make notes of any questions you might have."

Jeff opened the binder over both their laps, and Celia glanced through the pages. Dividers marked sections for condition, radiation, chemotherapy, home care, blood counts, clinical trials, resources and support. An overwhelming array of terms like anti-metabolites, nitrosureas, hyperpigmentation filled the pages.

"What's wrong?" Jeff said to her, and she realized she was shaking her head.

"Nothing," she said. "Go on."

"Today is likely going to be overwhelming." Marnie smiled sympathetically. She wore normal clothes too, her long, dark brown hair pulled into a clip at the back. "I can't stress enough how important it will be to keep a notebook throughout this process and write down all your questions. You'll find it especially helpful for when you get a chance to speak to the doctor about your son's condition."

Celia glanced up at the wall at the framed diplomas--one for nursing and one for a master's degree in clinical education. When did Marnie Helm decide this was her calling in life? Who would want the job of speaking to parents about their children's illnesses?

"You'll notice two of the tabs are for home care and blood counts," she said. "Those two sections contain a lot of specialized information you'll need to know when you take Caleb home. Things like what to do about pets, how much activity your son can engage in, when and why to be concerned about infection, how to know when to call the doctor."

Things Celia had no idea about. She had pictured home as a haven. She hadn't thought about it being a threat. Her stomach felt rotten, as though she were the one who had drunk the coffee.

"All that information is in the binder?" Jeff asked.

"Yes, but you may also want to sign up for one of the classes in the Resource Room. We have classes specifically addressing many of these areas." She smiled again and tilted her head to one side. "So, unless you have some specific questions, I'll give you Caleb's treatment schedule, and we'll talk about the next couple of weeks."

She passed them several pieces of paper. "You'll start Monday by getting Caleb fitted for a mask that will help to deliver the radiation to the correct part of his brain. The fitting will be done at Princess Hospital with a specialist called a dosimetrist. Princess Hospital has all the special equipment necessary for the fitting. They're just down the street. The second sheet I handed you is a map of the area with Princess Hospital marked on it."

Jeff rifled through the sheets and Celia pulled the binder into her lap and flipped open to the tab labeled "chemotherapy." She found the section about side effects and glanced over the list: fatigue, diarrhea, constipation, headaches, hair loss, skin reactions, nausea and vomiting, mouth sores, low blood counts, mood changes, inflammation, cognitive dysfunction.

How did they get here? How could this be her son's future?

"I have a question," she said.

"Of course." Marnie smiled.

"If Caleb receives chemotherapy and radiation treatment, what is the prognosis?"

Marnie's mouth made a thin line. "Most patients live a year. In rare cases, some live two."

In two years, Caleb wouldn't yet be eleven.

"And without treatment?"

Marnie Helm raised her eyebrows. "A few months, likely," she said. "There are no guarantees, unfortunately. Caleb has an extremely aggressive form of cancer, as I'm sure the doctors told you."

"These side effects?" Celia tapped the binder. "Some of them seem serious."

"Every case is different." Marnie hesitated. "But it's true some of the side effects of treatment can be uncomfortable and distressing."

The dim hallway again. The rows of doors. Celia was running.

* * *

Whoever designed Children's Hospital obviously did so with one goal in mind: make the place appear as much like a playground as possible, while still allowing it to function as the farthest thing from it. This design appeared to have the desired effect on the intended audience. Caleb, and every other child Celia had met there, seemed buoyed by the bright atmosphere. The place had the opposite effect on her. The décor was too obvious, like the friend who searched too hard for the right thing to say in the face of bad news.

Princess Hospital, by contrast, was downright antiseptic, although nurses had begun to decorate for the holidays. Nurses' stations had tacky little metallic banners and streamers, and miniature Christmas trees perched between stacks of medical charts.

With each step toward the radiology department, Celia found herself wishing for a moment to talk to Jeff alone. A horrible anticipation of what they were about to do gripped her, as though this first step was the trickle that would unleash a flood of waters waiting behind a dam.

Although Marnie Helm had told them a little about the procedure, before long a nurse and the dosimetrist sat them all down to explain more about the fitting. The dosimetrist put the chart down and faced them, his hands resting on his thighs, his heels hooked on the bottom rungs of the stool he sat on.

"Okay Caleb. I'm Dr. Jake. We're going to do two things today. We're going to put you on the table over there." He motioned across the room. "After that, we're going to take a CT scan to figure out exactly where the radiation beams should go to do the most good.

"The next thing we're going to do is make some marks on you called tattoos. Not the tattoos your mom says you can't have." Caleb grinned. "These will be little Xs on your body to tell the doctors exactly where to aim the radiation beams for the treatments."

"Will it hurt?"

"You might feel a little pinch when we make the tattoo, but the first part we just do with a permanent marker. That won't hurt. Sound okay?"

"Mmm-hmm."

"Then we'll make a mask. Have you ever made something with papier maché at school?"

"Not at school. We made a piñata at camp last summer."

"Oh yeah? What did you make?"

"A donkey."

"Well, good. That's kind of like what we're going to do this morning. But instead of a donkey, we'll be making a mask of your face. That way, when we give you the treatments later on, we'll have a perfect match of your face. It's the best way we've found to deliver the radiation to the area where the tumor is."

Caleb nodded, and Dr. Jake continued, "We're going to use a kind of plastic material. It has to go right on your face, so you need to be really still." At the mention of stillness, Caleb began to squirm.

"We can give you some medicine in a needle to help you to sleep right through the whole thing, if you think you won't be able to stay still. It's a little bit like what they gave you when you had your surgery."

The doctor glanced at Celia and Jeff out of the corner of his eye and returned his gaze to Caleb. "We can do this either way. Doesn't matter to me which way you want to go, but once we get started, we really can't stop until it's finished. If we don't use the medicine, you do have to promise to stay completely still."

Dr. Jake seemed to search Caleb's face for comprehension or signs of anxiety. "It's going to feel a bit like a warm washcloth is being smoothed out over your face, and it won't take long at all."

"But how will I breathe?"

"That's a good question." He smiled. "We'll put something like a straw in your mouth that you'll be able to breathe through."

Celia finally asked the question that had been burning in her since they'd arrived. "Can we stay?"

"No, I'm afraid not. The waiting room is just outside these doors, though, and the procedure from here on out will take less than an hour." He paused for a moment to make eye contact with each of them. "I'll give you all a moment to talk about things, and we'll get started when you're ready."

"What do you want to do, Champ?" Jeff said. Anxiety rose up in Celia's gut. Don't call him 'Champ.' It was like asking him to rise to the challenge.

Caleb didn't hesitate. "I don't want the needle."

"You're sure, sweetie?" She wanted to reach out and cradle him in her arms the way she had when he was a baby. Her arms ached with the wanting. "Whatever decision you make, Daddy and I--"

"I'm sure."

She stole a glance at Jeff, who was smiling proudly at Caleb. "Okay."

The memory of another table and another doctor rushed back to her. When Caleb was an infant, they decided to have him circumcised, and she thought she couldn't watch. Jeff went in the room with the doctor, and she stood outside. At the first cry from Caleb, she couldn't stand the separation, and burst into the room. She was still unable to watch--she stood behind the doctor during the procedure. When the doctor was done, she swept her baby up and nursed him to soothe his pain.

She stared at Caleb. His arms were crossed and his face betrayed no fear. How did her son become so brave? When did he become so old?

Jeff caught her eye and his brow furrowed. He nodded in Caleb's direction, and she realized tears were welling up in her eyes. She reached up and quickly brushed them away, forcing a smile.

Dr. Jake returned and began his preparations, and the nurse opened the door for them, nodding in the direction of the outer offices. "It won't take long," she said, smiling sweetly. Caleb didn't make eye contact with Jeff or Celia as they left.

She sat down in the waiting room with Jeff, who immediately began shuffling through magazines.

"What are you doing?"

"I was going to read *Scientific American*." He settled down in the chair.

"I know, but--"

"He's going to be fine, hon. I trust the doctor, don't you? And you saw how brave Caleb was."

"How can you just read?"

"Listen, Cel. It's all I can do not to think about what's going on."

She stood. She needed to move.

"Where are you going?"

"I'm just going to look around."

"At what?" He was right. The room was filled with nothing but chairs and people. Some toddlers played in a large area between the chairs inside a little plastic house. The entire waiting room ran a semi-circle around the atrium that was the center feature of the whole hospital. On sunny days, the light would pour into every floor--even here, one floor below the main level. But today's overcast skies allowed in little light to cheer the place.

"I don't know. I'll go find a magazine or something."

Jeff picked up two or three magazines and held them up to her, but she shook her head and walked away, launching her tour of the floor. The waiting room, the atrium, the restrooms, the elevator and the CT Simulator area, and she'd seen the entire thing. She walked to the area behind where Jeff still sat staring at his magazine, and climbed the stairs to the main floor. At least she could get a coffee or tea and keep her hands busy with something while she waited. She'd get Jeff one too.

She walked toward the aroma of coffee and passed a long wall where contractors were working. One by one, they peeled away the plastic protection from gold letters mounted on the wall and buffed them. Celia stopped to read the inscription:

I will remember there is art to medicine
as well as science,
and that warmth, sympathy and understanding

86

may outweigh the surgeon's knife
or the chemist's drug.
- Excerpt from the Physician's Oath

Her eyes blurred with tears as she saw herself standing in another doctor's office more than ten years earlier. Only a week had passed since severe cramping and bleeding sent her to the emergency room. She refused the dilation and curettage, perhaps in some vain hope that despite what the doctor said, life still fought to hold on inside her. Or perhaps simply because it felt wrong to have them clean her out, as though they were removing so much trash. If her baby couldn't live inside her body, let nature take its course. She didn't want to force something to happen. She supposed that was the same reason she couldn't quite bring herself to consider artificial insemination, even though it was the fifth miscarriage.

The visit to the doctor's office was more or less a formality. The third time, he'd given her all the statistics and laid all the choices before her. She already knew that after three miscarriages, her chances of carrying a baby to term were less than 50 percent. If statistics existed beyond the third miscarriage, no one told her about them. They had been through all the tests--for chromosomal abnormalities, structural problems of the uterus, infection, hormonal imbalances. They were handed another statistic: in 30 percent of cases, medicine cannot discover the reason why a couple is unable to conceive.

Nevertheless, she stood in her gynecologist's office that day, waiting for him to come and tell her what she knew already. He was running late, and she'd already studied his diplomas and the collage of patients' photos. Each picture displayed a couple in hospital gowns, husbands wearing masks pushed over their heads or dangling around their necks. They all held squealing pink babies and the sweat of pride and exhaustion gleamed on their bright faces. An ache stabbed in a place she didn't know how to identify--a place deeper than her womb--a chasm of need so profound, its hollowness had begun to swallow her up. Finally she looked at the doctor's family photos and read a plaque on his wall, an engraving in marble of the Physician's Oath.

When the doctor entered the room, she still stood reading the plaque. "It doesn't say, 'First do no harm,'" she said.

"What's that?" Dr. Morgan looked up from the stack of papers in his hands and peered at her over the rim of his glasses.

"The oath here," she said, and pointed at the plaque. "I always thought this said, 'First do no harm.'"

"Oh yes, that. Well, a patient gave it to me. Actually we all swear different oaths. Usually depends on the college you attend. You're thinking of the Hippocratic Oath, but even that doesn't say, 'First do no harm.' That's a quote from another manuscript written by Hippocrates. Common misconception," he said. "Now take a seat. Let's look at these results, shall we?"

She obeyed and tried to appear as though she were paying attention, but the truth was, more than a fetus died inside her during the last miscarriage. She and Jeff stopped trying after that. Caleb was a wonderful miracle who happened all on his own, without any effort, the following year.

All those years ago, she hadn't really paid attention to what Dr. Morgan said. But now, as she stood in front of the bright letters the contractors unveiled one by one for an audience they weren't even aware of, the thought sank in. "It doesn't say, 'First do no harm,'" she said aloud, to no one.

She thought of the list of side effects of the cancer treatments-- everything from nausea to cognitive damage. The doctors weren't proposing to heal her son. They weren't even promising not to harm him. She refused to sit back and just watch him waste away, robbed of life by something she couldn't put her hands on, something killing him from the inside out. But she didn't want to be the one to sign off on causing him pain, either. There had to be some other way.

The contractors stood back from their finished job, noticed her and smiled. She managed something she hoped passed for a smile in return and turned again in the direction of the coffee shop.

When she arrived back at the waiting room, Jeff sat in the same posture, reading *Scientific American*. He slapped the magazine shut and tossed it on the table when he saw her.

"I've read the same paragraph at least ten times." He accepted the cup with a long sigh. "Just what I needed."

He took a long sip, and settled back in his chair. She wanted to blurt everything out--how she was uncertain about radiation and chemotherapy. That she didn't know if she could watch their son face the side effects of those medications, know they were sending beams of radiation to his brain, giving him drugs to kill him cell by cell. She thought of poor Michaela from The House and all of the other kids she'd seen there, small shadows of the children they should be. Was it fair to put them through this treatment on the chance of extending their lives an extra six months or a year? There must be another way. But Jeff, who always knew what to do, who depended on scientific fact, who always took the next logical step without hesitation, would not be thinking the same things. They were worlds apart, and she didn't know how to speak his language.

A door swung open and a nurse leaned out and scanned the room, "Mr. and Mrs. Bennett?"

They stood.

The nurse smiled. "We're all done now. You can come in."

Caleb was dressed, and just coming out of a small restroom, his face scrubbed red, and the hair around his face wet and sticky-looking. Celia kissed his face and smoothed his hair.

He squirmed and glanced over his shoulder in the direction of the doctor. "Mom," he whispered.

"Sorry."

"So how was it, Champ?"

"Pretty cool, I guess," he said. "Dr. Jake said after the treatments are all done, I can keep my mask and paint it or do whatever I want with it."

Like burn it.

"They're going to attach the mask to the table for my treatments."

"The clinical educator gave us some information on Friday," she said. "If you want, we can read it back in our room."

Jeff winked at Caleb. "How about we stop for a banana split first?"

Celia scowled at Jeff. With Caleb still recovering and the cold weather outside, he wanted to go buy ice cream?

"What?" He shrugged. "I found some touristy information in the room. There's supposed to be a great little ice cream shop a block away. You can walk that far if we go slowly, can't you, Champ?"

Though she had been doubtful, Celia had to admit the ice cream shop turned out to be a wonderful idea. The ice cream was homemade and the smell of waffle cones lured in unsuspecting passersby from the street. For a few brief sunny moments they were a normal family again, at a

89

restaurant, enjoying a treat. Caleb ordered first. He chose a double scoop of chocolate and strawberry the strawberry on top, and just started in on the chocolate scoop when her cell phone rang.

Celia's mother had waited back at the room for them. "Are you coming back soon?" she said.

"Sorry I didn't call when we got out. Jeff took us out for ice cream."

Jeff assumed an expression of mock innocence and pointed at Caleb, a smirk on his face. Caleb grinned up at him and swatted his hand away.

"You getting lonely?" Celia asked.

She hesitated. "How soon can you make your way back here?"

* * *

Her mom was not a good liar. When Celia asked her why she wanted them back at The House, Adele dodged the question, said she had to go, and hung up. Something unusual was going on.

Celia understood the reason for her secrecy as soon as they walked through the door of their room. Adele sat in the armchair by the window, Sarah sat in the chair across from her, and Justin had already found one of Caleb's video games. He lay on his stomach on Caleb's bed, fingers moving furiously, mumbling to himself.

Before Celia could react, Caleb pounced on the bed and shouted, "Justin!"

Relief washed over her as Caleb transformed before her into just Caleb again. She giggled and hugged Sarah.

"I wouldn't let your mom tell you we were here," she said. "Surprised?"

"No, actually. This is just like you." Celia smiled. "And my mom's a lousy liar."

Adele straightened in mock indignation. "I take that as a compliment."

Sarah laughed, full and loud. "You should."

"Hey, wait a minute," Jeff said. "Shouldn't Justin be in school?"

"Oh well. Some things are more important than school." She squeezed Celia in a hug again.

On the bed, Caleb bent his head and Justin parted the hair to examine his surgery scar. "Cool."

"Hey, if you're here, who's taking care of Hershey?" Caleb asked.

"Your grandpa." Justin said.

"Who?"

Sarah stepped forward. "Oh don't worry, Caleb. We've got someone taking care of him who really loves dogs. We won't be here long. Like your mom said, Justin should be in school now, so we can't stay forever."

She turned and beckoned Justin. "Buddy, wanna come help me get those things we brought for Caleb? We left them in the car."

Celia followed Sarah into the hallway. She hadn't even opened her mouth when she said, "Listen, sorry Celia. We just decided on this last-minute and I wanted someone to take good care of Hershey. With Dan at the shop all day--"

Celia didn't know how to respond. An odd mix of emotions fought within her: surprise and anger. And horror--because she also felt jealousy. Although she never wanted to see her father again, and had been uncomfortable in his presence, Sarah had somehow resumed the trusted relationship she shared with him when she was girl.

Why was everything in her life so wildly out of control?

"I'm sorry," Sarah said, "I should have asked, but that would have spoiled the surprise. You know how I am about surprises." She smiled in apology and drew Celia into her arms.

Tears came easily. "I'm sorry too," Celia mumbled.

Sarah stood back, "What for?"

She laughed, through her tears. "I don't know. For being angry." She wiped her face.

"I honestly do have something out in the car for Caleb," Sarah said. "I didn't want to drag it up here in case we couldn't find you guys."

"Okay." Celia hesitated. "I need to talk to you."

"Definitely. I want to talk to you, too. And I guess you have some damage control to do." Sarah's gaze travelled over Celia's shoulder to the door of their room.

"Maybe," she said. "Maybe he missed it." She hoped so. Her mother wouldn't say anything to Caleb about her father, but her recently proven reputation for being incapable of concealing the truth made Celia uneasy.

She needn't have worried. Sarah's plan of distraction worked. When she returned to the room, she carried a huge cardboard box and set it on the bed in front of Caleb.

"What's this?"

"A box," Justin said.

"Duh." Caleb elbowed Justin and made a face. "Homework?"

"Well, yeah, some of it is, but open and see."

Caleb hesitated, but Justin grabbed Sarah's bulky ring of keys, poked the tape that sealed the top and began to run a key down the length of the box. Caleb grabbed the keys from him and finished the job. He opened the lid and Justin grabbed the box and tipped the contents all over the bed. Dozens of envelopes spilled in all directions. Caleb looked at Justin, his eyebrows raised.

"Open them and read them."

Caleb picked one up and tore open the seal. "It's from Nathan," he said. Nathan was a classmate of the boys' and played on their soccer team. He smiled as he read, then put the letter aside and opened another one. "This one's from Taylor."

"Practically everyone in the school sent one." Sitting on his knees, Justin bounced on the bed in excitement. "It started with the soccer team. Next, Mrs. Johnson made it a class project in writing a friendly letter. Then I guess she talked to the other teachers, because after that all these other ones ended up in the box.

"Check this out." He reached under the pile of envelopes and pulled out a large folded paper. He unfolded it to reveal a long mural that stretched the length of Caleb's bed and trailed along the floor. "Get well soon, Caleb!" was printed in green marker across the top in large letters, and the entire mural was covered in paint handprints and primitive crayon drawings.

"From the kindergarten class."

Caleb was quiet. His head slowly rose and he looked at Celia and Jeff. His eyes reflected uncertainty. Was he thinking what she was thinking? Was he wondering if he could do what they said and get well?

He studied the mural again, draped across his lap. "Thanks," he said. "This is great."

"There's one from Krissi Padula." Justin said as he dug through the pile again. "I think she likes you."

"Um, I'm kinda tired. Do you mind if we just watch TV for a while or something?"

Justin raised his head and studied Caleb, then shrugged. "Sure. What channels have you got?"

Sarah and Celia slipped from the room after the kids chose *Animal*

Planet, and Adele said she would stay with them while Jeff ran down the street for take-out.

"Thanks," Celia said, once the door closed behind her.

"You're welcome." Sarah smiled and put a hand on her arm. "What was that about, in there?"

"Caleb, you mean?"

"Yeah, he's so quiet."

"He knows."

"How serious it is?"

She nodded. "He talked to me about it."

They found a spot in the lounge on an oversized purple sofa and sat down.

"I really need to talk to you about this alternative medicine thing." Celia said.

"I'm so glad to hear you say that. That's one of the reasons I came."

"Don't get me wrong, I'm still cautious. I need to do some research, but yesterday they gave us this binder, and the side effects--"

"I know."

"And they can't promise much." She hiccupped, like a child in the aftermath of uncontrollable crying, and bit her lip.

"I know," Sarah said again, and moved closer to put her arm around Celia.

"But where do I start? Jeff's not thinking like I am. I need an education in this stuff, and I need it now."

Sarah put her hand on Celia's lap. "Don't worry. I have a friend. She lives here in Toronto. I've already spoken to her. We can visit her tomorrow if you like."

CHAPTER FOURTEEN

Alfie

Alfie sat behind the wheel and stared out the windshield. Scenes flashed before him--rolling countryside, big skies and fields of ripened wheat, tiny villages with church spires that reminded of years gone by. It had been a good life, treated him well. He had friends all along those roads.

A red Sunbird drove down the small cottage lane. Must be Osmond. Right on time. He caressed the dash, took a last look at the console, the sleeper, his radio. "I'll miss ya, old girl." He grabbed the envelope with the registration, ownership and repair receipts and climbed down out of the cab.

"Nice little spot you've got here." Osmond said as he extracted his wide frame out of the tiny car. He walked up to the rig and stood beside Alfie, hands in his pockets. "So this is your Peterbilt."

"This is her." Alfie forced emotion out of his voice. This was a business transaction, that's all--the beginning of something, not an ending.

"She's a 2002, you said?"

"That's right." Alfie inspected the man as he walked around the rig, as much as the man inspected the truck. He was about the same height as Alfie--average height--with a bright red face under a graying beard and a belly that rounded out over his belt.

"Why are you sellin' her?"

Alfie took a deep breath. "Not gonna to be haulin' anymore."

"Oh no?" Osmond raised an eyebrow and seemed to be fishing for more. Alfie wasn't interested in making any long explanations.

The man bent down to inspect the underside of the cab. "Retiring?" he asked from underneath the truck, his voice modified by the awkward position.

Alfie waited until he stood upright again to respond. "Something like that. Gonna try staying in one place for a while."

"Hmmph."

Whether that was a positive or negative assessment of his choice, Alfie couldn't tell.

Osmond put a foot on the running board and grasped the handle, poised to climb into the cab, but looked back at Alfie. "May I?"

"Be my guest." Alfie stayed on the driveway. He'd said his goodbyes.

"How long did you have her for?"

"Two years. Bought her at around 200,000. At 560,000, she had a complete overhaul: pistons, linings, heads, you name it. That was April or May last year. All the paperwork is right here." He tapped the envelope. "Bought her off a guy in Arizona when she was just a year old."

Alfie tugged on the visor of his baseball cap. "That's something to think about, too. She's mostly been driven in the southern States. She hasn't seen as much salt as a truck you might buy up here." If he was going to sell her, he was darn well going to get a good price for her.

"Yeah, I saw those Tennessee plates in the cab there. They were yours?"

"Up until a couple of weeks ago, yeah that's right."

Osmond leaned down and dusted off the knees of his blue jeans with a brisk stroke to each one.

Alfie raised the hood and Osmond climbed up to take a look.

"She looks good," he called down to Alfie. "Seems like you took good care of her. You firm on the price?"

"Firm." Deep down, Alfie knew if he were serious about this, he would negotiate. When does anyone ever pay the asking price on anything?

Osmond climbed down and dusted his hands off. "All right then. Lemme take a gander at the paperwork, and we'll get down to business."

Alfie stared at Osmond, unbelieving. "Okay," he finally said. "How about we go on inside. I'll make you a cup of coffee."

"Sounds good." Osmond turned toward the cottage. "So you were living in the States, were ya?"

"For more than 20 years."

"What made you move here?" The man's gaze cast out over the lake.

"Not that you didn't pick a pretty little spot."

Alfie opened the front door of the cottage and stood back to allow Osmond to enter. "Guess it's like one of those good ol' country songs. I came back for love."

Osmond chuckled from down deep in his belly, and the belly responded by shaking up and down as he did so. His face shone red and weathered from behind his graying beard. "So what're you going to do now?"

"Not sure yet." Alfie bent down and slipped off his shoes. "Come on in the kitchen, Osmond."

"Call me Jack."

"All right, Jack."

Alfie measured out the coffee into the machine while Jack sat at the kitchen table, spread out the contents of the envelope Alfie had given him and studied everything. He made notes in his own notebook.

When Alfie put two mugs on the table in front of him, Jack looked up, as though Alfie had interrupted him in the middle of deep concentration.

"Whaddaya think?" Alfie said.

"She looks good. I believe I'll take her. If I can get a buddy to drive me over here, I'll drop by tomorrow with a cashier's check. That suit you okay?"

"Sure." Alfie thought about watching his rig drive away from here. This was happening fast. He'd just placed the listing in the paper yesterday. He wasn't even sure he'd attract any attention in the small local paper. "Cream? Sugar?"

"Both."

Jack stood with his mug and walked toward the sunroom. "Construction project?"

"Yeah, long overdue. Just started, and hoping it'll be finished before the cold weather hits."

"You doing this yourself?"

"Yes, sir."

Jack ran his hands along the wood frame of the sunroom. "This is good work. You're looking for a job, right?"

"I guess I am." Alfie said, although he hadn't thought much about the next step yet. All this was new to him--the idea of commitment and staying in one place. Selling the rig was a logical first step, but a decision made more with his head than his heart. He'd only been hauling for two years, the rig less a treasured possession, more a symbol of the freedom he was leaving behind.

As though reading his thoughts, Jack turned to him. "You been trucking for long?"

"No, not really. A couple of years. Before that, I got work wherever I could." He'd been something of a migrant worker, often more concerned about the migration than the work, never staying in a single place longer than months at a time.

"You know, if you're serious about work, I know a guy does construction, renovations, that sorta thing, He's lookin' for an extra man for his crew."

"Oh yeah?"

Jack handed him a business card. He examined it and shoved it in his shirt pocket. "Thanks. I'll think about it."

The next day, a Ford Ranger drove up to the cottage. Alfie took the cashier's check without looking at it and watched his old life drive away.

CHAPTER FIFTEEN

Celia

Sarah stood in front of the door, her finger poised over the doorbell. "Wait!" Celia said.

"Are you having second thoughts?"

"No. Well, maybe yes, but I just wanted to say, no matter what we find out here, thank you."

Sarah rubbed her shoulder. "Sweetheart, don't mention it. I'm your best friend. Of course I care about what happens to you and Caleb. This is the least I could do." She raised her eyebrows and lifted her finger to the doorbell once more. "Ready?"

Celia's heart pounded, but she took a deep breath and nodded. She barely slept the night before, not knowing what to expect. She was trying not to pin all of her hopes on this chance encounter, but she needed answers.

Sarah rang the doorbell. A dog barked somewhere from the depths of the large brick house and moments later, a smiling woman opened the door. A fluffy white dog wagged wildly at her feet.

"Hi, Sarah," she said. "And you must be Celia. I'm Jaeda. So nice to meet you." She welcomed them in and hugged Sarah. Tall and slender, she had an olive complexion and jet black hair pulled into a long ponytail that hung down the middle of her back. She moved like Sarah, which made sense, since Sarah said they'd met at a yoga instructor's course.

Jaeda led them into a large room with a cathedral ceiling and a fire blazing in the fireplace. She motioned toward an overstuffed loveseat and sofa. Celia sat close to Sarah on the loveseat. Candles flickered on the mantle and the coffee table, and the room was heady with an earthy, spicy aroma. "Can I offer you something to drink? An herbal tea?"

"Sure. That sounds nice." Celia said.

Jaeda returned with a tray bearing a teapot, three mugs, a jar of honey and a small pitcher of milk. She tucked her feet under her as she sat opposite Celia and on the large sofa. The dog jumped up and sat beside her.

"So, Sarah tells me you have some questions about alternative therapies."

"I do. My son--he's been diagnosed with a --" Celia's eyes filled with tears. She opened her mouth, but no words came out.

"I know how difficult this is for you," Jaeda said. "Let me tell you a little of what I know about the subject."

She leaned over and poured three cups of tea. "Help yourself," she said.

"I practice a healing technique called Reiki which is a treatment that helps life energy to flow in a patient."

Celia swallowed hard. "Okay," she said.

"Reiki isn't used so much to cure cancer as it is a supportive therapy to help in the healing process. Even cancer clinics that use conventional therapies such as radiation and chemotherapy are beginning to use it for its healing benefits."

"I don't know," she said. "That sounds a little--"

"Out there?"

"Honestly, yes." She stole a glance at Sarah. What was she thinking, bringing her here? "I don't think this is what I'm looking for."

Sarah smiled and touched her arm, as though she thought Celia might get up and run away. "Jaeda, tell her more about the clinic where you worked."

"Sure." Jaeda smiled. "I worked for two years with a team of physicians and practitioners at an alternative cancer clinic. Their philosophy is to address the whole person, which is why they hired me to help. They address cancer from every angle: physical, emotional, spiritual."

"Spiritual?" Celia tried her best to keep skepticism out of her voice. Jaeda had offered her time, after all.

She put the mug of tea back on the tray and shifted on the loveseat, trying to resist sinking in.

Sarah leaned forward. "Tell her more about the doctors."

"Ah yes. The doctors are all from Europe or the United States. Some of them practiced conventional therapies for cancer treatment--chemotherapy and radiation--but they felt there had to be a better way to treat the whole person. These therapies have been proven to be effective in their treatment of cancer, but cause their own form of destruction." She stroked the dog next to her as she spoke.

"Right. I've been reading up on the side effects."

"And you're right to be concerned. The side effects are many, and some of them life-threatening all on their own."

She tilted her head to the side, as though surveying Celia from some new angle. "You don't seem sure about whether or not to pursue alternative therapy."

"I'm not."

"Tell me what you *are* sure about."

Good question. Did she know? She thought about the hospital, the uncertain, regretful voices of the nurses discussing a child in palliative care, Michaela's haunting image, the big binder with the list of side effects. "Seems like they're stabbing in the dark--the doctors, I mean. They don't really have a cure."

She waited for Jaeda to say something, but she sat silently, listening. Sarah sipped her tea gingerly, as though she were afraid making a noise would disturb the atmosphere in the room.

"I can't get past the feeling they're just experimenting on these kids. What they can do for them--the treatments they do have--cause so much suffering, but they're not a cure. Is it fair to subject a child to all of that for the sake of prolonging his life a few months?"

Celia put her hands to her eyes, an attempt to stem the flow of tears threatening to rush forth. Jaeda reached inside the drawer of a side table and produced a box of tissues.

"Maybe--" she hesitated. "Maybe I'm in denial. I guess I probably am. But I can't believe there isn't some way to cure this--not just a treatment--but a cure."

Jaeda settled back on the sofa, her voice was barely above a whisper. Yet she possessed an arresting confidence. "I believe there is. Just a moment." She stood. From beside a flickering candle on the mantelpiece, she picked up a framed picture and handed it to Celia.

"This is my son Parker. I'm hoping you'll get a chance to meet him. He should be home from school any minute now. He was diagnosed with leukemia. I am positive he's alive today because of alternative therapy. It might be the right choice for you and your son."

Celia accepted the picture from her and stared into the smiling face of the small boy.

"Okay," she said slowly. "Tell me more."

"Well, for starters, you're here alone. Is there a Mr. Bennett?"

"Yes--" Celia glanced in Sarah's direction. "He's not very eager to pursue anything but the standard medical treatment."

She straightened. "Neither was my husband."

Celia picked up her cup and sipped but the tea was still too hot. She wished for something to warm her from the inside.

"I will tell you this is not an easy road. From the moment I started looking into the treatment center, David--my husband--opposed me. In the end, I knew I had to make the right choice for Parker." She met Celia's gaze. "It meant the end of my marriage."

Celia didn't ask what she meant, afraid of her answer. She couldn't look into her eyes, couldn't match her intensity. She turned to her tea and forced herself to swallow a mouthful, sweet and citrusy, but it burned all the way down.

"You came to hear about the treatments, so I'll tell you. But my advice to you is to think seriously about how far you want to take this if your husband doesn't agree."

Flames flickered in the fireplace, but the room still seemed cold.

Jaeda crossed the room to a desk in the corner, picked up a file folder and opened it to produce a worn brochure. "This is my only copy, or I'd give it to you," she said.

Celia reached out for it and her hand shook. She hoped Jaeda didn't notice. The cover of the brochure showed a picture of a building surrounded by tropical trees and gardens. Above the picture, in large green print, were the words *Hope Healing Center*.

Celia's eyes met Jaeda's. "Where is this clinic?"

"Mexico. Tijuana."

"Tijuana." She didn't know anything about the place. But it wasn't the kind of place she expected to find her answer. "Is that a vacation spot?

Why would they locate a clinic there?"

Jeff would never go for this.

"Well, I'm sure the extra vitamin D hasn't hurt." She sighed. "Americans started these clinics. But the FDA won't approve their treatments. They're throwing their money behind conventional treatments--like you said--the ones that treat but don't cure."

"But if there's a cure, wouldn't everyone know about it?" Celia cringed as the contradictions flew from her own lips.

Jaeda was unruffled. "You know, I was skeptical at first, so I understand how you feel. But I take one look at my son these days, and all those early doubts seem so insignificant and needless."

A door slammed, laughter sounded from the hallway, and two boys came crashing into the living room just then, Parker--unmistakable from his photograph--chased another boy. Both boys giggled hysterically, their eyes wild.

"Hey, you guys. Slow down," Jaeda said. Parker came to a full stop and smiled at his mother in feigned innocence.

"Kenny's mother knows he's here?"

"Yep." His playmate stopped at the kitchen doorway.

"Come over here, honey, and meet our guests."

Parker obediently stood beside his mother.

"This is Mrs. MacKenzie and Mrs. Bennett."

"Hi."

"They're here to find out about Hope Healing Center."

"Oh." Parker made an effort at staying polite and still, but snuck a glance at his playmate out of the corner of his eye and snickered.

"All right. Run along and play now. Just don't bring the house down, okay?"

Kenny made a roaring sound and Parker took off after him again.

Celia smiled. "How old is he? I never asked."

"He'll be seven next March. He was five when he was diagnosed." She nodded in the direction of the brochure, and Celia turned her attention back to the blur of information while Jaeda spoke. "The clinic is all about an integrated approach to therapy. If you've been checking things out on the Internet, hundreds of alternatives exist out there."

"So what made you choose this one?"

"I read the research, compared the claims. And this clinic offered to hire me, which offset the cost of treatment."

"What are the treatments like?"

"Mostly, they're administered at home: supplements, some teas and formulas Parker takes. But we go to the clinic once a month--twice a month in the beginning--for regular checkups and some special therapies the doctors need to supervise. Portions of the therapy use medical equipment or injections we can't do at home."

Celia glanced at Sarah, uncharacteristically quiet beside her. Jaeda appeared to sense her unease.

"This is a lot to think about," she said. "And with a brain tumor, you feel like all the decisions needed to be made yesterday, right?"

Celia attempted a smile.

Jaeda leaned forward, her brown eyes earnest. "Take some time to make the right decision."

The right decision. Whatever that was. She scanned the brochure again.

"They have a website," Jaeda said. "It's very informative. I'll jot down the information for you before you leave."

Celia smiled, handed her the brochure, and her eyes rested on the file folder she tucked it into, held shut by a rubber band. Many of the papers sticking out appeared to be receipts.

"You mentioned the cost of treatment. What is that like?" She cringed in anticipation of the answer.

"Payment for each course of treatment is due up front. Treatments usually work out to about $20,000, give or take."

She coughed.

"Celia, if you have any doubts, let me assure you, this *is* the cure for cancer. They just can't say so because of all the legal ramifications with the medical boards of the various countries and what the law stipulates you can say."

Celia's head swam. The weight of decisions, the inevitable negotiation with Jeff, the uncertainties that lay ahead pressed down on her chest, pushing the air from her lungs. She was at the end of the line. The search for a cure ended here. If this wasn't the answer, where else could she turn? She had at least a hundred more questions. She didn't want to leave Jaeda--the one person who seemed sure of the answer. But as Jaeda picked up the file folder and set it on her lap, Celia realized no one else could make this happen for her. She had to do it herself.

"Jaeda, thanks so much for this," she said.

Sarah stood. "Yes, thank you." She and Jaeda exchanged another hug.

Jaeda hugged Celia then too. "You're entirely welcome."

She picked up a small notepad from a table near the wall, wrote in fat, round cursive, ripped off the sheet and handed it to her. "The contact information for the clinic," she said.

Back outside, Celia pulled her jacket tight around her neck. A biting wind had stirred up since they arrived, sending tiny, hard darts of sleet swirling in mad circles. They pricked against her skin like a thousand tiny thorns.

"Okay." Sarah let out a puff of breath into the chill air. "Ready?"

Celia nodded, staring down at the note she still gripped in her hand. All the hope she possessed in the world on a piece of paper three inches square.

CHAPTER SIXTEEN

Alfie

The ride into town felt longer than Alfie had imagined, but the morning was perfect for it--clear and cool with the promise of winter in the air. That promise kept him moving. He needed to accomplish a lot before the cold weather and snow settled in for the season. He'd pulled Adele's bicycle out of the shed and rode it the ten or so miles into town from the lake.

He stopped first at the bank, opened an account and dropped in the cashier's check. Then he pedaled to the car dealership. The salesman looked a little astonished that he rode up on a bicycle and paid cash on the spot for a two-year-old Chevy Silverado.

"Trade in?" the dealer said, and flashed a smile that belonged on a political campaign poster.

The papers were signed and the final handshake made. Alfie leaned down to pick up Adele's bike and put it into the bed when something fluttered to the ground. It was the business card Jack Osmond gave him. He read it: Peter Humphrey, General Contractor, Custom Home Renovations and Repair.

His stomach tightened. Why didn't he want to think about a job? He had married Adele, moved up here, sold his rig. Wasn't this the next logical step? He stuffed the card into his pocket again and deposited the bike in the truck.

He still felt strange going into the big box hardware store instead of Old Man MacGregor's place. He had to admit, though, it was convenient being able to find almost everything he needed in one place.

This time, he was looking for windows and a door.

He pushed the huge flat cart down the wide aisle with one hand and tugged at an envelope from his pocket with the other. He'd scrawled the measurements for the windows on the back. The business card once again came fluttering out with it. He looked up. "You tryin' to tell me something?"

He knew he wasn't ready for retirement, but would anyone hire him at his age? A pang of regret struck him. Maybe he shouldn't have sold the rig. He could drive truck and live anywhere, after all. And he already had two years' experience.

The window department was small, but he figured he would find everything he needed: triangle windows for the top near the cathedral ceiling and standard window sizes for the ones that ran around the whole room. He found a door, too, that would work nicely, and made a note of the price and product number. With the bike in the back of the truck, he'd take just some of the windows today. They would keep him busy for a day or two, anyway.

He couldn't wait to get home and begin this phase of the work. He tried to imagine the expression on Adele's face when he finally unveiled the room.

But after he was finished, then what? What would he do then? He realized with a sudden guilty stab the project wasn't just a surprise for Adele, not even just a way to atone for the past, but a way to keep himself busy. Something to keep him from going crazy while his life turned upside down.

He piled a few of the windows onto the cart and headed for his next stop: caulking. He found the aisle easily and searched the overwhelming selection for the kind he liked to work with.

"Excuse me?"

Alfie turned to see a young woman. Her belly pregnant and round, stuck out of a coat that fit her a season ago.

"Sorry to bother you. I'm here with this list of things I'm supposed to get, but I don't really know what I'm doing." She scanned the aisle. "I can't seem to find anyone to help me. Do you know anything about this stuff?"

Alfie smiled. "Sure. What are you looking for?"

"I'm supposed to buy caulking. That's all my husband wrote down. I didn't realize there would be so many kinds."

"What kind of project are you working on?"

She patted her belly. "A window for an addition. We're finishing the nursery."

"Exactly what I'm looking for--window caulking I mean." Alfie chuckled. "You're going to want to go with the latex caulking right here."

He picked up the tube of caulking and ran his finger across the label. "See? You can get this stuff in all kinds of colors. But if it's for windows, you probably want white, do you?"

"Yes, I think that's right. I mean, the frames of the windows are white."

"Do you plan to paint the frames?"

"No, we're leaving them white."

"Well, it doesn't really matter, anyway. Buy the white, and you can always paint over it." He pointed at the canister again. "See right here? 'Can be painted to match adjoining surfaces.'" He smiled and handed her the tube.

"Thank you so much." She smiled. "I guess you must do this for a living, do you?"

He opened his mouth, ready to say no, it was just a hobby, but he said instead: "Yeah, you could say that."

Back at the house, he picked up the phone and dialed the number on the business card. "Hello. Peter Humphrey?"

"This is Pete."

"This is Alfie Hanson speaking. Jack Osmond told me you're looking for someone. I have quite a bit of experience."

CHAPTER SEVENTEEN

Celia

"Have you been to the CN Tower before, Dad?"

"Uh-huh. With your mom." Jeff sat in the back of Sarah's Pathfinder dodging elbows and arms with the boys. Celia sat up front. They'd taken the Pathfinder to accommodate everyone, and so they could leave their car in long-term parking. Big wet snowflakes fell against the windshield and melted on contact.

They'd decided to do something to celebrate Caleb's birthday. The weather was cool so they wanted an indoor activity. The CN Tower was close to the hospital, and seemed like the perfect solution. Celia and Jeff had settled on this idea the previous afternoon. She still hadn't told Jeff about her excursion the morning before to meet Jaeda and Parker. On the way home from their house, she and Sarah stopped to pick up birthday presents for Caleb, and she didn't let on to Jeff they'd done anything more.

"You've been to the CN Tower, Mom?"

"Actually, I've been twice. The first time was with Auntie Sarah, when I was just a little older than you. With our school, right Sarah?"

"That's right. We even stayed overnight in a hotel together. We went to the CN Tower and the Eaton Centre."

"As I recall, I was a chaperone for that trip," Adele said.

"Funny. I don't remember that." Celia laughed.

"Neither do I." Sarah joined in the laughter.

"Do you remember how long we waited in line?"

Sarah groaned.

"Will we have to wait in line, Mom?" Caleb said.

"I don't know, sweetie. I hope not. We waited so long that day because a whole lot of school groups were there on the same day."

She could still picture Sarah in her little pleated skirt. When they'd finally reached the top and looked out at the observation deck, Sarah bumped up next to her and said, "Wow, look how small everything is, huh Celia?" She nodded, but she felt just the opposite--that she was small, and everything else all around was immense and uncertain.

"When did you and Dad come?" Caleb asked.

"Oh, let's see. Daddy had a business trip. I came with him."

The trip had come right after one of her miscarriages, and he didn't want to leave her home alone. He'd thought a change of scenery would do her good. The whole trip remained a bittersweet memory.

"We stayed right down there." Jeff pointed down a street toward the Royal York Hotel.

"And we went to the restaurant at the top of the CN Tower at night for dinner." She remembered the evening like a scene from a movie, as though those events happened to someone else. She didn't remember what was on the menu or what they talked about--just a warm glow, a sweet, romantic memory.

They took twenty minutes to find a parking spot. Sarah was fairly particular about where her car was parked, but at the same time, she refused to pay the crazy downtown parking prices. They ended up a good four blocks from the tower. Obviously she hadn't considered the distance Caleb would need to walk.

They unloaded, and just as Sarah's *faux pas* dawned on her, Jeff offered Caleb a piggy-back ride. Celia couldn't remember the last time he'd done that.

Once inside the tower building, Caleb and Justin crowded the elevator door. Jeff insisted they look at all the historical pictures of how the building was constructed, all the statistics about how the height of the tower compared to other famous structures.

"Come *on*, Dad," Caleb wrenched on his arm. "Let's go already."

"Yeah, Mr. Bennett. This stuff is boring. Let's go up the elevator. They have a glass floor."

"Yeah, Dad. Let's go see."

Celia tugged at Jeff's hand, smiling. This stuff wasn't boring to him. He loved architecture.

"Okay, all right. But you guys are missing school. You may as well learn something."

Both boys rolled their eyes, and burst out laughing. Caleb tugged on Jeff's arm again, and they all lined up and boarded the elevator with several other people.

"Is it as tall as when you're in a plane?" Justin said.

"No way. A plane goes way higher--right, Dad?"

"Yeah. Way higher. A plane can go up to 40,000 feet. The tower's not even 1500 feet."

Celia stared out at the view, remembering their last visit there. The city seemed a lot larger and smoggier now. But nothing ever measured up to a memory. The kids were remarkably quiet--not as unusual for Caleb as for Justin. They both stood against the windows and gawked down at the ground. Justin had an expression of complete wonder on his face.

"Too bad about the weather. We won't see nearly as much." Celia said.

She smiled at Sarah, who smiled back. But suddenly Sarah's eyes filled with panic, and she grabbed Celia's hand. Celia followed her gaze to the boys behind her, in time to see Caleb's eyes roll back in their sockets and his body go limp.

"Caleb!" She grabbed desperately at Jeff, who was already reacting, and managed to catch Caleb with one arm, saving his head from hitting the floor. Six or seven other pairs of legs moved aside to give Caleb more space. Celia crouched down and cradled his head in her lap. She looked up to meet the gaze of the elevator operator. He stared at them with an odd expression, as though trying to determine if this were some child's sick prank or a real emergency.

"He has a brain tumor!" Celia spit out. The operator flipped a panel open and pushed a button, bringing the elevator to a jerky halt. Then slowly they changed directions. Celia's stomach did a flip. It was the first time she'd said those words.

The operator used the phone in the elevator. By the time they reached the ground and walked out of the elevator, Jeff carrying their son like a baby, ambulance sirens already wailed in the distance. Adele held Caleb's coat. Celia took it from her and draped it over him to shield him from

110

the cold. As she did, his eyelids fluttered and he reached up to put one arm around Jeff's neck.

"Dad?" he said, his voice quiet.

"Yes, are you okay, son?"

"I got dizzy."

"Okay, well an ambulance is coming to take us to the hospital. We'll have the doctors take a look at you, okay?"

"Mmm hmm." He relaxed his arm again.

The ambulance arrived and Jeff helped load Caleb in. Jeff told them briefly about the situation. They made a call and decided to take Caleb straight to Children's Hospital.

Jeff grabbed Celia's arm. "I'll drive with Sarah and Justin. You get in."

The ride to the hospital brought back horrible memories. As they jostled their way through traffic, she focused her attention on Caleb, willing herself not to look at the oxygen tanks, defibrillator, medicine bottles and syringes.

Caleb stayed conscious. By the time they arrived at the hospital, curiosity had taken over any remaining weakness he may have felt. "What's that for?"

The paramedic glanced over his shoulder in the direction Caleb pointed. "That's a blood sugar monitor."

"What does it do?"

"Have you ever heard of diabetes?"

"I think so."

"Well, people with diabetes have to keep track of their blood sugar levels. That machine measures them."

When they arrived at the emergency room, Caleb was obviously fully alert, but the paramedics insisted on transporting him by gurney.

Sarah had somehow managed to keep up--only a few cars' distance behind the ambulance. She dropped Jeff, Adele and Justin off at the emergency room entrance. Justin looked awkward and small. Adele seemed to sense this as well, keeping him close to her side. Together, they kept pace with the gurney as an orderly pushed Caleb through the entrance.

They waited for a moment at the emergency room door for a nurse to release a set of automatic doors. Justin leaned close to Caleb, a smirk on his face, "Did you fake it?" he asked. Right away he seemed to feel self-conscious or guilty, and pulled closer to Adele.

A stab of pain ran through Celia. Justin shouldn't see this. None of this should be happening. Not again. Not in the first place.

It seemed to take forever for someone to see Caleb in the emergency room. He and Justin sat talking, and the rest of them stood around impatiently, unsmiling, keeping a vigil of anxious silence. When a doctor finally appeared, it was Dr. Nazar, accompanied by a nurse.

"Tell me what happened," he said. "You went for Caleb's simulation appointment yesterday morning, did you not?" He checked his chart.

"Yes, but today, we thought we'd go to the CN Tower." Guilt washed over Celia. Had they pushed Caleb too far, made him use too much energy?

"Today is his birthday. The social worker suggested an outing--"

The doctor said nothing.

"We were in the elevator. On the way up. He passed out, I guess," Jeff said.

Dr. Nazar checked Caleb's pulse and listened with his stethoscope, glanced at Jeff and nodded, holding up a finger while he listened.

"There we go." He patted Caleb on the back and removed the stethoscope from his ears.

"His eyes rolled back in his head, and he just collapsed." Sarah said.

The nurse took Caleb's blood pressure; the doctor shone a penlight at him and peered in his eyes. He leaned against the gurney with both arms and smiled at Caleb. "You feeling better now? Not going to scare your mother anymore?"

Caleb grinned. "No."

Dr. Nazar stood up and faced Celia and Jeff. "The thing we have to remember is that Caleb's tumor surrounds the brainstem. As such, it can have any number of side effects not directly related to the cancer itself."

"Like what?" She winced at Jeff's question. Did they want to hear the answer? With Caleb here?

"Hearing loss, vision impairments, dizziness, loss of balance, difficulties breathing, virtually anything the brainstem controls."

"Will they be permanent?" Jeff asked.

"These side effects can come and go, or they can stay throughout the course of the disease. Frankly, it's unusual for a minor change in elevation to trigger such an event, so it could be coincidence, but it's not

112

impossible the elevator ride exacerbated the existing problem. You said Caleb experienced a loss of consciousness before, isn't that right?"

"Well, yes. That's how we found out about the problem in the first place. But it was related to his respiration the first time."

"Ah yes, that's right," he said. "But at the time was he physically exerting himself?"

"The boys were playing soccer." Jeff motioned in Justin's direction.

"Hard to say. Could be this dizziness will come and go for him. Just keep that in mind and make allowances. Next outing, take a stroller or a wheelchair."

"So he's okay?" Celia's question sounded ridiculous, even to her own ears.

"He'll be okay. Just take it easy for the rest of the day. The next time you see your social worker, ask about how , to make permanent arrangements for a wheelchair." He scrawled something on a prescription pad. "In the meantime, ask the nurse to direct you to the department responsible for leasing them on a daily basis. Where are you staying?"

"Ronald McDonald House." Jeff reached out to take the slip of paper.

"If you're walking back there now, that would likely be the best way for you to transport Caleb."

A wheelchair. First the bandage, and the small shaved patch on the back of his head that was starting to grow in, then since their visit to the oncologist, chemotherapy drugs. Already they were making his face puffy. Next the trach tube, and now a wheelchair. This disease was making more and more inroads into Caleb's life, making itself harder and harder to ignore.

Jeff didn't wait for an objection. He headed straight for the nurse and asked directions to obtain a wheelchair.

Once they had Caleb settled in and were on their way from the hospital, a heavy cloud seemed to settle over all of them. Even Sarah seemed awkward and quiet. She and Justin walked to The House before going back to their hotel. They formed a morose parade along the wet sidewalk from the parking lot, Jeff in front pushing Caleb, Celia and her mother walking behind him, and Sarah and Justin bringing up the rear. The wet snow of the morning had turned to drizzle.

Along the way, Sarah talked quietly to Justin. "We'll go back to the

113

hotel for a swim."

"But what about Caleb? We came to see him."

"He needs to rest, honey. We'll go for a swim now, and I'll take you to the Hard Rock Café for dinner."

Celia hoped Caleb couldn't hear them. Sarah walked to the front door and hugged her. Justin stood awkwardly at the sidewalk, waiting.

Celia's mother hugged her too. "I'll go with Sarah for a while, give you some time alone, give Caleb a chance to rest," she said. "Call me if you need me."

Inside, Celia settled Caleb in bed with some books and Jeff's laptop without protest. Jeff stretched out for a nap on the other bed.

"Sweetie, I'm going to go to the kitchen and fix up a can of soup and some crackers." None of them had eaten since breakfast. "I'll bring it back for you."

In the kitchen, Celia met Leigh. "I thought I heard you folks getting in." She squinted at her. "Is everything okay?"

In spite of her efforts to hold herself together, a stream of tears began to flow. Leigh opened her arms and held her. "I know, honey. I know," she cooed. It felt right to accept her comfort--even more than from Sarah.

"Caleb collapsed in the elevator at the CN Tower."

"Oh my gosh."

"Yeah. We spent the rest of the time in the emergency room. We just got back."

She was silent a moment. Celia got out a can of soup and started rummaging for the can opener.

"Cancer sure is inconvenient, isn't it?"

"Inconvenient! I guess you could say that." For some reason, instead of crying, Celia laughed. She laughed, and Leigh laughed with her, a giggle that worked its way into something deep and hearty, shaking her ample chest.

Celia wiped her eyes with her sleeves. "I need to get Caleb something to eat. I'm sure he's starving."

"I've got restaurant leftovers," Leigh said, opening the fridge. "Does he like spaghetti?"

She smiled. "It's his favorite."

"I ordered it for Michaela--she's on Prednisone again and going through one of her hungry stages--but by the time it arrived, she was feeling nauseous, so no one's even touched it." She dumped the container onto a plate and shoved the plate into the microwave.

Celia stared at the microwave and the plate of spaghetti turning around and around inside. She marveled at how matter-of-fact Leigh was about Michaela's illness, how it had assumed the general landscape of their lives and become this thing that was so--normal. She shuddered.

"You okay?" Leigh asked.

She smiled. "No."

* * *

Back in the quiet of their room, Caleb had fallen asleep. He didn't stir when Celia came in, but Jeff sat up and smiled at her. She set the plate of spaghetti on top of the dresser and Jeff patted the bed beside him.

She curled up next to him.

"Rough day, huh?" he said.

She glanced at Caleb again to be sure he was genuinely asleep. "Caleb said something to me the other day."

"What was that?" Jeff's chin rested on her head and moved when he spoke.

"We were reading Harry Potter. I don't remember exactly what, but he talked about being afraid of death."

Jeff raised up on one elbow and looked her in the eye, the furrow deep in his brow. "He said that? Really?"

She nodded and tried to put into words what she wanted to say. Her heart pounded. "Jeff, I'm not sure about chemotherapy and radiation."

"What do you mean?"

"I mean, I'm not sure it's the right course to take."

Jeff sat up fully now, and so did Celia. They faced each other on the double bed, cross-legged.

"I don't know what you mean, Celia. It's the *only* course to take."

"Did you look at the binder the Clinical Educator gave us the other day? I mean, really look at it?"

"Sure, we looked at together, in her office--that Marnie woman."

"The list of side effects ran a mile long. Some of them were categories of side effects, with subcategories that took a page to write about."

Jeff's gaze drifted off to nothing in particular. He took a deep breath. "So what are you saying? We don't treat him at all? They were talking a difference of at least six more months with treatment. *Six more months.* Six months of his life we wouldn't have otherwise. And who knows? Maybe during that time, they'll come up with some new research, some drug trial we can take advantage of."

She searched Jeff's eyes. Did he really believe that? Did either of them think there was any chance that could happen?

"I'm not proposing we stand by and do nothing. I'm just not sure chemo and radiation are the right things to do. They're not a cure."

"But there is no cure." Even as he spoke the words, pain wrote itself in his expression.

Celia held his hand.

"What if there was?"

Jeff stared at her in silence. "What are you getting at?"

"Yesterday, when Sarah and I went out to buy Caleb his birthday presents, we also stopped in on a friend of hers, this woman whose son also had cancer. She took him to this alternative medicine clinic."

"What does that mean?"

"To be honest, I'm not sure myself. I haven't had enough time to investigate things. All I know is, he received his diagnosis almost two years ago, and you should see him, Jeff. He's doing great."

"Sounds like a bunch of new age quackery to me."

Celia thought about Jaeda, her references to Reiki, the spiritual elements of disease, the herbal tea and the candles and was glad she hadn't asked Jeff to come along to meet her.

"I don't think so. The treatments sound scientific enough. I looked at the brochure."

"Where is it?"

"She couldn't give me her only copy. But they have a website."

"Where is this clinic?"

She sighed. "Mexico."

"Mexico? Are you serious?" Jeff stared at her long and hard without saying a word. Finally, he shook his head. "This is our son's life. I don't want some quack doctors experimenting on him. Chemo and radiation, they're proven treatments--"

"Proven to do what? Cure him? No!" Her volume had risen. Caleb rolled over and moaned softly.

"I'm sorry." Her eyes filled with tears. "Will you at least consider this?"

116

"I'll take a look at the website, but we don't have a lot of time to think about this. His radiation is supposed to start next week."

The phone rang and she jumped. Jeff picked up the receiver before the second ring. Caleb slept on.

"It's for you," he said. "It's Sarah."

"Listen, Cel, Justin and I have been talking, and we think maybe with Justin here, it's a bit too much for Caleb. I know we were still supposed to do cake and everything, but we're going to drop our presents off in a few minutes. We'll take our time tomorrow, but we're going to head home."

"But Caleb's really looking forward to it--"

"I know, hon. I'm sorry. But I think this is for the best."

"Okay."

"See you in a few minutes, okay?"

"All right. Bye."

"What's wrong?" Jeff asked when she hung up.

"They're going to leave now. No birthday party."

"Too bad." He scanned Caleb's sleeping form.

"We were talking about something--" Whatever energy had been propping her up seemed to have drained out of her.

"I'm not sure, but there is something I've been meaning to talk to you about. I've got a client who's been pressing me for a meeting. I can't put him off any longer--"

"But the radiation--"

"I know. I promised to stay for that. Why don't we find out if we can get the radiation schedule pushed back a couple of days?"

She remembered then what they had been talking about. "Alternative medicine. What about that?"

"Okay well, I'll drive up to Ottawa for this meeting, and I'll try to check out this website and maybe make a few phone calls while I'm away. What do you think?"

Behind Jeff, the window ran with rivulets of water. She couldn't remember the last time she'd seen the sun.

CHAPTER EIGHTEEN
Alfie

Alfie squinted in concentration, as he ran a line of caulking around the window. "Well, Hershey, my boy, looks like I'm gonna need to make another run to the hardware store. This is the last of those windows I picked up the other day."

Hershey's brown eyes followed Alfie's movements and he seemed to listen with intense interest. Alfie enjoyed his company. He smiled at Hershey, but the dog barked and took off up the incline toward the road.

Alfie dropped the tube of caulking and took off after him. "Hershey. What are you doing? Come here, boy!"

"Don't worry," a male voice called from the front of the house. "It's just me."

Alfie crested the little hill. Hershey lay prone, one leg up, receiving a good scratching from Jeff.

"Well, hello! You come to get him?"

"No, but Sarah should be coming through any time now to pick him up. I'm headed up to Ottawa for a meeting. I'll have to go back to the hospital later this week. Thought I'd stop in though, and see how you were doing." Jeff straightened and looked around. "Guess you have the run of the place, eh?"

Alfie grinned. "Come, see what I've been up to."

Jeff trudged down the hill beside Alfie. Hershey's tail thumped against Jeff's leg. He barely managed to restrain himself from jumping onto his master.

In sight of the sunroom, Jeff let out a low whistle. "Wow, Mr. Hansen, nice job. You've truly outdone yourself. Adele's going to love it."

"It's Alfie, remember? And I hope so."

"Oh, she will. How are you going to finish the outside?"

"I'm thinking some board and batten. The rest of the house is so much older, I don't want this part sticking out like a sore thumb." Alfie motioned toward the door. "Can you stay for a coffee?"

Jeff glanced at his watch. "Yeah, sure."

"Cream and sugar?"

"A little cream, if you've got it."

"Not sure. Been pretty busy here, haven't done too much about groceries." He walked through the framing and into the house through the sunroom. "A door will go here, so Adele can walk out to the garden."

"Nice."

Once in the kitchen, Alfie scooped coffee into the machine. "How is Caleb doing?"

Jeff leaned against the counter. He sighed and pressed his lips together. "Not so good. He had an accident. Passed out on the elevator at the CN Tower. We were supposed to be celebrating his birthday."

"Adele told me. Is everything all right?" He regretted the words as soon as they left his mouth. Of course everything wasn't all right. "I mean, how is he feeling now?"

"He's better. The doctors say these kinds of things can just happen. Kinda hard to be prepared for them. The thing is, the tumor is pressing against a part of the brain that controls a whole lot of functions."

Alfie stared off in the direction of the lake. In addition to the concern he had for his family members, he was going to be living for a long time with regret about not having been part of their lives before now.

"Wish there was something I could do."

Jeff nodded. "Join the club."

"Here's your coffee. Pull up a chair."

"Thanks." They sat across from each other at the small kitchen table.

"Now, on top of everything, Celia's got some crazy ideas about alternative medicine."

Alfie swallowed. He probably shouldn't mention his conversation with Sarah.

"Oh? What do you mean?"

"Well, to be honest, I haven't given the whole thing much serious consideration yet, although I promised I would look into things while I was away. Celia gave me some website to look at. A clinic in Mexico, if you can believe it."

"Actually, I do know what you're talking about. There have been clinics in Mexico for years now. Saw a few of them when I lived south of the border."

"Well, maybe you can tell me what in blazes they are doing down in Mexico. If they're legitimate treatments, why not open up a clinic here in Canada or in the United States somewhere, or even Europe? Don't you think it smacks a little of the shady, running them down there?" Jeff's emotion seemed hard for him to contain, like a bottle of soda, shaken. He stood and leaned against the wall.

"If I'm not mistaken, their argument is it's expensive and difficult to get treatments approved in the States where the FDA is running the show. Move the clinic to Mexico, you avoid all the red tape."

"Avoid the FDA. Sure. So you can try any quack therapy you want and call it medicine."

Alfie lowered his head. Imagine him being the mediator, the reasonable one. Adele would get a kick out of this. "Think you're gonna need to check this out for yourself, son."

Jeff sighed.

"Can I offer a little advice?"

"Sure." Jeff slumped back into the chair and sat across from Alfie again. He took a long sip of the coffee and grimaced as he swallowed.

"I mean, I realize I'm probably the last person anyone would come to for advice on relationships--"

Jeff smirked. "Shoot."

"If this is something your wife feels passionately about, what is the harm in letting her pursue it?"

"My son's health, for one thing."

"Of course. But don't you think Celia's just as interested in that as you are?"

Jeff looked over Alfie's shoulder, out at the lake, took a deep breath and let it out. "Well, yes, of course."

"Trust her. Let her pursue this thing. She'll know if it's not right. She won't put Caleb in harm's way. In the meantime, you've put an investment of trust in your marriage. In her. I think it'll pay off."

"I don't know. She doesn't seem entirely rational to me. I suspect for one thing, that Sarah's been talking to her. You wouldn't know--not having had much to do with Sarah all these years. I appreciate that she and Celia have been friends for a long time, but frankly, she's a bit of a flake.

"These Mexican places? She thinks they could cure Caleb. It just seems to me that if there was a genuine cure, people would be shouting from the housetops and doctors would be lining up to administer it to their patients. It wouldn't be available only at these barely-heard-of clinics in a developing country."

Alfie nodded slowly. "That's fair. But what if they *do* have a cure? What if they can cure Caleb? Isn't that something that should be investigated?"

"We don't have a lot of time to work with here."

"I know." Alfie rubbed a toe over a dent in the linoleum of the kitchen floor.

Jeff sat back in the chair, stared out at the lake again. "Then there's the money. There'd be flights to Mexico, and you'd better believe those treatments wouldn't be covered on any health plan."

Alfie rose from the table, took his cup and set it in the sink. He gathered some papers from the top of Adele's rolltop desk in the corner and laid them out on the counter. "An investment, remember?"

Jeff snorted. "Yeah, right."

"Okay, suppose you tell Celia no chance. You won't pursue this. Then what?"

"Then we go ahead with chemotherapy and radiation, like every other family whose child is diagnosed with this cancer."

"And what's the outcome for those families?"

Jeff frowned.

"And if you do that, what happens to Celia? How will she feel a year from now, two years from now? Do you think she'll be able to swallow that kind of regret? Thinking there may have been something she could have done to save her son, but *you* were the one who stood in her way?"

Jeff still said nothing. Out on the lake, a flock of geese made a noisy ascent into flight.

"I know about regret, Jeff. It can eat you up." He held out a small piece of paper to his son-in-law. "Here. Take this."

Jeff inspected it. A check.

"Alfie, I can't accept this."

"Yes you can. I sold my rig the other day. I've got a surplus. Can't think of anything I'd rather spend it on."

Jeff shook his head. "I can't. How will I account for this to Celia?"

"Is Celia asking where the money would come from to treat Caleb?"

"Well, no--I don't know. She didn't specifically mention the costs."

"Her son--her only child--is in harm's way. She'd do anything. Maybe even take money from her loser of an old man."

"Alfie--"

"Not another word." Alfie turned to pour another cup of coffee, but turned back again and faced Jeff. "If you decide not to pursue alternative treatments, use the money for something else. Pay for a new drug, for transportation back and forth to the hospital, a hotel in the city-- whatever expenses are extra. "I know it`s gotta be tough. Right now, it's just about all I can do, and I want to do something."

CHAPTER NINETEEN

Celia

Celia still wondered at Jeff changing his mind as quickly as he did, especially when he clearly still had reservations. He did his best to be supportive, but he obviously didn't hold as much hope in the outcome as she did. She had only a few days to go to Mexico, gather the information they needed and come back before Caleb's rescheduled radiation treatments were to begin.

She had prepared herself for everything. She had made a call to the clinic and booked an appointment to speak to Dr. Findlay, the doctor who had created the protocol used at the Hope Healing Center. She said goodbye to Jeff. He was to head home for the next few days to work on a project for the company in Ottawa. She said goodbye to her mom, who was going to stay with Caleb at The House until she returned. And she called Sarah with the good news.

She didn't know how to leave Caleb, though. This was, after all, all about him. But when the taxi pulled up to Ronald McDonald House, she couldn't help feeling as though she were abandoning him. She kept reminding herself: only a couple of days and she would be back again, bearing hope.

Later, standing in the boarding area, looking out on the tarmac, she closed her eyes and saw them waving to her from the front window at The House. A circle of steam formed in front of Caleb as he pressed against the window, beaming and excited. Jeff stood beside him, the muscles of his face propped up in a smile--for her benefit or Caleb's, she wasn't sure.

"I'll call when I get there," she promised.

Now she steered her carry-on down the narrow aisle, hoping when she found seat 23A there would be no one already sitting in the seat beside it. She was in luck. She stored her luggage in the overhead compartment, sat down in the window seat and tried to control her breathing and the pounding of her heart.

Full of jitters, she felt the way she'd felt back in college, taking an exam. Or the time she gave a speech about literacy at Caleb's school for a fundraiser she helped organize. How long would it be until they offered refreshments? A glass of wine might help.

She watched the line of passengers filing onto the plane. Their eyes scanned the seat numbers, registered success, and began arranging themselves, stowing luggage and pulling out books, MP3 players and in-flight magazines.

She found herself muttering a little prayer under her breath, *Please don't let anyone sit here. I just want to be alone.* Not that she believed those kinds of things worked. She had prayed once, a long time ago, the prayer of a little girl who wanted desperately to see her father again. As the months passed, she learned that the idea of a God who answers prayers is just a fairy tale.

This prayer worked no better. A young woman with long black hair and puffy olive features stopped at Celia's row of seats. A flight attendant rushed to help her stow her bag in the overhead compartment, and she sank into the seat beside Celia. Once she was thoroughly ensconced, the woman looked at her and smiled shyly, hands resting on her belly.

At least she wasn't a salesman or something.

Celia smiled. "How far along are you?"

"Five months." She rubbed a small circle over her swelling middle. "I can't believe how big I am already."

"Your first?"

She nodded. "You have children?"

"One. He just turned nine."

A flight attendant took his position at the front of the plane and the pilot's voice announced itself over the intercom, "Good afternoon, ladies and gentleman. This is your pilot speaking. We'll be taking off in just a moment on runway three…"

"I'm Celia, by the way." She held out her hand.

"Sonja. Nice to meet you." She reached awkwardly across her middle and returned the greeting.

The airplane began its takeoff. Celia stared out the window. Nearby passengers assumed an expectant hush as the giant 737 thundered down the runway and began the ascent. When the plane had leveled off, chatter resumed around them. The back of her seat jerked as the passenger behind lowered his tray table.

"Do you have a picture? Of your son?" Sonja said.

Celia nodded, dug around inside her purse for her wallet, and flipped it open to display the family portrait they had taken last Christmas. How long ago that seemed. She ran a finger over the image of Caleb's face, the ache building again.

"He's lovely," she said.

"His name is Caleb," she said, still looking at the picture, her voice thick. She closed the wallet and turned back to face her seatmate.

"A boy." Sonja sighed softly, and smiled. "I think this is a boy too. That's what everyone says who sees me. Because I'm all out front."

Celia laughed, remembering all the ways people predicted the baby's gender. Did you eat the heel of a loaf of bread or not? How beautiful did you look during pregnancy? What direction did a needle move when suspended over the pregnant belly? All of them had been suggested to her. But she had been certain from the beginning that Caleb would be a boy.

"You're not going to find out?"

"My husband doesn't want to. He wants to be surprised." She bit her bottom lip. "I would kind of like to know."

She rubbed her middle again, smiling, the dreams of a future alive in her eyes.

She adjusted uncomfortably. "Sex doesn't matter, though. The most important thing is that he's healthy, right?"

Sonja's words hit her right in the face. She hadn't even seen them coming, although she supposed she should have. She wished she were sitting beside that proverbial salesman, discussing computer chip sales or paper clips or feminine hygiene products--anything but this.

"Right," she said. "That's the most important thing."

She turned toward the window, hoping Sonja hadn't seen the tear that slid down her face and stained her blouse.

* * *

A small plastic statue of a soldier stared at Celia from the dashboard. A rosary around its neck swayed to the jostling rhythm of the taxi.

In the rearview mirror, the driver eyed her suspiciously, as though he didn't approve of a woman arriving alone late at night in his town.

"What brings you to Tijuana?"

She'd had to answer this question already on the plane. After the rest of her uncomfortable conversation with Sonja, she'd changed planes in Phoenix. She sat next to an American retiree and his wife who lived in Hermosillo, the next stop on the trip. Apparently, every flight to Mexico was busy at this time of year. The next flight, she sat beside a businessman. He'd been kind enough to point out the dome of the Cultural Center and the huge bullfighting ring as landmarks while the plane made its wide circle over Tijuana before descent.

"Business," she said.

The driver apparently didn't buy her confidence. "Where are you from?"

"Canada. I'm Canadian."

He appeared immediately set at ease by this information. "Most of the tourists here in Tijuana are from America. They come here to taste of the--well I'm sure you've heard of the reputation of our town."

"Actually, I don't know much about Tijuana--only that Americans buy their Viagra here." She laughed self-consciously.

"True. America's favorite drug store. All the drugs are cheaper here. I was thinking of its other reason for fame. Sin City, people say." Celia couldn't tell if he was proud or ashamed of it. "These Americans, they come here to do things they wouldn't do in their own cities."

"What do you think of Tijuana?" She slid across the seat to the passenger side so she could see his face--a kind face, she decided--like a father's, or a grandfather's. Deep lines etched his brown features, little gullies running down his face, around his eyes and across his forehead.

"Ah well. Tijuana is in my heart because she is my home. I know she is ugly, but I love her. A child may know his mother is not attractive, but he still loves her, and for that, she is beautiful."

Celia smiled.

"Will your 'business' give you time to enjoy the sights?"

"Probably not." She had only one reason to be here.

126

"Well, if you do, this street on the right here, Avenida Revolución, is the place all the tourists go. You need a couple of days for looking here. Eight blocks of shops with a little bit of Mexican flavor."

She gazed down the long, wide boulevard. A large metal arch at the end of the street illuminated the sky.

The driver assumed his warning look again. "Don't go there at night, señora. This place is not the same at night."

"Thanks. I'll keep that in mind." She forced a smile. Maybe she'd eaten something disagreeable on the plane, but she had an unsettled feeling in the pit of her stomach. If she was being honest with herself, though, she had to admit she had been feeling the same way since before any food or drink was served.

The dashboard soldier gawked back at her. "Does he mean something? The soldier?"

"Him? That's Juan Soldado--Soldier John. He's a patron saint of Tijuana."

"What is he the patron saint of?"

He looked over his shoulder at her, a crooked smile on his face. "That would be a little hard to explain. I guess I would say he's the patron saint of finding a better life."

A better life. That was what she was here for.

She smiled and didn't attempt to hide her cynicism. "So does he answer your prayers?"

"*Sí, señora*, I believe he does."

The car rocked to the left. "Your hotel, *señora*." The driver pulled under a wide carport in front of the hotel, lurched to a stop, and opened the door for her. He tipped his hat. "I hope you find what you are looking for in Tijuana."

She lifted her lone bag, stepped out of the car, and handed him some American money. "I do too."

* * *

The next morning Celia awoke with an almost giddy sense of anticipation. Today she would visit the clinic--this morning was the morning of her hope.

She showered and dressed, thinking about the little plastic statue in the taxi. Patron saint of a better life. Could there be any truth to the designation? It had been a long, long time since she had prayed and

127

actually believed someone was listening. She laughed to herself. It couldn't hurt. *Well, Juan Soldado, give us--give Caleb-- a better life.*

Just before leaving the room, she placed a call to Ronald McDonald House and spoke to her mom and Caleb. After that, she ate a quick breakfast of fried eggs and Corn Flakes at the hotel restaurant. She left most of the eggs on the plate. They floated in grease, and her stomach still seemed queasy.

Her appointment at the clinic wasn't until the afternoon, but as soon as possible, she wanted to fix it in time and space. She had a nagging fear that it wasn't real or that she might miss her appointment. She wanted to make sure she knew the way.

When she'd called to schedule her meeting with the doctor, she'd asked for their recommendation on a hotel close by, so she knew it was within walking distance. The clerk at the hotel desk gave her a map and drew lines to show her the easiest route.

She walked by innumerable little shops and stalls, half of them still closed, metal doors pulled down and tightly locked up, graffiti mutely defying their security. A large sign posted at the end of one of the streets read, *Welcome to Tijuana...A well behaved tourist is a welcomed tourist.*

She took everything in, at each new sight thinking of Caleb, and what he would think of all of it. She shared so many experiences with him, it was strange not to have him here. Sadness threatened with a burning lump in her throat, and she forced herself back to the moment.

A few people stared or smiled as she walked by. One old woman sitting on the sidewalk with a cartful of handmade linens, carpets and shawls dyed brilliant colors waved and nodded, her puckered mouth likely absent of most of its teeth.

Most people didn't seem to pay any attention to her at all. She hiked on until she came to Avenida Revolución. It was unmistakable as the same street she'd seen the night before. The arch and the broad boulevard with its bright signs silently screamed for attention. She glanced at her map. She could walk down this street without making a significant detour from her route. Maybe she could find Caleb a souvenir.

In addition to the crowded little shops selling "authentic" Mexican trinkets, dozens of merchants with carts of goods stood all along the street. Some had been hitched to white donkeys made to look like zebras with painted black stripes.

She steered into a strange little shop, filled with a mixture of beautiful handmade goods and cheap, plastic trinkets and picked up one of the sombreros to finger the embroidery around its edges. Just the right size for Caleb. Footsteps scuffled in front of her, and she looked up into the smiling face of a man.

"Anything else? I've got a lotta nice stuff here, *señora*."

She smiled and reached for her purse. "Thanks. This is fine." Behind him on the wall hung a poster of the soldier from the taxi--a boyish face, his hands at his belt.

The shopkeeper followed her gaze. "You know about Juan Soldado?"

She smiled. "A little. He's a patron saint, right?"

"I sell you a poster with the story. You know his story, *señora*?"

"Not really, no."

"Here." He handed her a laminated copy of the poster, faded and bent from much handling. "He was falsely accused of a crime. He was killed by a mob before the truth came out. Now, he is the patron saint of the border. For those who seek a better life."

"You mean, for illegal immigrants?" She said the words without even thinking. Once they were out, heat rose in her face.

But the shopkeeper didn't seem to be the least bit insulted or self-conscious. "*Sí, señora*, and the legal ones. There is a shrine for him at Panteon Numero Uno."

She looked at the poster. There were more details. He had been a soldier. He was executed by firing squad. He had been accused of the rape and murder of a young girl. The patron saint of a better life met a tragic end, suffering as a criminal.

She paid for the sombrero and rushed from the store. No more detours.

She hurried along the streets marked on her map, paying no attention to the shops or their merchandise. Finally, she turned down a street to find a quiet collection of old buildings in various states of decay. Most were stucco, long ago painted bright colors, now faded, the stucco missing in spots. Nothing looked like a medical building. No signs or shingles hung over any of the doors to identify a clinic. She grasped the small scrap of paper Jaeda had given her a world away. The address, Numero 340A. The building was easy enough to find, but locked. She stepped away from the door and looked around, but only one window faced the street, and it was too high to reach. Enough people milled around the street or stood in doorways of buildings to deter her from trying to climb up to peek inside. As she mulled this over, she heard a woman's voice behind her.

"Are you looking for the clinic?" Olive skinned, she spoke with a Spanish accent, but like almost everyone else she'd met in Tijuana, her English was practically flawless. She wore a simple long black skirt and white blouse and she had wrapped a dark red scarf around her shoulders and over her head. She pushed it back to reveal hair so black it seemed blue--like the feathers of a raven.

"Yes, I am."

"You have an appointment?"

"Well, actually, not until this afternoon. I wanted to come early to--" How could she explain her need to see this place? What had she been hoping to do?

The woman didn't seem to notice she had become lost inside herself. "When no appointments are booked, they don't open early." She stepped past Celia up the three small, concrete steps to the door, and pulled on it, wiggling the doorknob. Still locked.

"You work here?" Celia asked.

She smiled shyly. "I do." Seeming to read her unspoken thoughts, she said, "But I don't have a key."

She stepped down from the door to the sidewalk and scanned the street in both directions. "Would you like to join me across the street for a coffee? The clinic should open soon. I am scheduled to begin work in about fifteen minutes."

Celia hesitated. But the woman smiled again and pointed across the street to a small café, dark in contrast to the bright sunlight washing the dusty street. A few men sat on barstools watching a television mounted high over the bar. "My appointment isn't until two o'clock," she said. What else would she do until then?

They crossed the street, each of them seeming to feel the same shyness with one another. "I'm Teresita," the woman said finally. "You're American?"

"Celia." She smiled. "I'm Canadian."

"Really? We don't get many Canadians at the clinic. Mostly

130

Americans."

"Why?"

"I don't know. Maybe Canadians prefer to go to Europe for treatment. There are clinics there, too."

They found a table close to the low open windows overlooking the street. Teresita glanced once again in the direction of the clinic before pulling the shawl from around her and sitting down across from Celia.

A short, stocky man with a beer belly shuffled to the table and spoke in Spanish to Teresita, who interpreted to Celia. "Would you like a coffee?"

"An espresso?"

"*Si*, good." She turned back to the man and placed the order.

"How long have you worked at the clinic?"

"A few months only," she said. "I worked at another clinic before, but it was closed down."

"Closed down?"

"Sometimes the border extends beyond what it says on the map. The United States is sometimes able to pressure the government here in Tijuana to close down the clinics."

Celia didn't know how to respond. Finally, she asked, "Do you mean to say there's more than one clinic in Tijuana?" She thought about the time she'd spent searching for an answer. Perhaps hope was more plentiful than she'd dreamed.

"Oh, at least a dozen." She looked down at her hands and smiled shyly. "It's a good job." Her gaze traveled across the street to the clinic door, and back again.

Their espressos arrived. Teresita looked at her cup, but didn't pick it up. She had been studying Celia closely. Her eyes narrowed. "Excuse me for saying this, but you must be doing something right, already."

"What do you mean?"

A cluster of tourists wandered by on the street. They stopped near the door of the clinic as they consulted a map and continued on.

"You look so healthy. I've been wondering how long you've known you have cancer."

"Oh. The treatment isn't for me. It's for my son. I'm here to check things out."

"Oh! But you didn't take one of the healing tours?"

"Healing tours?" Celia held her cup but stared at Teresita. "What are

131

you talking about?"

"You stay in San Diego. Someone comes to pick you up and takes you on tours of the clinics. So you can choose the right one for you. I'm not sure how much it costs, but I've heard it's quite affordable."

Panic rose in her gut. What did she think she was doing here, all by herself on the word of a friend of a friend? She wished Jeff could have come along with her. How would she convince him this was the right move?

"Can I ask you what's wrong with your son?"

"A brain tumor." This was the second time she'd spoken the words aloud. Both times to strangers. "Maybe, since we're still waiting, you could tell me more about the therapies the clinic uses. That's what I came to find out anyway."

"I don't know very much about medical things. I only handle office administration. I'm not a doctor." Teresita touched her hand. "But I've seen many people get better. Many people cured."

She took another sip of her coffee, and Celia ignored the fleeting, nervous glance out of the corner of her eye toward the door of the clinic. She stared straight at her, drawing hope from her like water from a well.

"I know they will suggest a change in diet, and there are a lot of supplements. We prepare a tea for some clients. And with some people they use machines. I think they would probably use them on your son-- with some kind of magnets or electricity."

She gazed at Celia intently, as though she knew how tightly she held on to each word. "I'm sorry I can't tell you more. But I do know people get better."

She must have seen them before Celia did, the way fear slowly dawned on her, robbing the color from her face, the hope from her eyes. Two men in dark blue uniforms and badges approached the door of the clinic. One tried the doorknob. The other made a fist and banged on the door. When no one answered, the first officer produced a small hammer and a bright orange paper and nailed it to the door. More banging. Then, seemingly satisfied, they walked away.

Celia fumbled with her wallet, found a five dollar bill, slammed it down on the table, and was only seconds behind Teresita crossing the street and in front of the door.

The words were all in Spanish. "What does it mean?" Dread like tentacles wrapped around her throat and cut off the air.

Teresita looked back at her , the fear in her eyes erased now by a flat, empty expression. "It means that the clinic is closed. For good."

CHAPTER TWENTY
Alfie

Alfie walked through the doors of Ronald McDonald House and approached the receptionist. "Excuse me. Could you tell me where Caleb Bennett's room is? He's a cancer patient."

"Are you a family member?"

"Uh, well, yes, I'm his grandfather."

"Oh, Adele's husband?" The girl smiled.

Alfie rubbed the insides of his boots together. "Uh, yes."

"Caleb's room is upstairs on the third floor. Just take the elevator down there on your left." She pointed down the corridor. "You're looking for room number 312."

Alfie started off in the direction the girl had indicated, then turned back. "Actually, would it be okay if I left this suitcase right here with you?"

The girl tipped her head to the side. "You can go on up. It's alright. Are you parked out front or something?"

"No, in the parking lot next door."

"I'm sure they're looking forward to seeing you. Go on up. Room 312."

"Thank you."

Anxiety rose in the pit of his stomach. Adele had asked him to bring her some clothes, some books and personal things from home. She had been here longer than she expected, especially now with Jeff back to work and Celia in Mexico. But she'd asked him to be discreet: come up to the room, drop her things outside the door and leave.

She would try to keep an eye out for him. But if she didn't happen to notice, or was out of the room getting a coffee, he might not even be able to see her. It seemed odd that for the second time, he would be this close to the grandson he'd never met, and yet not able to catch even a glimpse of him.

Alfie found the room without difficulty. He deposited the small suitcase onto the floor and noiselessly turned to walk back down the hallway again. He hoped the woman at reception wouldn't notice him leave. Surely, she would wonder why he left so quickly.

"Alfie," Adele's said in a loud whisper. She stood at the door to the room and beckoned with a finger. "He's asleep."

He smiled and folded Adele in a hug. "Good to see you."

"Good to see you too. I'm sorry I've left you all alone."

"Oh well, I had Hershey to keep me company for a while." He planted a kiss on her forehead. "Not quite the same, though."

He nodded toward the room. "How is he?"

"Not doing too badly. We went for a little walk this morning around the block. I bought him a doughnut at the coffee shop on the corner. He gets tired out pretty easily, though. He's sleeping now."

She stood back from him and gave him the once-over. "You're looking thin. I'd better hurry back so I can feed you."

"I'm just staying busy, that's all."

"Doing what?"

"Puttering around mostly. While Hershey stayed at the house, I took him for walks everyday. I told you I sold the truck, right?"

"Yes."

"I saved this to tell you in person: I got a job."

"You did? Already? Doing what?"

"I'm working for a contractor--renovations, that kinda thing. I already worked a day last week."

A noise came from the room. "Grandma?"

"Oh dear," she whispered. She called in Caleb's direction, "Coming, sweetheart."

She stepped inside the room.

"Grandma, who are you talking to?" Caleb's voice sounded closer. The door opened, and he stood in the doorway, woozy from sleep.

"Grandpa?"

Alfie froze and stared at Adele for a stunned moment. Paler and thinner than his image from the photos in Celia's scrapbooks, he still reminded Alfie of his mother at his own age. A lump developed in his throat.

Adele opened her mouth, staring at him helplessly.

"I shouldn't be here," he finally said.

Adele closed her eyes and took a deep breath. "Don't be silly. This is ridiculous. Caleb get in bed. Your grandfather would like to formally meet you, but you've had a big day already.

"Come on in the room, Alfie. Let's sit down and visit awhile."

"Really, I should probably be going."

"Nonsense. What's done is done. This silliness has been going on far too long as it is." She pulled tightly on the sheet and blanket on Caleb's bed and tucked it firmly around him, then sat on the edge of the bed.

With some hesitation, Alfie slid into one of the deep armchairs near the window.

"Now Caleb, what made you think this is your grandfather?"

Caleb hadn't stopped staring at Alfie since his first glimpse. "When Aunt Sarah and Justin came to visit, I heard Justin say something I don't think I was supposed to. Mom and Aunt Sarah didn't seem to want to talk about it.

"But I've asked Dad about him before. All I knew is he went away a long time ago. I guess Dad didn't think I was big enough to know any more than that.

"You are my grandpa, though, aren't you? I can tell. You look like my mom. Sort of. I mean, you're a man and you're old, but you look like her."

Alfie chuckled. "You're right, Caleb. You're pretty smart to have figured all that out."

"Why are you here?"

He and Adele exchanged glances.

"Your grandfather and I have been writing letters to each other for a long time. We've stayed in touch for years. About a year and a half ago, we started talking on the phone a lot. When I went away on vacation, I went down to visit him, and--"

Alfie held his breath. Would she tell Caleb they'd gotten married?

"And now he's come to visit me," she concluded. "Only we didn't

136

expect you to be in the hospital when we got back."

"Wow. So it's really you." He looked at his grandmother. "Mom's going to be upset about this, isn't she?"

"Don't worry. I'll talk to your mom."

"Why doesn't she want me to see you?" Caleb frowned.

Alfie took a deep breath and let it out forcefully. "Caleb, obviously I haven't been the best grandfather in the world. Here you're nine years old, and I'm just now meeting you. I did the same kind of thing with your mom too. I left our house when your mom was only eleven. Your mom probably doesn't think I'm the best example in a grandfather, and I guess she'd be right.

"I'm trying to change now, but you'll have to cut your mom a little slack if she has a hard time believing me."

"Okay," he said slowly.

Alfie rushed to change the subject. "So Justin was right. I took care of Hershey for a while. He's a great dog. Did you get him when he was a puppy?"

"Yeah. I got him for my birthday when I turned six. I miss him."

"I'm sure he misses you, too. But if it makes you feel any better, he did a great job keeping me company while your grandmother was away here with you. He loves being by the lake, doesn't he?"

"Yeah. Did you know he can do tricks?"

"Well, no, I guess I didn't." Alfie smiled. He couldn't believe he and his grandson were in the same room, sharing a conversation.

"He can roll over and beg and shake a paw. You should try."

"If I ever get the chance, I will."

"I guess Grandma's told you why I'm in the hospital."

"Yes, she has."

An awkward silence grew in the room.

"So, how long have you been here?" Alfie said finally.

"Since October. The accident happened on the last day of September at the soccer shoot-out. They brought me here to Toronto the day after."

The last day of September. He and Adele had been in California. He sought Adele's gaze, but she didn't seem to realize the significance of the date. He had to tell her. Surely this couldn't be a coincidence.

"They say I'm going to die," Caleb said simply. Adele drew a breath.

"Maybe Jesus could heal you." The words were out of his mouth before Alfie even knew what he said.

Adele looked at him sharply.

"What do you mean, Grandpa?"

What did he mean? Where had those words come from? "I guess, like in the Bible."

"In the Bible? There are kids getting healed of cancer in the Bible?"

"I'm kinda new to reading the Bible myself, but there are stories of healing in the Bible. I know at least one story of a kid being healed."

"From cancer?"

"I'm not sure."

"I have a Bible here, in the room. It's in my drawer. Can you find me the story?"

Adele stood up. "Caleb, I think it's time Grandpa left, and you had some more rest."

"But I want him to read me a story." Caleb handed him the Bible. He fumbled with the pages and searched Adele's eyes. She had good reason to be uncomfortable. Celia would not be happy about this conversation. But he couldn't just ignore Caleb.

"Caleb, your grandmother's probably right, huh? I should let you rest. You've had a lot of excitement today." He laughed. "Me too."

Caleb smiled but didn't relent. "I'll rest right after you leave. Read me a story first. Please?"

Adele sighed and shrugged as if to say the damage had already been done.

Alfie leafed through the pages. A story about Jesus should be in one of the first few books of the second half of the Bible, from what he remembered. When the padre had talked to him about making a decision to turn his life around, he'd taken him to the book of John. He turned there now, but after reading over several pages, he couldn't find any references to healing. The words were different, too, from the Bible he read. So many "thees" and "thous."

He glanced up from the pages at Caleb's expectant face and closed the Bible. "What if I tell you the story, as best as I can remember."

Caleb leaned forward. "Okay."

"All right. Here goes." Alfie cleared his throat. "There was this man. He had a sick son."

"What was he sick of? Cancer?"

"I'm not sure. I don't think it says, but he was about to die." Adele put her head down. What could she be thinking? "So this man asked Jesus to come to where he lived, to heal his son."

"So did he? Did Jesus go?"

"Actually no, he didn't."

Caleb frowned.

"He told the man he didn't need to. That if he went home, he would find his boy already healed."

"No way. So what happened?"

"The man believed what Jesus said to him, and before he even got home, one of his servants met him and told him his son was alive and well. The man wanted to know when the boy got well, and they figured out it was the very same time that he talked to Jesus."

Alfie handed the Bible back to Caleb who held it a moment, as though weighing it in his hands.

"Okay, now your grandfather really does need to go." Adele stood, took the Bible from Caleb and slid it back in the drawer. She adjusted Caleb's pillow and pulled his covers up. "I'll go walk him to the elevator, and you, young man, need to get some rest."

In the hallway, Alfie paced back and forth in front of the door.

"Adele. The last day of September. September thirtieth."

"September thirtieth?"

"That was the day you sensed something was wrong. What did you call it? An impression. And we prayed. We were praying for Caleb. Could be the very moment of the soccer shoot-out."

Adele narrowed her eyes.

"Okay," she said at last. "I get why you're excited about that, but why did you tell him Jesus wants to heal him? What were you thinking?"

"I--I don't know. It just came out. But don't you see? Maybe Jesus does want to heal him. You had the impression to pray for him, right?"

"Yes, but--"

"And the story from the Bible. I never thought about this before, but Jesus said those words and then right then and there, the kid is healed, while Jesus is miles away. That's kind of like you and me praying in California for Caleb back in Point-du-Fleuve."

"Yeah, okay, but Caleb *isn't* healed." She lowered her voice and tears pooled in her eyes. "He's dying, Alfie.

139

"I already have a lot of explaining to do because he knows about you. Now I'm also going to have to account for the things you've said. Celia will be furious."

CHAPTER TWENTY-ONE

Celia

Celia stood in the quiet street outside the closed door of the clinic for a long time, unsure about what to do next. Finally, she ran back through the Avenida Revolución, with its gaudy displays, color assaulting her from every direction, nausea and panic building inside.

She had opted for a lower budget hotel, with no internet access in the rooms. Jeff had the laptop, anyway. She asked at the front desk and found out the hotel had a room for business services: two computer stations, a printer, a pay telephone that used credit cards and a work area. A man sat at one of the stations, his brown suit jacket hanging over the back of the chair as he viewed a webpage. He glanced over his shoulder when Celia walked in the room and turned back to the computer, his eyes never meeting hers. She sat down in front of one of the computers and began to search. She tried to think of the things Teresita had told her. Healing tours. Tijuana clinics. Cancer cures. She searched everything she could think of.

She waded through the quack watch links, and the news articles describing the phenomenon of Tijuana clinics--the ones documenting several recent closures. Finally, she found a phone number in San Diego for a woman who ran healing tours. And a webpage that listed clinics of various types, including more than a dozen cancer centers.

She scrambled to the phone, dialed the San Diego number and swiped her card. Her heart beat in her throat as the ring tone sounded in the receiver. After a click, a machine answered. She left a message and went back to the computer and printed out the clinic listings. Where should she start? A closer look at the list revealed that two of the clinics noted closures. She glanced at her watch. Already after one o'clock.

She gathered her things and headed for the front desk. She would take the practical, if not very scientific, approach. She found the concierge--a young man who flirted with the female staff when he thought none of the guests were looking. He had been, nevertheless, very helpful that morning when she left for the Hope Healing Center. She plopped the list in front of him on the front desk.

"Which of these addresses is closest to here?"

"Hmm..." His glance flitted from the list up to her face, and back again. He pointed a stubby finger at the paper. "Well, these two are in Rosarito Beach. It's true that's still in Tijuana, but not close to here."

An expression of triumph crossed his face. "This one. This one is very close." She peered at the map where his finger had landed. The Hope Healing Center.

"Forget that one," she practically spit out. She grabbed a pen from the desk and made a huge angry 'X' through it.

"Well, in that case," he said, with a tentative glance at Celia. "I guess your best choice is this one. They give only a U.S. California address here, but I know this one because it is close to my home."

He took the pen and scribbled a street name beside the name of the clinic. "Tell the taxi driver you want La Costa. I'm not sure of the street number, but it is at the corner of La Costa and Tijuana Street. A large medical clinic. You can't miss it."

"Thank you," she said, and snatched the paper back.

"Ma'am?"

"Yes?"

"Good luck." He smiled the piteous smile given to the suffering, and she turned to walk away. Then she remembered something. She had been using U.S. dollars since she arrived. She hadn't taken the time to change anything into pesos and had handed the last of her American money to the taxi driver who'd brought her back to the hotel. She would need more before heading out again.

"Is there an ATM close by?"

"In the gift shop, ma'am." He pointed across the lobby.

She nodded and followed the direction of his finger to the little store filled with more of the trinkets she'd seen on Avenida Revolución. As she approached the ATM, she realized she didn't know the balance in their checking account. Jeff hadn't been working, and he had pretty much been handling financial affairs from his computer the whole time they'd been staying at The House. She didn't want to leave him without cash. She decided she had better take a cash advance from her credit card.

She flipped her wallet open and stared at the slot where it should be. Empty. Her mind began spinning through her day--breakfast, Avenida Revolución, the clinic, the café, the taxi, the business center, the payphone.

She raced back across the lobby and down the hall toward the swimming pool, fitness room and the business center.

Men sat at both of the computer stations. Neither of them looked up as she entered. She searched beside the phone, under the desk, on the workstation. She scanned the first computer station, and stared at the man, who didn't turn in her direction, but nonetheless seemed to sense she was looking at him.

"Excuse me, sir. I've lost something."

"*Si, señora?*"

She gestured awkwardly. "May I--may I look here?"

He smiled, a little too warmly, and moved only slightly. She choked back the queasy feeling in her stomach. Was this her thief?

She leaned in front of him, peeking under the keyboard, running her fingers around the sides and back of the workstation. Nothing.

"Thank you," she forced herself to say.

"*De nada, señora, de nada,*" He said, leering at her.

She left the business center and stood in the hallway, staring at the list with the big 'X' and the scribbled notes from the concierge. The smell of chlorine wafting down the hall from the swimming pool pervaded the air in the room.

Hope slipped away. Defeat grasped at her--clawing her down into some horrible pit she would not escape from. She thought of Caleb and how she had failed him. How could she have come all this way, find herself this close to the answer for him and let it slip away?

She checked her watch. How much damage could someone do with a stolen credit card in half an hour? She turned to the list again. What should she do now? Should she walk to the next clinic on the list? At least if she walked, she wouldn't need money. But how long would that take,

143

and what could become of her credit card in the meantime? If she didn't do something about it, how would she pay for the hotel tomorrow when she checked out?

She folded up the list, slipped it back in her purse, and headed for her room. The fight drained from her. She wanted to board the plane, go back to Caleb, wrap her arms around him and never let go.

* * *

Lively music and noisy men filled the hotel cantina. At nearly five o'clock, it seemed this was the place to unwind from the business day. Several of the customers wore suits. They crowded around the bar in raucous clusters, their collars open, their jackets undone or slung over the backs of chairs.

Celia would have preferred somewhere she couldn't hear any English at all--somewhere she would not have to listen to the sounds of a world she recognized. She had been warned, however, that cantinas outside the hotel often allowed men only--not the place any "proper lady" should find herself.

Right now, however, she cared more about not caring. She wanted to numb the place where defeat had taken up residence. A tear dripped into her sangria. Her third--or fourth. She shrank into the dimly lit corner. Shrank away from the world.

Earlier, when she had returned to her room, the answering service held a message from someone who ran the healing tours. In the message, a woman said she'd be glad to arrange a customized tour for her. Celia was in luck. She had an opening in two weeks--rare to find one so quickly. Call as soon as possible, she said. She suggested several clinics to consider visiting, unless there were specific places she had already decided on.

Clearing up the credit card had taken the better part of two hours. As it turned out, a lot of damage could be done in a half hour. Almost six thousand dollars' worth of unauthorized purchases had been made on the card--airline tickets, various store purchases Celia didn't recognize--all in Tijuana. The company's security department would look into them, they said, and get back to her. She needn't have worried about the hotel. Her card had been swiped when she checked in, and had been pre-authorized for the expense. In the meantime, her card would be frozen. She really should call Jeff with the news, in case he tried to use it. But she couldn't bring herself to look her defeat in the face.

A live band set up on the small stage opposite the bar. A few more women filtered in. The men at the bar had all lost their jackets now and rolled up their sleeves. The party was heating up, it seemed. She ordered a Bailey's, and sank back against the dark, cool wall of the cantina.

The band began to play: mariachi and Gipsy Kings numbers. A cry went up at the bar, and two or three of the men found partners, weaved through the tables to the stage and started dancing. Their hips swayed and shook to the rhythms. Women threw their heads back in laughter.

Celia tried to picture herself on that dance floor--as though the vacation she and Jeff had once planned to Mexico had actually happened and they were there together. She imagined herself carefree and given over to the music, oblivious to anything but the pulse of the drum, the enchantment of the violins, and the earthy sensuality of the voices.

"Dance with me, *señoreeta!*" One of the jacketless men swaggered in front of her, his eyes glazed with drink or lust, or both.

"No, thank you."

"Come on, sweetheart. You're so gloomy, back here in this dark corner." He grabbed her hand and tugged. "Get up and dance with me, baby!"

His hips began to sway smoothly from side to side, a solo salsa, while he held her hand. "You know you want to," he shouted, as the music swelled.

People started to stare in their direction, some smiling and laughing, others tentative, seeming to wonder which way this was going to go.

"I really--I don't--"

"It's easy, I'll show you."

"It's not that. I--really--No. Thank you."

"Come on," he said, as though he hadn't heard her at all. He snatched up her other arm, and gave one final, decisive yank, pulling her to her feet, and clutching her body to his. "Follow my lead."

He smelled of beer and sweat and the suffocating scent of a musky cologne. He kept his eyes on Celia's and steadily moved, swaying hips coaxing her to rock in rhythm with his body. The room began to whirl, bile collected in her stomach, excess saliva in her mouth. She stomped on his foot, ran past the laughing swarm at the bar to the closest bank of elevators and punched the button, thankful that the door opened immediately. She didn't turn to see if anyone followed, or if anyone looked in her direction. She didn't care. She needed out. She couldn't wait to pack her bag and go home tomorrow.

* * *

Tiny rivers of water took a frantic course down the windowpane as the plane curved and descended on Toronto. A dismal air hung over the city, dull patches of gray and white and brown dotting the landscape. Fog hung low, muting everything. The pilot announced rain in Toronto, but there would be snow where Jeff was, farther north in Ottawa. Celia closed her eyes. How would she face him and Caleb, or her mother, empty-handed? She'd called Jeff the night before and told him about the credit card. She hadn't said anything about the clinic. She didn't know what to say or how to say it. She was thankful he hadn't asked.

The plane hit the runway with a thud. Little clicks sounded all over the plane as people readied themselves for arrival, defying the lit seatbelt sign. Passengers bent over, extracting bags shoved under seats. Soon a line of passengers crammed into the aisles.

Celia stayed in her seat next to the window as the bustling people on the tarmac pulled luggage off the plane and prepared to fly all over again. When the line had dwindled to just a few passengers, she picked up her carry-on and filed off the plane. She claimed her luggage, had nothing to declare, and in no time at all, walked through the wide doors and into the waiting area. No one would be there to meet her, with Jeff still in Ottawa until the end of the week, and her mom at The House with Caleb.

Then she saw him.

"What are you doing here?"

146

CHAPTER TWENTY-TWO

Alfie

"Looks good Alfie, real good."

"It does, doesn't it?" He grinned and extended his hand to Pete. "Thanks for helping me out with this."

Pete shook his hand. "Don't worry about it. It'll just come off your paycheck." He poked a friendly elbow at Alfie's ribs.

"Naw, just kidding. Truth is, I have a little of the romantic in me. Ya can't tell anyone else that, though."

"Secret's safe with me."

Pete was a good guy. Alfie was certain Pete hadn't been sure of him when he first started on the crew--probably thought an "old man" like him wasn't capable of pulling his weight on the job. He started Alfie on a probationary basis. But it didn't take long for him to tell Alfie he was welcome to stay on as long as there was work. Pete openly admired his workmanship.

They peeled off their work gloves and stood back to admire their work. Alfie had done a lot of the work himself. But at a certain point, with the frame up, and his vision of the finished project firmly in mind, he'd decided to ask for help. Pete had worked with him to install the last of the windows and then the two began work on the board and batten siding. Halfway through, the weather threatened snow, and for a whole day little snowflakes filtered down from an ashen sky.

Adele would be back tomorrow, after Celia returned from Mexico. Some of the siding and the shingles would have to wait, so they'd done their best to seal things up against the weather. He would work on installing insulation the next day before she arrived.

It felt good when he'd been able to help Jeff make Mexico happen for Celia, although he was certain she had no idea about his role in things. It felt good too the progress he'd made on the sunroom. If only he hadn't messed things up so badly for Adele the day he went to Toronto.

"Know where I can get a really big bow?" Alfie asked.

Pete laughed. "That'd be awesome. She'll be blown away, for sure, no matter what."

"We finished none too soon, I'd say." Alfie's attention had moved to the clouds, low now and laden with snow.

"Yeah, I should probably be headin' on outta here. Haven't got my snow tires on the truck yet. I was planning to take care of that this weekend."

All evening long, as Alfie worked on the inside of the sunroom, he watched out the windows as the snow fell. At first, the soft flakes melted into dots of water, but after a while, the snow turned thicker and dryer, and a layer of white began to accumulate.

It had been years since he'd lived in a cooler climate and enjoyed the rhythm of the seasons, complete with snowy winters. He smiled as he thought with anticipation about nights around the fireplace with Adele, snowy tramps through the woods nearby, the steely surface of the lake on a snowy day.

But then he thought again of how upset she'd been after his visit to Ronald McDonald House the other day. Her voice had lost its warmth when he talked to her on the phone, carried instead the strain of worry. She said she'd cautioned Caleb not to say anything to his mom until after she'd had a talk with her. But Adele shouldn't have to handle his responsibility.

He shoved another piece of insulation into place between two studs and gazed out at the lining of snow that gathered in the sills of the windows. The words of a poem he'd memorized as a child floated back to him: *the only other sound's the sweep of easy wind and downy flake.*

And then the rest of the words: *the woods are lovely, dark and deep, but I have promises to keep, and miles to go before I sleep.*

Promises to keep. Yep, that was it. He couldn't let Adele handle this situation alone. It wasn't her fault. He would own up.

He knew what he had to do.

*** ***

Smiling travelers and those welcoming them home packed the terminal. A few people, already burdened down with luggage, wore colorful souvenir sombreros on their heads. Lovers kissed, families hugged, and a few proud returning sun-worshipers rolled up their sleeves to compare suntans with the members of their less-fortunate welcoming committees.

While he'd driven, the snow had turned to rain, but it had nevertheless slowed his progress, since the flight's arrival coincided with rush hour. He scanned the crowd to make sure Celia hadn't already exited from the huge doors marked with a giant Do Not Enter sign. Unless she'd left the building, she didn't appear to be here yet. He found a spot at the railing looking at the doors that belched forth a never-ending stream of passengers, his heart pounding, and waited.

Finally, she exited the doors, jostled in the midst of a large crowd heading through the customs exit, seemingly all at once. She held her head high and searched, he guessed, for the airport taxi service counter.

He stood right in front of her before she glanced his way.

"What are you doing here?" she said.

"I came to pick you up."

"I've arranged my own ride." She pushed past him and yanked on the handle of her luggage as though it were the leash of a reluctant dog.

"I know, but I cancelled it, and paid the cancellation fee."

She whirled around. "What? Who asked you?" She shook her head in obvious disgust.

"I wanted to talk to you."

"I have nothing to say to you." She turned around and resumed her march to the taxi counter.

"Where are you going?"

"To Ronald McDonald House. I'm sure I can get another taxi."

He touched her arm. "Please. Please let me drive you home."

"I'm not going home. I'm going to The House."

"Okay, please let me drive you to Ronald McDonald House. Please, Celia. I--I need to tell you something."

"Fine. Tell me here." Her lips made a thin line.

"Here?" Alfie scanned the noisy crowd again. At least a dozen languages floated by as people navigated their way through the mass of bodies.

149

"Look. I've had a long day, and a pretty lousy flight. I want to go and see my son, and you're not welcome."

"I don't want to stay. I just want to talk to you. Why don't you let me help you with the luggage? You can get in my truck, and I'll drive you to Ronald McDonald House. We can talk in the truck."

"Driving downtown in traffic at rush hour will take a minimum of 45 minutes, and I have no desire to sit in a vehicle with you for any period of time." She spat the words. "Say what you have to say, or don't. I'm leaving in a taxi."

"I came because of Caleb." Not entirely the truth, but he was desperate.

"What about Caleb?" her eyes narrowed.

Alfie took a deep breath and let it out forcefully. He made one last attempt. "Would you please come with me?"

"No."

He sighed again. "Your mom asked me to deliver some clothes and things, and--"

"And what?"

"I tried to be discreet. Caleb had been asleep. But he woke up and saw me." She said nothing and he held her gaze. "He knows. He knew right away I was his grandfather."

"I can't believe this. How hard is it for you to just stay away? You did it for years, after all."

"I'm sorry, Celia, honey, I truly am. I didn't mean for it to happen."

"Sure." She nodded briskly. "Fine. Thank you. You've said your piece."

She wheeled around and her suitcase fell over on its side. She bent down, straightened it and marched away.

"There's more."

"Don't you think you've done enough?" She called the words over her shoulder. She didn't even turn around.

In this sea of faces, no one stared or paid even a passing notice to her anger or his grief. Small consolation. He hoped he had at least spared Adele bearing the responsibility for the situation. Maybe in those 45 minutes, Celia would cool down and think clearly. Maybe the good news she surely brought from Mexico would outweigh her momentary emotion.

***

Adele arrived in the middle of the morning the next day. She carried her own bag and quietly hung her keys on the rack by the door. Alfie had just come from the shed where he had stacked a winter's supply of firewood. He was bringing in a load of split logs to start a fire, when the front door clicked shut behind her.

He stood just inside the back door, dirty and sweaty, with an armful of wood. She did not seem especially happy to see him.

"I'd planned a better reception," he said. "But I'm afraid I can't hug you right now, and I'm not sure you'd want to anyway."

She set the suitcase down, but clearly some burdens were not so easily relinquished.

"What were you thinking?"

He deposited the load on the hearth dusted off his hands and clothing.

"Last night, you mean."

"Yes, of course, last night."

He walked slowly toward her. "I didn't want you to take responsibility for something that was my fault. I was hoping by the time she reached you, she wouldn't be so angry."

"I've never seen her so furious."

"I'm sorry, honey, I thought I was doing the right thing."

She took his hand and led him to the sofa. A sigh escaped as she settled into the cushions. "I think you are the target for all her anger right now. She's angry about you, she's angry about what she can't fix, she's angry about Mexico--"

"About Mexico? What happened?"

"I don't understand. I don't think she understands. Things didn't work out at all. The place wasn't even open anymore, from what I understand *and* her credit card was stolen."

"Oh." He sat back and let the weight of this new misfortune set in.

The two of them sat and stared at the cheerless fireplace.

"I guess I should get the fire going now. You must be cool," he said finally. "But first, can I show you something? I had this all planned a little differently, but you'll see it sooner than later."

"What?"

"Come with me." He took her by the hand and led her to the back of the house, off the kitchen, where the smell of fresh-cut lumber still

151

pervaded the air.

"It's not finished yet, but it's as far as I could get while you were gone, with a little help. I wanted to surprise you."

"Oh, Alfie, it's beautiful!" She hugged him and tears ran down her face. She held him tighter, and sobbed until his shirt soaked with her tears.

CHAPTER TWENTY-THREE

Celia

"Jeff! Did you hear me? Get me another towel." Celia shouted at him over the sound of running water and the coughing that shook Caleb's body.

Jeff appeared at the doorway, tired, beaten. "No towels. We've used them all."

"You stay here. I'll go look." She stroked Caleb's sweaty head once more, ignoring the clump of hair that caught in her fingers and fell to the floor when she did. She scrambled up from the bathroom floor.

"I'm telling you, I looked everywhere," Jeff said. He folded to his knees beside Caleb.

Celia brushed past him and ran down the hallway toward their room. She ran her fingers through her hair and stared down in horror. She was still clutching the clump of Caleb's hair. She hadn't wanted him to see it on the floor and intended to throw it in the garbage. But she'd forgotten and for a brief moment, thought the hair was her own. She wished it were. She wished she were the one going through all of this, and not her baby.

In the room, she opened every drawer and closet, for once disregarding the fallout of unfolded underwear and wrinkled clothes. In desperation, she threw open their suitcases. Nothing.

A faint knock at the half-opened door startled her.

"Celia? That you?"

"Yes, I'm sorry. Did we wake you?"

Leigh's bright face appeared at the door.

153

"Naw. I was up prowlin' around. Just finished updating my blog so folks at home'll be able to stay in touch with what's what." She took in the upturned suitcases and disheveled drawers. "Need anything?"

Celia sighed. "A towel."

"Oh dear. One of those nights, huh? Hang on. Lemme get you a stack. I'll bring them down to the bathroom. You go take care of your kiddo."

Celia obeyed, but when she arrived at the bathroom, Jeff had already used paper towels to clean up the mess, and had somehow managed to clean Caleb up as well. Caleb lay asleep, his arms in a circle around the toilet seat, his head resting in the crook of one arm.

"He can't have anything left in him." Jeff wadded up a piece of paper towel and fired it at the garbage can.

"I think he's had dry heaves for the last half hour, at least." They knelt down on either side of Caleb. Celia rubbed his back. "What should we do?"

"We can't leave him here."

"He's exhausted. I don't suppose he'll wake up anyway."

"The change of position could upset his stomach again." The dark circles under Jeff's eyes were almost as pronounced as the ones under Caleb's.

"Oh dear. I didn't change his sheets yet."

"I'll help you." Leigh stood at the door, the stack of towels in her arms.

Celia stood and shrugged at Jeff. "I guess wait here. I'll come back when everything's ready."

In the room, Leigh moved with the decisive movements of the experienced. She yanked the soiled sheets from the bed, spread out a towel on the floor, washed out the trash can and set it beside Caleb's bed.

Celia pulled the clean sheets from a drawer. "How do you keep going?" Her voice cracked, and a tear escaped down her cheek.

"It gets easier." She produced a tissue from her pocket, checked for cleanliness, and held it out to Celia.

The sheets snapped as Leigh flung them out over the bed and let them float into place. Celia tucked them in around the bottom. "There's an art form to those anti-nausea meds. You'll get the hang of things eventually. We always found it was better to have Michaela take 'em before the treatment. Course, not a lot you can do when the treatment is to the brain. Sometimes the stomach has to get rid of whatever's in there, meds or no meds."

She held the two corners of the top sheet together in her hands and regarded Celia. "You asked how I do it. I'm sure I couldn't if not for prayer. Our whole church back in Berry Mills prays for us every day. I expect I couldn't keep going without the good Lord watchin' out for us."

She resumed bed making. "First time, though, it was rough. I remember being glad my Bill was here with me. I think I woulda dissolved into a puddle of tears on the floor without him."

The room prepared, Celia turned to leave, but Leigh touched her arm. "You know, Celia, I'm sure it's not my place to say. Word is you went to Mexico looking for some kinda special treatment. Bill and I, we prayed and prayed about what to do for Michaela. We considered giving her no treatments at all."

Leigh surveyed her and smiled. "You seem surprised.

"Thing is, she's happy at home. She's got her granddad and her mawmaw and everyone else who loves her. All the travel is wearying. We wondered if she wouldn't be better off without all of this.

"In the beginning, it was harder. I didn't understand, and I asked God 'why' a lot."

Celia held her breath. She was sure she didn't want to hear whatever followed an opening like this.

"Someone shared a poem with me. It talked about how we don't always understand what God is doing, but the good and the bad is all part of His plan. We may not understand everything while we're here on this old earth, but one day, it will all be clear."

The room was suddenly stuffy, too hot. "Are you saying you think cancer is part of God's plan for Michaela?"

Leigh smiled again. "Well, I don't think I've put it just that way before, but yeah, I guess it basically boils down to that. Because of her cancer she's already had a lot of opportunities to share her faith in Jesus with her school friends--"

Revulsion filled her. "You honestly believe God did this to your daughter? And that's okay with you?"

Leigh looked down, fingering the tissue she held in her hand. "Believe me. I'm sure I've had some of the same thoughts as you. Why my child? Why not me? Why is this happening to my family? But the thing is, we can't see the bigger picture--"

Celia shook her head. "She could die."

Leigh's eyes met hers. She had no smile now, just a calm even voice. "No, Celia, she will die. We know that, and Michaela knows that."

She touched the tissue to the corner of her eye. "But what is death, anyway? When Michaela dies, she'll go to heaven. No more pain. No more suffering."

She bent and swiped a hand across the bed to smooth it, picked up the remaining towels and offered them to Celia. "You can keep these as long as you need them."

Celia wanted to run screaming from the room. How could anyone talk about her own child like this? Words she couldn't articulate swelled up inside her chest until it hurt.

"I'd better get back to Caleb and Jeff."

CHAPTER TWENTY-FOUR
Alfie

Christmas Day should have been perfect. The tantalizing aromas of spiced apple cider and Christmas dinner filled the house. Adele had a crock pot cooking with quail, carrots, yams, and strips of bacon laid across the top for flavor. A fire crackled in the fireplace.

But Alfie spent the day alone. Adele had set the large crock cooking with dinner, and a smaller one with the cider and tiptoed out of the house before he was even awake. Celia made it clear he was not welcome for Christmas celebrations. Adele felt badly, but Alfie insisted she spend the day with the family.

"You've always spent the day with them, and they're expecting you." Neither of them said what both were thinking: this might be the last Christmas anyone spent with Caleb. On the tag for the gift she bought for him she wrote, "From Grandma and Grandpa."

She compromised by not heading up until Christmas morning. They had their celebrations on Christmas Eve instead. "It will be a German Christmas," she said. "Just like when you were growing up."

She gave him a sweater and a framed watercolor she had painted of the Grand Canyon. He gave her a bottle of her favorite perfume and a box of laminate flooring wrapped in a bow for the sunroom--the finishing touch. The meal bubbled away in the crock pot as he got busy with installation. Over the last month, he'd been able to finish up all the work on the place. Pete had been back to help with the shingles and the siding. He'd installed the drywall himself. All that remained to be done was the floor.

However, about halfway through, at what should have been dinner time, he wandered into the kitchen, lifted the lid on the pot and sniffed deeply. Outstanding. Too bad he wasn't hungry. He sampled the cider, but opted instead for a bottle of wine.

He sat down in the living room in front of the fire, uncorked the bottle, and pulled out Adele's scrapbooks--the ones Celia had made for her. After a couple of glasses, he thought better of skipping the meal altogether and stacked a plate with a little of everything. He sat at the kitchen table and gazed out over the choppy, blue-gray lake.

He made another stab at the floor in the afternoon, but his heart wasn't in it, and he worked neither hard nor fast. The sun was dipping down over the lake when finally, into the silence, he said, "Enough of this," grabbed his coat and walked out the door.

* * *

The Royal, once Port Sandford's oldest hotel, was established in the late 1800s by some wealthy citizen of the town. Right about the same time, half a continent away, Donald Smith drove in the last spike on the Canadian Pacific Railway.

These days, The Royal was the last hotel in town. The only place to find people on Christmas Day with nothing better to do than sit around, shoot the breeze, and drink enough to forget why they weren't somewhere else.

He blinked as his eyes transitioned from the snow-white outdoors to the dimly lit, dark wood-paneled bar. He found a seat and ordered a beer.

"That can't be Alfie Hansen," came a voice from the corner of the room.

"Well, I'll be--" The voice came closer, and its owner sat down across from Alfie.

"I don't believe it."

Alfie smiled. "Brewster." No one called Bruce Stewart by his real name.

"What has it been--twenty years? No, more--thirty?"

"Been a long time." Alfie said. "What have you been up to?"

"Aw, now lemme see. You knew Gladys left, right?" From the heavy stench on Brewster's breath, he clearly had a head start. Gnawing discomfort ate at the pit of his stomach. He shifted in his seat.

158

"No, you two were still together when I saw you last."

"Aw well, she took up with some guy from over to Belleville way. Met him at work, I guess."

Alfie shook his head in sympathy. An urgency coaxed him to get up and leave, but his beer arrived, and he smiled, thanked the waitress and took a long, slow drink.

"Whatever happened to your ol' lady? Doesn't she live around here? Runs a flower shop or somethin', ain't that right? You're not still together are you?"

Alfie shifted in his seat again, and took another slow drink, avoiding the question.

"Hey, Brewster." A tall woman with mahogany-colored hair slid up to their table. "Who's this handsome stranger? You holdin' out on me?"

"Alfie, this is Brandy. Brandy, Alfie."

"Pleasure to meet you, Brandy." He nodded at her.

"Aren't you going to move over, Brewster, make some room? Or maybe I could sit here with you, Alfie. You seem like the friendly type."

Brewster rolled his eyes.

"So where have you been all these years, man?"

"Oh, here and there. Down in the States mostly, Mexico some."

"Sounds interesting," Brandy practically purred.

"Anything'd be more interesting than this one-horse town." Brewster said, his words slurring together.

The waitress passed by the table again and Alfie ordered two more beers. "You want anything?" he asked Brandy.

She raised her eyebrows and the corners of her mouth turned up slyly. "Well, if you're buying, sure."

She turned to the waitress. "Another of what he's having."

The waitress appeared unimpressed. "A Labatt's then?"

"Labatt's Light. A girl's got to watch her figure, right?"

"Me too." Brewster said. "Regular, not light."

"Excuse me a moment." Alfie moved to stand, and Brandy gave him just enough room to squeeze by her.

"You all right man?" Brewster asked.

"Yeah, I'm not sure. Something I ate, I guess. I'll be right back." He found the men's room, splashed cold water on his face. What was going on with him? He stared at his reflection in the mirror. He thought it would be good to be here again. But it was like putting on a favorite old pair of shoes and discovering they didn't fit anymore. He splashed more water on his face and went back to the table.

He squeezed by Brandy again. The beers had arrived in his absence, and he threw his head back and tipped the bottle high in an effort to let the cool liquid douse whatever had him agitated.

"My, my, we're thirsty," Brandy said. She inched closer to him, and her hand rubbed his thigh.

"Well folks, hate to drink and run," Brewster said. "Good seeing you again, man. I've gotta go, though. Ol' lady's got Christmas dinner ready about now, I expect."

Alfie raised an eyebrow.

"Oh yeah, forgot to tell you. I'm with someone else now. We ain't married or nothin', but we been together almost 10 years." He picked up a pen from the bar and scrawled a number on a napkin. "Gimme a call sometime, man."

Alfie nodded, mid-swallow. "Later, Brewster."

"I thought he'd never leave, didn't you?"

Alfie shifted in his seat again, the uneasiness in his gut stronger now, more insistent. He swallowed hard.

"You all right?"

"Yeah, yeah, I'm fine," he said in a raspy voice.

Brandy glanced around the place. "Some real history here."

"Yep." Alfie looked around at the woodwork, the pictures and the furnishings, some of which hadn't been replaced since the '70s. The place reeked of old smoke.

"They say they're gonna sell the place, auction off the contents."

"Is that a fact?"

Brandy's hand slid around him now. She leaned in close and whispered in his ear. "What do you say we get ourselves a room and make a little history of our own?"

Alfie turned to face her now. "So that's what you had in mind."

"As if you didn't know, you naughty thing." She giggled. "The bartender's a friend. I'll get a key. You wait right here."

Alfie swallowed back the rest of his beer. Brandy sashayed by the table and held out her hand. He took it and followed her up the creaky staircase. He gripped the wide wooden banister with his other hand.

They reached the room, and Brandy inserted the key into the door. "Merry Christmas," she whispered in his ear. "This is a lot better than sitting at home alone, don't you think?"

The sensation that had been building in Alfie all evening hit him like panic in his gut, as though someone had thrown a bucket of cold water over him.

"I--I can't do this," he stammered. "I gotta go."

He turned and ran down the stairs, and out into the cold night.

CHAPTER TWENTY-FIVE

Celia

Sarah stood at the door with an enormous pot.

"Homemade chili," she said. "Sorry it's not turkey. I wanted to do it up right, with all the fixings. I didn't think you'd have time. As it turns out, neither did I."

"Thank you. This is so sweet. Come in." Celia pulled the door open farther and stepped aside.

"I'd love to." Sarah glanced over her shoulder toward the car. "I've got to get back home, though. Justin's not well."

Celia leaned out the door and waved in the direction of the car. "Oh, what a shame. So he won't be able to visit with Caleb later?" Caleb had talked of nothing else on the drive from Toronto to Point-du-Fleuve.

"No, I'm so sorry. We'll see how he's doing a little later in the week. Of course, we have Dan's family visiting until next week." She shrugged and wrinkled her forehead in a what-are-you-going-to-do expression and held out the pot.

Celia accepted it. "Well, perhaps the two of us can get together then. It's been so long."

"I'll call you." Sarah hugged her, pot and all, and skipped down the steps and along the snowy walk to the car.

She closed the door against the cold and carried the pot into the kitchen. They'd have the chili for supper tonight. She didn't tell Sarah that a turkey already sat in her sink, thawing for tomorrow. At two o'clock in the afternoon, Caleb still rested in bed. The trip in the car had done him in. They had considered flying from Toronto to Ottawa, but

Jeff wanted to come pick them up so he could be on hand for Caleb's last treatment. The idea sounded good to her.

The trip to Mexico had robbed them in so many ways--literally and financially, but emotionally too. She and Jeff still talked around things. They hadn't discussed Mexico since she'd returned home, beyond the most cursory of details. She hadn't questioned his sudden change of heart when he encouraged her to go, in case his decision was some lapse in judgment and he would change his mind. Things felt so distant between them, but she wasn't sure how to bridge the gap. Everyday, Jaeda's words played in her head: "It meant the end of my marriage."

But Jeff hadn't opposed her, in the end. He had given his blessing--or at least he had let her go. During the silences in their phone conversations when she could have asked him about his motivation, she held back in fear. Certainly digging deeper or admitting the depth of her failure would reveal something she didn't want to know.

Jeff had probed for more about Mexico a few times. Something usually came up, however, to provide a good excuse to delay the conversation until a later time. Once, Caleb needed medication. Another time, he tired early in the day, and she needed to get him to bed early. A third time, they ended up in another crowd around the table in the Ronald McDonald House kitchen.

She had thought through the circumstances around the clinic's closing innumerable times, trying to make sense of things. Jeff would never understand. He would write her experience up to a justifiable government crackdown on quack medicine. She was convinced an alternative existed, even though they were now left without one. She didn't need to hear from Jeff on the subject, adding to the pain of her failure.

She drained the sink and filled it up again with water to help the turkey thaw. She was staring out the kitchen window when Jeff stepped beside her and gazed out at the tree line.

"Think I should just go out and get one without him?"

"Oh, no, don't do that." She turned around to read his face, to assess how serious he was.

"He can still help with the decorating--"

"I know, but it's not the same."

"He's not going to feel up to it anyway."

163

He was right. It was totally impractical, but she couldn't let this slip away, too. "You can pull him on the sled, can't you?" Even as she made the suggestion she wondered if Caleb would go for the idea. When was the last time he'd been pulled on a sled to go get the Christmas tree? When he was two or three? Ever since those first early years, no matter how deep the snow was, he strapped on his boots and snowsuit and waded into the deep drifts to help his father cut down the tree.

Jeff didn't answer. Just stared out the window at the bush, seemingly lost in his own memories.

"Well, maybe I'll chop some wood for a while. But there really are only two hours or so before dusk and--"

"I know."

After Jeff went outside, she tiptoed up to Caleb's room, peeked through the sliver between the door and the doorframe, watched the covers rise and fall over his chest. She went back downstairs and puttered around in the kitchen. She cleaned the crumbs out of the toaster, organized under the sink, scoured under the stove elements, pretending to care about order and cleanliness. Finally, she shuffled through the pile of mail on the dining room table--the stuff Sarah had deemed non-essential. She found a women's magazine dated back to October, picked it up and flopped onto the sofa. She couldn't get past the first paragraph of the articles. Topics like how to clean your kitchen in 20 minutes flat, how to make a Halloween centerpiece your kids would love, how to know if your relationships were destructive. Panic grew inside her.

She climbed the stairs again, forcing herself to walk, willing her pulse to slow. Caleb was tired, but why was he sleeping this long, especially given how much he looked forward to the day's events? True, she'd just have to disappoint him about Justin, but he could still go to cut down the tree with his dad.

Undeniably, the last week had taken too much from him. He'd lost weight and seemed weaker. But with the exception of the days immediately following surgery, he'd never slept this long the whole time they'd stayed at the hospital or at The House. She peeked through the door again. He lay still on his bed. Too still? He'd stopped breathing before. Is this how her son's life would end?

Quietly, in his home on Christmas Eve...surrounded by his family... survived by his parents, Jeffrey Elliott Bennett and Celia Elizabeth

Hansen Bennett...

Her thoughts swallowed up sound and her eyes filled with tears. She checked the ventilator, then crept closer to the bed, till her face hovered an inch from Caleb's. She peered at the stoma site and the trach, to make sure the ventilator was properly attached. She strained for the sounds of air entering his body, but couldn't hear for the rushing in her ears. He smelled of the curious mix of shampoo, laundry soap and vomit from when he'd fallen into bed after scrambling to the toilet almost twelve hours ago.

His breath caught, and his eyes opened wide. "Mom?"

She stood up, swiped away tears and forced a laugh "Sorry, sweetie. I --I just wanted to make sure you were warm enough. I didn't mean to wake you."

He glanced sleepily around the room, taking in the familiar surroundings he hadn't seen for months, and blinked into the light peeking around the shade. "What time is it? Where's Dad?"

"He's out chopping wood. He's been waiting for you."

His eyebrows furrowed in a question.

"To get the Christmas tree." She pulled up the shade and let light flood the room. "Are you feeling up to helping?"

"I don't know. Maybe. I'm kinda tired." His eyelids closed again.

"Are you hungry?"

"Nope."

"You should have a little something. A piece of toast?" She smiled. "I'll pop one in the toaster and tell him you're coming."

She closed his door behind him to give him the privacy a nine-year-old needed. She leaned against the wall and waited for the blood to drain out of her ears, the flush to leave her cheeks, and the tears to pour down them. She let it in--the thought she'd been holding back for months. The thought she'd been shutting out with the sheer force of will. Her son was going to die.

It hadn't been today, but one day, perhaps a day very much like this one. No one could tell her exactly when. But one day, she would come to his bed and he would be gone.

* * *

"I'll get it!" Caleb ran down the hall, green felt reindeer antlers clipped to his head. "Deck the halls with boughs of holly," he screeched, hopelessly off-key.

Celia resisted the urge to scold him about exposing himself to the cold as he flung open the door to greet her mother.

Celia stepped behind him and ushered her in. "Come in, come in. It's cold outside."

Adele smiled and hugged them. "Smells wonderful in here."

She carried a clothes hamper filled with presents. She'd been quiet when Celia told her she didn't want her father to come. Guilt hovered in the air between them, but Celia shoved it away, reminding herself how much more uncomfortable things would have been if he had come. She surveyed the room and smiled at the same little family who had gathered together to celebrate Christmas at their house since Caleb was only weeks old.

"You haven't decorated the tree yet?" Adele asked.

"Nope. I was waiting for you, Grams." Caleb had tired quickly the day before and hadn't been able to cut the tree down with his dad. He stood at the sliding glass door that emptied out to the back yard and shouted directions to his father as he tromped about in the stand of trees. "Not that one. It's too small. Go left."

He'd awakened this morning with no trace of nausea and with energy to rival any nine-year-old.

Adele rolled up her sleeves. "Let's get started."

Steam clouded the windows. Jeff had put his Boy Scout training to good use with the fire blazing in the fireplace. The turkey, yams and potatoes cooked in the oven, lending the house a warm glow. Celia peeled off her sweater, leaving only the T-shirt she wore underneath, and knelt down on the floor beside them in front of the box of ornaments.

Caleb thrust a hand in and pulled out the first one. "This is my favorite." He held up a tiny, hand-painted soldier.

Celia smiled. The trim little warrior had been one of her favorites when she was a child. He gave the ornament to her and she turned it over in her hand. "This was Grandma's, wasn't it?"

"Mmm-hmm. She brought him with her from Germany. This one too." Adele pulled out an amethyst-colored ball and held it up for Caleb to see.

"I like the soldier better."

"Ah yes, but this one is special. They call it a kugel. This is one of the first kinds of ornaments they made for trees in Germany in the late 1800s. This one belonged to my mother's grandmother."

Caleb blinked at her.

"About five hundred dollars on eBay," she said.

"Whoa! Just for that one?"

She laughed. "Yes, just for this one." She stood and reverently hung the ball high on the tree.

"Hey, cool. Here are the pinecone ones." He busied himself hanging the entire assortment of them--red, green, purple and silver--one after another. Too many red ones ended up all clumped together. Normally Celia would rearrange them later when he wasn't looking, but she wouldn't. She wanted everything just the way he did it. This was Caleb's tree.

She turned back to digging, found one cradled in its own individual box and pulled it out gently. A delicate ballet dancer hung from an evergreen wreath. Every year, she hung her next to the soldier. She held her up and she spun inside the wreath, taking her back to the first year the little ballerina hung on their tree.

Celia's father had made a holiday tradition of giving her a new ornament every year. The year she turned seven, she was completely obsessed with ballet. She had started lessons that fall and had just learned the five positions. Her father took her to all of her lessons.

"You look like a princess in your little costume," he would say.

"It's a tutu, Dad."

"Whatever you call it, you're beautiful in it, Princess."

That Christmas, he bought the ballerina ornament for her. How beautiful she looked, twirling on the tree.

Celia became quite serious about ballet, and had dreams of one day joining the National Ballet of Canada. Her instructor, Mme. Parot had high hopes for her.

But when her father left, so did the budget for lessons, and she had to give up the ballet. She was angry at her mother, at first, of course. She didn't understand why she made her quit. So the ornament hung hopefully on the tree for a few years after, Celia's silent reminder of how her mother had ruined her ambition. By the time she had grown old enough to understand the role her father played in the denial of her dream, she stopped putting her on the tree. She dug her out a few years ago, when she and Jeff took Caleb to the Nutcracker for Christmas.

The little dancer spun gracefully one way and slowly back the other, the memories rising bitterly in Celia's throat. She stilled the movement with her fingers, and the ornament quietly back in the cotton-lined box. She wouldn't hang her this year. She glanced up at Caleb and her eyes met her mother's. She had no idea how long Adele had been watching, but judging by her expression, she'd taken in enough to understand her daughter's actions. Adele's brows narrowed over cloudy eyes, but she said nothing.

Celia tucked the fragile little package into the bottom of the box of ornaments, found another one and pulled it out. This one, though not as yellowed as the ballerina's box, held as many memories.

Adele had finished hanging the first box of antique ornaments and turned as Celia cradled the box. "What's that one, honey?"

"This is the first ornament I bought for Caleb."

"I'm not sure I remember."

"I do." Caleb reached inside before she had the lid off all the way, pulled the ornament out and held it up. "Something's wrong with this, Mom."

Celia held out her hand to take the ball from Caleb. "Let me see."

Sharp edges lined the fragile ball where the top had broken off. The break extended down the side, splitting in half the image of Caleb taken in the hospital the day he was born.

"Don't worry, Mom. I'll bet Dad can glue it or something. Right Dad?"

Tears had already collected in her eyes. Tears Caleb must have seen.

"Caleb, why don't you put the presents from Grandma's basket under the tree?" Adele said. She moved closer to Celia as Caleb took her up on her suggestion. "Are you okay, sweetheart?"

"Yes." A tear leaked out of Celia's eye and splashed down her cheek, and she wiped her face with the back of her hand. "This is stupid, I know. It's just--"

"It's not stupid. I understand." Adele put her arm around her shoulder and squeezed--so hard it almost hurt--a welcome discomfort obscuring the pain in her heart.

"Ta da!" Caleb stood back from the tree. "Now turn on the lights."

Poised at the outlet, cord in hand, Jeff plugged in the tree and lights sparkled through the antique glass ornaments. Even the plastic ones looked beautiful. The lights blurred, as their magnified brilliance shone through the remains of the tears in Celia's eyes.

"Stunning," her mom said.

"I should check on the turkey." Celia hurried to the kitchen.

Adele bustled in behind her. In the other room, Jeff cranked up Bing Crosby to fill in the silence. They soon had the meal spread on the table with twice as much food as they were likely to eat any year. Too bad Celia had lost her appetite.

Fortunately, Caleb's appetite had regained vigor. He cleared his entire plate and asked for seconds of stuffing and mashed potatoes.

After dinner, he dove into the presents. They had tried not to spoil him, or make this Christmas different from any other. But Jeff did most of the shopping in the evenings after work from lists Celia emailed him from the hospital, and he'd obviously had some great ideas of his own. Clearly, more gifts sat under the tree than any previous year.

Her mother gave her a scrapbook of pictures she took on her trip on Route 66, complete with personal notes beside each picture describing the significance of each shot. She captured roadside attractions, absurd kitsch from souvenir shops, breathtaking flowers, and the Grand Canyon with equal dignity and uniqueness of perspective, each one a marvel. Celia stared at each photo, aware of the obvious absence of her father in the selection her mother had made. The first real twinge of regret tugged at her. She had denied her mother Christmas Day with someone she cared about.

Hours later, Jeff scooped Caleb up from the floor, where he'd fallen asleep, his hand still poised over the buttons of the remote control for the Jeep Jeff had bought him. He carried him upstairs. It would have been the perfect Christmas, had it not been marred by Celia's own selfishness and the thought she couldn't seem to shake all day: What would Christmas be like next year?

* * *

"Comfy?" Celia fluffed the pillows she had stuffed behind Caleb to prop him up.

"I'm fine, Mom." But even as he said the words, his eyes blinked sluggishly.

She shook her head. "I didn't think you were ready for this." She and

169

Jeff had argued about Caleb going back to school. Jeff sided with the social worker, who had suggested they try to keep things as normal as possible for Caleb, and allow him to attend school. As a compromise, Jeff suggested sending him for half days.

She didn't agree. "What if he gets sick because of someone at school?"

"You heard the doctors say that casual contact with someone who's sick isn't the issue. The real concern would be if one of us were sick. Besides," Jeff hovered with a handful of olives over the pizza they were making. "Caleb wants to go."

"Caleb doesn't like those. Not on this half."

"I didn't forget," he said, sounding wounded at the reminder.

"Since when do we allow something just because Caleb wants to do it?" All his logical arguments aside, she didn't want to give up precious moments with her son just so he could learn long division or the proper structure of a paragraph.

"I'm not suggesting this simply because Caleb wants to. This is something the social worker recommended. Doesn't your friend Leigh send her kid to school?"

"I didn't ask."

"And even if the social worker hadn't suggested, it's what I think is right for our son. You know I have his best interests at heart."

Celia didn't say aloud the thought that leapt into her mind--that maybe he didn't know as well as she did what was best for their son. It was an awful thing to think about her own husband. In all their years of marriage they'd functioned as a unit, a well-choreographed dance. Now they were out of sync.

In the end, Celia's thoughts didn't seem to matter. She lost the argument, and Caleb started school the first day after the Christmas holidays.

She pulled the covers up around Caleb's chin, minding the stoma site and the trach tube, and tucked the blankets under the mattress.

"I'll be okay. I'm just a little tired."

She sat down on the bed beside him and rubbed his leg. "Do you want me to read you something before we plug in the ventilator?"

"Naw. But you can stay and talk to me for a bit."

"Okay." She smiled. Like her, he liked company. "Did you have a good day?"

He'd been home an hour and had eaten most of a turkey sandwich, but she'd been buzzing around preparing his lunch and his room, and hadn't sat down to talk to him.

He adjusted the covers, pulling them lower. "It was kinda weird. Seeing all the guys. It looks like the team is gonna be in the finals." Sadness clouded his face.

"I know." She rubbed his leg, as though she could rub away the unhappiness.

"I missed a lot of school."

"More than two months."

"Social studies and English were a cinch. French too. But math was hard."

"Maybe I can help you?"

"Mrs. Sewell said I could do extra homework to take back to Ronald McDonald House with me." He stared at the glow-in-the-dark stars on the ceiling. "But I'm just going to get behind again."

Celia turned away and stared in the direction of the bookshelf. Almost a decade of sweet, sleepy memories lined the shelves from *Goodnight Moon* to *Where the Wild Things Are* to *Harry Potter* and everything in between. She wished for any of those quiet moments back again, struggling with what to say, until Caleb broke the silence again.

"I didn't get to talk to Justin much."

"I guess not. You had to leave at lunchtime."

"I wanted to stay." Regret trailed in his voice, as though he wanted her to give him permission to stay longer the next day.

"But you're tired."

She expected a denial, but he sunk deeper in the covers. "A little."

"He got a new snowboard for Christmas."

"Who?"

"Justin."

Caleb loved it when they went skiing on family vacations. They took at least one weekend every year to go to a resort--usually Mont Tremblant. They'd even talked about Whistler for this year. Would they ever get the chance? She had to fight back the tears lurking under the surface, like floodwaters threatening to break through a flimsy dam.

"Mom?"

"Mmm-hmm?"

"I want to ask you something, but I don't want you to get upset."

She patted his leg through the covers. "You can ask me anything--or tell me anything. You know that."

"This is different."

"What, sweetheart? What do you want to ask?" She lay down beside him on top of the covers, staring up with him at the glow-in-the-dark constellations on the ceiling.

"Do you think this is as good as I'm going to feel from now on?"

The suffocating sensation gripped at her chest again. "What do you mean?"

"I mean, when I went to school today, I thought I felt totally good." He fingered his blankets, in the comforting the way he had when he was a toddler. "But I got tired pretty fast, and when I saw everybody else--"

"What about everyone else?"

"At recess. Everybody ran around outside the whole time. I did for a while, but I had to stop."

"You were too tired?"

"I guess so. My legs didn't want to go."

"Well, don't forget before the radiation, you had to recover from surgery and pneumonia. You haven't been active for a long time."

"I know."

Quiet settled over him, and she held her breath, not sure where this conversation would take them, wishing once more for *Goodnight Moon* or *Guess How Much I Love You*. Wishing he was little enough to listen to those stories again. Wishing she could gather him up in her arms and rock him as she had when he was a baby. Wishing for a hundred other moments besides the one they were in, yet relishing the sweetness of this one too. She closed her eyes, willing away the bitterness that threatened to encroach.

"I wonder if this is the best I'll feel, until--"

She turned to gaze at his face as he stared at the ceiling.

"Until I die."

She went numb. How would the storybook mothers handle this one? Or the parenting experts? None of the self-help books or magazine articles she'd read in all these years had ever discussed how to talk about death with a nine-year-old. Much less his own death.

"You're not crying, are you mom?"

"No," she lied.

"Make sure Justin gets my hockey stuff. He always liked my Maple Leafs jersey and my autographed puck."

"Caleb--"

"I know the doctors think I'm going to die, mom. I've known for a long time now." The words spilled out simply and easily, as though he were talking about his score on a math test, or the weather, or what to have for breakfast. How long had he wanted to have this conversation? She didn't want to ask.

"I've been reading the Bible. I think that Jesus can heal me. I've been trying to figure it all out. But if I don't figure everything out in time--"

She drew a deep breath. She couldn't decide what was more agonizing--to listen to him talk about the fairy tale of healing or to hear him talk about death. "What else do you want me to know, then?"

"I don't know. That's all for now, I guess." He hunched down in the covers, turning toward her, his face inches away from hers on the pillow, and closed his eyes.

She watched him until his breathing slowed to a soft regular rhythm, the rhythm of sleep.

CHAPTER TWENTY-SIX

Alfie

"Look at this," Adele called from the door. She'd just come home from working at the shop, and she held a stack of mail in her hand.

Alfie emerged from the kitchen.

"Hey, smells good. Are you cooking?" she said.

"Barbecue. What do you have there?" He held her close and kissed her and the mail crumpled between them.

She walked with him into the kitchen. "Barbecue? In January?"

"Anytime is the right time for barbecue, baby. Marinated chicken. Wait 'til you taste it." He plunged a fork and knife into the corner of a chicken breast, cut off a piece and held it to her lips.

"Oh my, that's good. How long have you been home from work?"

"We finished early. So what is that?"

"Oh, right. An invitation to Vanessa's wedding. I found it in a pile of unsorted mail at the shop. I can't imagine why they would send something there and not the home address. The wedding's this weekend."

"This weekend?" Alfie squinted. "Who's Vanessa again?"

"Sorry, that's right. You don't know her. Vanessa is Patricia's daughter. You remember when we came to this cottage when Celia was small, she used to play with Sarah, of course, but she also had a little cousin Patricia, my brother David's daughter? They called themselves 'The Three Musketeers.'"

"That Patricia?"

"That Patricia." Adele leaned in for another bite and Alfie fed her

174

again. "This is kinda sexy."

Alfie smirked. "Wait 'til you get a load of my salad. So Patricia has a daughter old enough to get married. Wow. Are we old?"

"No. Will you go with me?"

"Go with you?"

"To the wedding. Will you be my date, Mr. Hansen?" Adele fanned herself with the wedding invitation and fluttered her eyelashes.

"How could I resist?" He pulled the dinner dishes from the cupboard and set the table, then looked up abruptly. "Wait a minute. Celia will be there, right?"

"I don't know. Probably. I mean they were very close. Not so much in recent years, since Patricia married and moved away, but I can't imagine her missing this."

"I probably shouldn't go, after all."

He pulled her chair out and motioned for her to sit. He sat across from her.

"You remember the day in the chapel in Arizona when I told you I chose you? I meant what I said. You are my husband, and I would like you to come to this wedding with me."

"I definitely can't refuse, when you put it that way." He smiled and stabbed a fork into the chicken on his plate.

Adele surveyed the table and laughed. "My goodness, what's the occasion?"

"Nothing special. I love you."

"I love you, too." She leaned over and kissed him. "Oh! I almost forgot. Someone called after you left for work this morning. He had an odd name. I wrote it down."

She went to her desk in the corner. "Here it is: Brewster. Does that mean anything to you?"

Alfie cringed. "Yes."

"How do you know him?"

He put down his fork and knife and pushed back his plate. "Adele, I need to be honest with you."

He told her the whole story of Christmas Day, tempted to leave out the details, but including every one.

"I'm sorry," he said, finally. "I made a bad choice. I know it's probably not a lot of consolation, but I left. I didn't go through with it. I couldn't.

And I felt miserable the whole time, like a fish out of water."

Adele said nothing, just walked out of the room. She went into the bathroom and closed the door. Alfie sat at the table, frozen to his spot, afraid to move--afraid to do anything. He wanted to give her the time she needed. Even getting up and clearing the table seemed like the wrong thing to do. The candle burned lower and dripped on the tablecloth. Still he didn't move.

Finally, the bathroom door opened, and she came and faced him, her eyes red and swollen.

"I forgive you," she said. "Never let it happen again."

She turned, went into their bedroom and closed the door.

* * *

The day of the wedding dawned clear and cool. Adele and Celia both cried. Celia sat beside her mother with Alfie on the other side and avoided him for the entire ceremony.

"Mr. Hansen, so good to see you," Sarah gushed, and threw her arms around his neck.

"Good to see you too." He beamed. One had to appreciate a girl like Sarah. Dozens of other wedding guests had either walked the other way or expressed open shock at seeing him here today. Sarah made everyone feel like they belonged.

While Adele visited with Celia and some of the cousins, Sarah took him by the arm and made it her job to acquaint him with everyone in the room.

She pointed at a white-haired woman in the corner. "That's cousin Greta. Do you remember her? She's the one who always falls asleep at family gatherings and snores loud enough for everyone to hear. Wonder if she'll be at it again. Oh, wait, look. She's nodding off already."

She leaned in conspiratorially and nodded in the direction of an elderly man. "Uncle Amos. What a name, eh? He's the one who always drinks a little too much and wants to make speeches."

"And here is one of my favorite people. Aunt Edna. How are you, honey?" Sarah leaned toward Aunt Edna's ear and raised the volume of her voice. "You remember Alfie Hansen, Adele's husband, don't you?"

The little eyes behind the bifocals widened. Finally she spluttered, "Glad you came. Better late than never, isn't that right?"

Sarah's laughter rang in the church like music.

Finally Celia approached. "Sarah, if you don't mind, I'd like a word with my--with--him."

"Sure sweetie. I think they have you and me sitting together at the reception. I'll see you later, okay?" Sarah weaved through the crowd away from them.

Alfie cleared his throat, pulled his hands from his pockets and shoved them firmly in again. "Hello," he said.

"This is not a friendly chat."

Okay. That's clear.

"Caleb has begun to talk about--" She lowered her voice. "About healing. Somehow he's gotten this crazy idea 'Jesus' can heal him."

Alfie's brain fired in a hundred directions. Cornered, all the words jammed up inside him. He'd better man up and take responsibility.

"I told him a story from the Bible when I went to Ronald McDonald House."

"Okay. Putting aside the fact that you should not have even been there in the first place, can you explain to me how that kind of a thing just 'happens?'"

"No. It doesn't just happen. I made a comment about Jesus being able to heal him."

"What would possess you to do that?"

He had to force himself to concentrate. Angry or not, his beautiful daughter stood in front of him, and this was the longest conversation he'd had with her in 27 years.

"Well, for one thing, I believe it."

"What?" Her voice was getting louder, higher-pitched. People had begun to stare and whisper. Alfie didn't care about any of them. He searched for the right thing to say to reach her somehow, make her see he was different than the man who left so long ago.

"I said I believe it. Look, I can understand why you would have a hard time believing I've changed. But I have, Celia." He closed his eyes and shook his head. "I can't tell you how much I regret leaving, and all the years I let pass by--"

"That has little or nothing to do with this. Why would you hold out some kind of pie-in-the-sky fairy tale to any sick child, much less your own grandson?"

"I didn't intend to make the comment. It just came out."

177

"Seems like you've got a big problem with self-control. I guess I shouldn't be surprised."

She turned to leave. He caught her arm. "Can I tell you one thing?"

Celia shook her arm free, regarded him suspiciously. "What?"

"When your mother and I drove back from California, one morning she had what she called an impression. You can ask her. She thought something was wrong and asked me to pray with her. Do you know when that was?"

"I don't ca--"

"September thirtieth."

The color drained from her face. "That--that doesn't mean anything."

"I respect you, Celia. I can tell you're a good mother, and you're trying to protect your son--"

"You're right. Which is why I'm going to tell you one thing: Stay away from my son."

CHAPTER TWENTY-SEVEN

Celia

Celia flung the curtains open and let the warmth flood in and toast her to her bitter core. She stood at the window to their bedroom overlooking the river, watching black water bubble through fissures in the icy surface. She closed her eyes and concentrated. She would enjoy their lives today. She wouldn't think about the future. She would embrace today.

Caleb had survived the whole week back at school and even pushed for a full day on Friday to work on a special social studies project. Now, he sat in his room planning places to visit when they returned to Toronto. He'd emailed Michaela to find out if she and Leigh would be interested in taking in a Maple Leafs game. Celia folded clothes into their suitcase on her bed while he shouted suggestions from his bedroom.

"What about the Science Centre?"

"Yeah, maybe." She hesitated to commit to anything. He'd been energetic all week, but no one could predict how the radiation treatments might affect him. "Are you dressed yet, sweetie?"

"Almost. In a minute."

"Hurry up. We want to stop at the library for some books, remember?" She figured quiet afternoons of reading might be a more realistic plan. "If we have time, we'll stop by and visit Justin."

"Okay. Hey, what about the zoo?"

"In January?"

"The brochure says it's open."

"We'll see." She folded the last of her shirts, grabbed socks and underwear and a pair of slippers, tucked them into the side pockets and zipped the lid. "Are you ready yet?"

"Almost. Hey, Mom, can you read this for me?"

"Well, you'll have to bring it here," she yelled back. "Or can you spell it?"

Caleb stumbled into the room, holding a pamphlet. Something was wrong. He pointed at the words and looked back at Celia, confusion in his expression.

"Caleb sit down," she said, trying to keep the panic out of her voice. He sat down on the edge of the bed. "Look at me."

He turned his head in her direction and fixed his eyes on her. His right eye remained that way, but his left eye wandered lazily, seeming to float inside its socket, until it gazed off far to his left. Her stomach churned.

"Mom, what's wrong? Why can't I see properly?" Terror wedged itself into his voice.

"Look at me again," she commanded. He did, and his eye corrected itself, stayed that way a moment, then drifted slowly left again.

"Mom?" His voice shook.

"Listen, daddy's already left for the hardware store to buy a bag to throw the Christmas tree away."

Caleb started to whimper.

"Caleb!"

"Mom?"

"Sweetheart, you're going to be okay. We're going to go to the hospital, to the emergency room. We're ready to go, right? We can leave now."

"I don't have my socks on."

"Okay. You stay here. I'll go get them."

She ran into his bedroom and rifled through his drawer. She couldn't think. Despite her assurances to Caleb, fear choked her. She forced herself to breathe. In. Out. What color were his pants? His shirt? Why couldn't she focus? She grabbed a pair of blue socks, hoping they matched whatever he was wearing, and ran back to her bedroom.

"Okay, sweetheart, can you walk?"

Caleb stood up, took three steps and started listing to the left.

"You're too big for me, baby. I can't carry you all the way to the car. Link your arm through mine, and lean on me. I'll help you down the stairs."

They made sluggish progress, Caleb's growing alarm slowing them more than his instability. Celia helped him with his seatbelt and challenged the speed limit all the way to Pontiac County Hospital, an all-too-familiar sick feeling in her gut.

The emergency room was filled with patients and bad memories. As the doors slid closed behind them, quiet resignation settled over Caleb. They registered and passed an hour in the waiting room while grown men with small cuts, teenaged boys with sprains, and children with coughs and runny noses preceded them in triage.

Finally, a petite nurse called Caleb's name from her post behind a computer. She ushered them down the hall, chart in her hand, her keys and I.D. badge jangling from a strap around her neck.

"Have a seat in here," she said, directing them to a small examining room. "Dr. Fischer is the emergency room doctor today. He'll be right with you."

She turned to walk away, but Celia called after her. "Excuse me?"

"Yes?" she said, glancing at her watch, as though she wished her shift was over.

"Caleb's most recent records are from Children's Hospital in Toronto--"

She smiled. "You can discuss those details with the doctor." She turned and walked down the hall.

"I guess we won't be able to visit Justin today." Caleb said, swinging his feet over the edge of the examining table.

"Maybe not. We'll see what the doctor says, okay, sweetie?" She read and re-read the posters on the wall: the hand-washing reminders, the admonitions against smoking, the ads for new vaccines.

"Good afternoon, Caleb. I'm Dr. Fischer." Short and stocky with a salt and pepper beard, his smile revealed yellow teeth. "What seems to be the problem?"

"Caleb has--" She took a breath. "We've been at Children's Hospital up until a couple of weeks ago."

"He was transferred there in October, after an MRI performed here. Is that correct?" He looked from the chart back to Celia over the rims of his glasses.

"That's right," she said, relieved she wouldn't have to say the words "brain tumor" out loud again. "They confirmed the diagnosis the ER doctor--I'm sorry. I can't remember his name--made at the time."

"That was me, actually."

"I'm sorry--I--"

"Quite understandable." He smiled. "So what brings you here today?"

"Caleb's eye--it--well, you can see--"

Picking up the scope, he moved to examine Caleb, and shone it into each eye, in turn.

"We're due back at Children's Hospital Monday for his next round of radiation."

"Hmm. I see. Can you look up at the ceiling for me?" Caleb followed his instructions. "That's it."

He stood back and looked at Caleb. "Follow my finger with your eyes, please." He moved his finger slowly from side to side and up and down, like the stereotyped image Celia had of a priest at mass. "Mmm-hmm." Caleb's eye followed sometimes, sometimes drifted in its socket, as it had at home.

The doctor glanced in her direction and back at Caleb. "What do you understand about why you've been at Children's Hospital, Caleb?"

"I have a brain tumor wrapped around my brain stem. It made me stop breathing." With some new kind of horror Celia realized that hearing Caleb say the words wasn't nearly so frightening as it had been the first time. She was getting used to it.

"That's a very good assessment, Caleb. Have your doctors told you any other effects your condition might have?"

"Just about anything, they said."

The doctor let out a short breath of air. "That's just about right. I think this is your tumor sending out another of its little messages. Since you'll be seeing your doctors again on Monday, we won't run any more tests here. I'll just send them a copy of my notes."

"And his eye?"

"I'm afraid he'll have to put up with its tricks until Monday, at least." He motioned with his finger. "Could I talk to you for a moment, Mrs. Bennett?"

"Of course. I'll be right back, sweetheart."

The doctor led Celia a few feet away from the examining room, and lowered his voice. "I think the tumor is likely growing. Of course, I can't confirm without an MRI, but no point in ordering anything here." He glanced back at Caleb in the other room. "If his doctors at Children's Hospital want a test done, they'll order one when he gets back to Toronto."

"Will they be able to fix his eye?"

"I'm not sure what they'll do. They might be able to order him some glasses to address the problem, temporarily. Of course, the only real fix is to shrink the tumor--"

"Thank you, doctor." It was the right thing to say, and yet there was nothing right about it. What was she thanking him for?

The doctor nodded, his lips drawn into a thin line, and walked slowly away. As she turned back to the examining room and Caleb, the doctor greeted the next patient.

Celia wished for a moment that she could be more like his father--call him "Champ" and put a brave face on things, stuffing the sorrow somewhere else.

Oh no! Jeff.

In her frantic race to get Caleb to the hospital, she'd completely forgotten to call him and tell him what was going on.

"Caleb, let's get home. And let's get out of here. I need to call Daddy and tell him where we are."

Back in the car, she dialed Jeff's cell phone number. No answer. She tried their home number. No answer there either. She hung up without leaving a message.

In the twenty minute drive from County Hospital to Point-du-Fleuve, Caleb fell asleep. Poor kid. He hadn't even had lunch.

He didn't wake up again until she'd pulled into Sarah's drive. He opened his eyes and looked around.

"Hey Mom. My eyes are better!"

Celia turned around in the seat to face him.

He looked all around, making circles with his eyes.

"Great." She hoped it would stay that way.

Dan stepped out of the house and threw salt on the walk.

"Hi, Dan. How have you been?"

"Can't complain," he said, unsmiling. He glanced over Celia's shoulder at the car. Caleb waved.

"They're not home."

"Oh?"

"Went out earlier."

"Okay--" Dan had never been particularly easy to like. He and Celia had gotten along reasonably well, Sarah the oil that lubricated their conversations. "Well, I just dropped by to drop off her chili pot."

She opened the trunk, lifted it out, and started to carry it up the walk to the front door.

"I'll take it," He reached out for it. "Walk's slippery."

"Okay, tell her thanks. I'll call her later, I guess."

Dan waved, apparently signaling the end of the conversation.

She climbed back in the car.

"Aren't we going in?" Caleb asked.

"No sweetie, they're not home. Mr. MacKenzie is the only one home right now."

"But I saw Justin look out of the window upstairs."

Celia squinted up at the window. There was no one there. She studied Caleb's face again in the rearview mirror.

"Think your eye's playing tricks on you again?"

"No, Mom. He was there. I saw him."

"Well, sweetie, he can't be. Mr. MacKenzie said they went out." She bit her lip as she threw the car into reverse and backed out of the drive. She needed to get him home as quickly as possible. The short nap in the car seemed to help his eye. She wanted to make sure he had all the rest he needed.

Caleb stared at the upstairs window as they drove away. "I saw him, Mom. I know I did."

* * *

Ronald McDonald House welcomed them back with its unique technicolor charm. Celia plunked her suitcase down in the room--a purple and pink one this time--exhausted from the five-hour drive. In some perverse way, she recognized this as their new routine, and she greeted this stay in a different way than she had the last time. Perhaps because Caleb didn't seem scared anymore, or perhaps in anticipation of the fun they had planned with a family who understood what they were going through. Whatever was responsible for the new outlook, she had let her guard down. She actually looked forward to visiting with Leigh. So she wasn't ready for what was about to unfold. Neither was Caleb.

"It's a girly room!" Caleb whined.

"It's not a girly room. It's nice. Look at the nice big window--facing--east I think. We'll be able to see the sun come up." Celia smiled up at Jeff. "Can you see the sun come up in Toronto?"

Jeff put down the last of the suitcases and looked at his watch. "I guess if I'm going to beat rush hour, I should just turn around and head back now."

"You sure? That's an awful lot of driving for one day. Why don't you stay the night?"

Jeff frowned at his watch again. "No. I'll grab a coffee and a bagel or something and head back while I know the roads are good and clean."

A wave of guilt washed over her as she realized how relieved she was that he was leaving and it would be just her and Caleb tonight.

Jeff bent over and kissed Caleb goodbye. "Be strong, Champ. I'll call you every day."

"OK, Dad. I'll cheer the Leafs for ya."

Jeff rubbed Caleb's head. "Sorry I'm going to miss that. Catch a puck for me, okay?"

"Right, dad. I'll get right on that." He rolled his eyes, and Jeff laughed.

Jeff checked his pocket for his wallet, picked the keys up off the dresser and leaned in for one last kiss from both of them. "See you in two weeks. Love you both."

He hadn't been gone from the room five minutes when a knock sounded at the door, followed by Michaela and Leigh's rosy smile.

"Whaddaya know? We're neighbors--right next door. Heard you come in." Leigh threw her arms around Celia as though she were some long-lost cousin.

"Good to see you." And it was.

Celia took a good look at Michaela. Despite herself, she drew an audible breath. Michaela had lost weight, if that were possible. She wore a kerchief over her bare head, and the lines under her eyes were so dark, she looked as though she'd been punched. Her eyes seemed to bulge from her thin face.

Leigh followed her gaze. "I know it. Darn good thing I can sew. I've taken those ruddy pants in three times since September."

Michaela stepped over to sit down on one of the beds with Caleb, and he pulled out the remote control Jeep he had received for Christmas. Celia had been dubious when he packed it and made him swear to keep

185

it in the room.

Michaela continued to arrest Celia's attention. She rested her arm on Caleb's shoulder as she stepped carefully and unevenly toward the bed.

Leigh lowered her voice. "She's taken a real turn. Guess the tumor must be growing again, 'cause her balance is all wonky. She needs to lean on someone or she'll fall right over, poor thing."

Leigh rubbed Celia's back. "And how are you?"

Guilt stung. Her daughter obviously in worse condition, she was nevertheless quick to focus on her and Caleb. How could she be so calm in the face of Michaela's illness? Something made Celia wish for that kind of peace. Or numbness.

"I'm fine, I guess. We had a nice time at home, for the most part. Hey, where's Emily?"

"Left her home this time. She was still breastfeeding, but I finally weaned her over the holidays."

She spoke a little lower. "If it hadn't been for Michaela--well, I woulda just kept right on, but--" She shrugged. "Feels a little weird without her. Like I lost my left arm or something."

"Did you have a good holiday?"

"Mmm-hmm. A real nice time. Christmas is my favorite time of year. We had lots of visitors. Michaela saw all her aunts and uncles and cousins."

"Sounds exhausting," Celia said.

Leigh laughed and swatted playfully at her arm. "You're funny. We had a lovely visit with everyone."

"Is anyone else here we know?"

"I don't think so. Rosa and the Coopers are all home. Doctors say Rosa's daughter may be in remission. The Coopers were here for Andrew's transplant, so hopefully they won't be coming back at all."

Just as well. After feeling a little friendless during the holidays with Justin so busy, Caleb was already laughing with Michaela, confiding in someone his own age. Caleb had given Michaela the remote control. She steered the Jeep around, giggling as it disappeared under the bed, and spun back out, then crashed into the dresser and spun its wheels.

"You guys are gonna to be able to go to the Leaf's game, Saturday?" Caleb said.

"Yeah, my mom says we can stay a couple of extra days so we can go."

186

"Cool."

"So don't get sick, okay? It would be a bummer if we couldn't go." Michaela passed the remote control back to Caleb.

"Okay," Caleb said. "I promise."

* * *

"Your fingers are cold," Caleb said.

Dr. Oster smiled. "Sorry. Forgot the hand warmer today. I warmed my stethoscope, though." She cocked her head, leaned in and listened to Caleb's breathing. She didn't have to tell him anymore to breathe deep or how many times. He just did it.

"Well, your breathing is clear, which is a good start." She reached over and picked up the scope. "Now, let's have a look at this eye, shall we?"

Her tone changed as she peered in concentration through the scope at his eye. "Why don't you tell me what you remember about how this happened."

"I was in my bedroom looking at travel stuff."

"Brochures," Celia said. "For attractions we can visit this week."

"Mmm," she murmured. "Eyes up and to the right. No, toward the door. Good."

"All of a sudden things went blurry. I had that feeling in my stomach like when you go over a big hill in the car, you know?"

"A little nauseous?"

"Sort of. And dizzy."

Caleb kicked his legs as they hung over the examining table.

"Keep still, Caleb. And look down."

"Sorry. Okay."

Dr. Oster stepped back, and crossed her arms. She stared at Celia. She'd been gracious when she'd returned from Mexico. She never asked about what changed her mind. She simply ordered the continuation of Caleb's chemo and the start of radiation therapy. Now, her expression said she'd rather be communicating this news to someone else. Jeff, perhaps.

"It's the tumor, isn't it?" Celia's words came out flat and matter-of-fact, and surprised her at the dull way they bounced off the ecru walls and lay there in the room.

"I'm afraid so. We'd have to order another MRI to know for sure, but the left lateral rectus muscle is paralyzed. This sometimes happens in children with the kind of tumor Caleb has. My guess is the growth is outpacing the effect of the radiation. It's growing faster than we can slow it down, if you will." She put the scope back in its tray, lined up in perfect order with everything else. "We can do something about the radiation dose--"

Celia groaned. The treatments had been more than Caleb could handle the last time. All the vomiting. How could he keep going through this? He'd gained back over Christmas only about half of the weight he'd lost during the first round.

She glanced back at Caleb. Those eyes had been the source of so much joy for her, from the first time she'd stared into them. Facing this wasn't easy. But in a moment of horrible selfishness, she realized it was harder when she couldn't look into his eyes and see him looking back at her.

Dr. Oster spoke again. "It may not stay this way. You said his vision returned to normal after rest?"

"Yes. After he fell asleep in the car."

"Rest may continue to help. We can also try introducing a drug that will reduce the intracranial pressure." She bent over her desk scribbled on a pad. "Let's get him started on this, and see how it goes. You know where the pharmacy is, right?" She smiled as she handed Celia the prescription.

Her son was a medical experiment.

* * *

Caleb, good to his word to Michaela, had fewer reactions to the radiation therapy this time, although they were more violent. The rest of the week, the vomiting and dizziness, though much worse than before, kept him up only two nights. On Thursday night, he needed to be admitted as an inpatient in the hospital to have intravenous fluids administered to combat dehydration. The new drug seemed to work, and Caleb's eye floated back to its proper place.

Celia kept herself going by focusing her attention on Caleb's immediate happiness, not thinking about where any of this would take them. As Caleb grew cranky and irritable from the treatments, drugs and fatigue, she fussed over him more. She indulged his every whim, mentally flinging out every bit of parenting wisdom she'd ever accumulated. She didn't belong to their world anymore--those other parents. Their rules didn't apply.

She hung onto Leigh like a lifeline. The nights before he was admitted, when not awake bending over toilets with Caleb, she leaned against the wall outside their rooms, confiding in Leigh. In the safety of their friendship, she vomited out all the awful thoughts that chased their tails inside her brain. Leigh would nod, pat her hand and offer her prayers. Sleep was like a hobby she no longer had time for.

She fought against the sickening sense of calm that threatened to settle over her. The sensation of seeing the rest of the world through plastic wrap, insulated from everything swirling around her by a protective film. Caleb had admitted his thoughts about death. What was left to protect him from?

By Saturday, Caleb felt more like himself again, and doctors released him from the hospital. He paced around the room, impatient for the hockey game to start. He sat on the edge of the bed and picked up the remote control for his car. He drove the Jeep around the room in a circle, and brought it up short by Celia's feet. She sat in an armchair in the corner of the room reading the same paragraph of a magazine article over and over.

"What time is it?"

"Five minutes later than when you asked me the last time."

Frost swirled in frantic patterns on the window pane. Only a few inches at the top showed the natural light. The dull gray weather outside didn't make for much of a view anyway and the temperature had snapped cold in the night. Otherwise, she would have suggested they go for a walk to wear off some of his energy.

"Why don't you lie down now and have a nap?"

He sighed. Even as a toddler he'd hated nap time, and grew out of taking them at only two years old. They were a necessary part of life now, but he still resented them. Reluctantly, he pulled down the covers. "Make sure you wake me up early."

"Okay, I will," she said, grunting back at him in the same insolent tone he'd used with her.

The corners of his mouth betrayed a smirk. "I just don't want to miss the puck dropping."

"Don't worry. I'll wake you up." She stood and smoothed the covers over him, tucked them tight and hooked up the ventilator.

At around three o'clock in the afternoon, while Caleb still slept, she knocked on Leigh's door. She hadn't seen either her or Michaela all day long. She went back to their room, found a pen and a scrap of paper, jotted a note for her, and stuck it to her door. *Caleb's napping. I'm going to catch a few winks too. Knock on our door when you get back.*

Celia awoke to a dark room, a rectangle of light outlining the door. She stretched on the bed and realized she'd never changed into pajamas. What time was it? She slowly emerged from the fog of sleep to realize it was afternoon, not morning, and she'd been napping. She glanced at the clock. It was already quarter after five. She sprang out of the bed. Why hadn't Leigh come to the door? Had she been sleeping so soundly she hadn't heard her? She crept out of the room and went to Leigh's door again. The note still dangled there. She tore it off and crumpled it in her hand. She knocked quietly at first, then louder, when she didn't answer. Where could she be? If they didn't eat supper soon and dress, they'd miss the start of the game. The kids would be disappointed.

She went back to the room and woke Caleb. "Better get up and get dressed for the game, sweetie. I fell asleep, and it's late."

"Aw, Mom! It's after five. You promised."

"Don't worry, sweetheart. It'll be fine. Hurry up and get dressed. We'll heat up some soup or something now, and get a snack at the game."

She surveyed her rumpled clothes in the mirror, and decided she'd better change. She ran a brush through her hair. One side was flat and hair stuck out in odd directions. But it was getting long enough--from sheer neglect--that she could make a respectable-looking ponytail at her neck. She tied it back and changed her clothes. "How about your hat sweetie?"

"Right here," he said, pulling the rim of the bucket hat low over his eyes. Hair had begun to grow back, but with the chemo starting up again, even the little bit left looked patchy.

"Don't you think you should wear something a little warmer?"

"I like this one."

Celia sighed. "We're going to need to stop by the front desk to find out if anyone's seen Leigh and Michaela. Then we'll go and grab some supper."

"OK. Where did they go?"

"I don't know. Let's go check."

190

Caleb usually scolded her for not taking the stairs--something his Phys Ed teacher taught him. Today, he headed straight for the elevator and pushed the button. She said nothing, simply followed his lead, afraid to ask questions.

On the main floor, they walked straight to the entrance and the desk where the reception volunteers usually sat. Celia had never met the woman on duty before, a small woman with bifocals and a permanent wave. She smiled warmly.

"Anything I can help you with?"

"Well, I hope so. I'm Celia Bennett and this is Caleb. We're staying in room 310, right next to Leigh McDonald and her daughter Michaela. We were supposed to go to a Toronto Maple Leafs game with them tonight, but we haven't seen them all afternoon--"

"Oh, yes. I think have a note about that." She hunted under papers on the desk.

"They left us a message?"

"No, there's just a note--" She turned to the computer and jiggled the mouse, tilting her head back and looking at the screen through the bottom part of her glasses. "It's a status note. Says they went to the hospital this morning."

Her heart pounded. "You mean Michaela was admitted?"

"Doesn't say."

"Did they check out of Ronald McDonald House?"

"No." She tipped her head back down, peering at Celia over the rims of the glasses. The rest of the message was in her eyes. Something was wrong.

"Do you have a room number? We'd like to go see her."

"Sorry." She smiled sympathetically. "That's all the information I have."

Afraid to look into Caleb's eyes, Celia grabbed his hand and whirled around, already heading for the elevators. "Let's get our coats and see if we can go find her."

She reached for the elevator button, but Caleb stood in front of her. "She wanted to go to the game, Mom. She made me promise." His eyes filled up with tears.

He knew.

CHAPTER TWENTY-EIGHT
Alfie

Alfie pulled up to the address Pete had written down for him. He didn't see Pete's truck yet, so he left the engine running and sipped his coffee while he kept an eye on the road for his boss's vehicle.

Pete had asked him if he would volunteer his time today.

"I probably should," he told Adele. "After all, I couldn't have finished that sunroom on time without him."

"What's the hesitation?" He'd stopped by Adele's shop on the way home. She was finishing the flower arrangements for a wedding. Stem by stem she selected each flower, snapped off excess leaves and located its perfect place in the bouquet.

"You make that look so easy."

"You're changing topics. Why don't you want to do it?"

"I wouldn't say I don't want to do it. I'm just not jumping at the chance, is all. Pete said something about this being a church thing."

"A church thing?"

"He said a group of volunteers from his church do good deeds by doing odd jobs, renovations, that kind of thing for seniors or people who can't afford it. Kinda like extreme makeover, church edition."

She laughed. "Seriously, though, that sounds wonderful."

"Kinda does, I know."

"So remind me why you don't want to get involved?" She squinted and turned the bouquet in her hand, plopped it into a vase and picked up ribbon for a bow.

"Never been a big fan of church." He measured lengths of ribbon, cut them and laid them on the table for her.

"I know. I find that a little strange about you."

"What?" He put the scissors down and gave her his attention.

"You'll read your Bible, but you don't like church."

"That's different."

She put down the bow and put her hands on her hips. "How, exactly?"

"I can't explain it."

Adele had finished the bouquets then, packed them away in the refrigerator, and started her closing-up routine. She forgot about the conversation. Just as well.

He had another objection, too. One he couldn't even tell her. Ever since his last collision with Celia, a plan had been brewing. He'd been waiting for a day like this--one when Adele had other things to occupy her and he was off work--to drive up to Point-du-Fleuve. He wanted to see Celia, all by herself. He wanted a chance to explain himself, put it all out there for her to see, how he knew he'd messed up, but he'd changed. He wanted to make her see, whether or not she could forgive him, that he had the answer for Caleb--that he knew the way his grandson could live.

A truck drove up, stopped at the three-way stop up the road, and drove on.

In the end, he couldn't think of an excuse to justify saying "no" to Pete and still get him out of the house long enough for the eight hours he'd need to drive to Celia's home and back. So he'd asked Pete about the project--a kitchen for a senior lady in the church with health issues that made it difficult for her to get around. They were going to make things more accessible.

He finally agreed to join the group. He figured if he brought the subject up again, Adele would dig deeper into his reasons for not wanting to go.

Pete said the place was in sore need of a renovation. "Probably hasn't been updated since the lady was married, and she's 75."

His boss's black Silverado pulled up and Alfie waved. They got out of their trucks and stood in the driveway talking while they finished off their coffees. "I wanted us to be the first ones here so I can show you the job and what we're going to do. You can help lead the team of volunteers."

They rang the doorbell. A small, white-haired woman answered, wearing a housecoat. She blinked at them through her bifocals, and recognition registered and her face broke out in a wide smile. "Oh, you're here. Aren't you dears."

"We're going to be making a lot of noise and tearing things up in here today, Mrs. Winters, do you have somewhere to go?" Pete said.

"Yes, thank you, sweetie. My daughter's coming for me in about an hour." She tottered off down the hall. "Kitchen's through those doors. Help yourselves. I'm going to get dressed."

They sat down at the kitchen table, and Pete pulled out the plans. "We're going to lower these countertops and make longer top cabinets. She can put the stuff she rarely uses up high. Lower down, we'll make sure she can reach all the things she uses regularly. Instead of cupboards below, we'll install drawers that glide in and out so she can see everything and not have to stoop down.

"If we lower the countertop, a regular stove won't come flush anymore, so someone's donated a modular oven and stovetop." He pointed at the plan. "They'll go here and here."

"And your church is doing all this?"

Pete nodded. "Some of the donations are made by individuals or businesses in the community, who like what we're doing, but yeah."

Alfie surveyed the plans. "Why?"

"We want to be the kind of church when people have a need, they think of us first. Plus, when people work together, it feels more like a community than if we only ever see each other on Sunday mornings."

"The church that works together stays together?"

He laughed. "Something like that, I guess."

The doorbell rang. "I got it, Mrs. Winters. Probably the rest of our team."

"So this is the right address." A balding man with a trim beard strode in, followed by several others. One young woman, her long hair tied back in a ponytail under a baseball cap, took up the rear, until the tiny room was full of volunteers.

"Okay, let's get busy." Pete clapped his hands. "Mrs. Winters is still in the house, so let's start by doing some of the quieter jobs. Grab those boxes and we'll unload all her dishes and things into them. There's paper for you to wrap things with--we don't want to damage any family heirlooms.

"Oh, yeah, and this is Alfie. He works for me, and he's joining us today to help with some of the more skilled labor. You got any questions, you can ask me or him."

"Good to meet you, Alfie." The man with the beard stood closest to Alfie. He shook his hand firmly. "I'm Doug. Doug Atkinson."

"You're gonna forget all these names," Pete said. "You met Doug. This is, Bob, Tony, Rich, and Kim."

The team set to work. Later in the morning, Mrs. Winters left with her daughter and the work began in earnest. They removed cabinet doors, unscrewed cabinets from walls and moved appliances. Good-natured chatter flowed as they worked. Some of the team went outside to dump the waste in an industrial container, but a good amount of it was being reclaimed for other projects. They were planning to use parts of the countertop for the church nursery. The stove and fridge would be donated to their next project.

Around mid-morning another team of volunteers showed up with doughnuts and coffee for break and a tray of sandwiches for lunch.

"I've never seen anything like this," Alfie said.

"Anything like what?" Doug asked, swallowing down a doughnut.

"This isn't what I think of as church."

"So what do you think church is all about?"

"Well, God, I guess. Religion. Preaching, singing, that kind of thing."

"Those things are all good--part of our worship." Doug's hand hovered over the box of doughnuts as he weighed his options. "But they're not church. Church is people."

"And people have needs," Kim said. "They need love, and love is an action."

"That's right," Doug said. "Someone can say they love you all day, but if they never show it--"

"Doesn't mean a whole lot." Alfie said. He thought of the woman at The Royal, and how close he'd let himself get to breaking his commitment to Adele. What had that said about his love for her? The pang of guilt stabbed at him again.

"I don't know. You all make it look so easy. It ain't easy--least not for me."

"What's not easy?"

"Loving, caring, being--holy--I guess," he said.

195

"You gotta be careful where you get your ideas about God."

"What do you mean?" Alfie considered the doughnuts now and picked a cream-filled one.

"A lot of people talk about God, but they've never looked close enough at the Bible to know who he is. They borrow ideas from culture, or they blindly believe what's been handed down from generation to generation--tradition--not truth."

"So who do you say God is?" Alfie didn't mask the challenge lurking behind his words.

Doug laughed "Nothing like skipping straight to the ultimate question, eh?"

Alfie laughed. "Well--"

"Are you married?"

"Yeah."

"What if I asked your wife, 'Who is Aflie?' What would she say?"

He cringed. "Not sure what you mean."

Doug tried another approach. "What would she have to base her opinions on?"

"The things I say, I guess. My actions too." His heart sank again as he thought of all the actions in the past--all the things that had communicated anything but love. It made going forward seem all uphill.

"So that's what God did. Instead of just telling us what a great guy he is, he spent all of history demonstrating his love. Culminating in this one completely unselfish, unconditional act of love when he sent his son to die on a cross for us."

Alfie was overwhelmed. He'd read his Bible some--he'd made a commitment to changing, living better, turning his back on the past, but evidently there was much more to this than he had understood.

He was quiet.

"Hate to break up the party," Pete said. "But we should get back at 'er."

For a group of non-professionals and volunteers, the team worked with amazing speed and efficiency. By day's end, the renovation was almost entirely complete. He and Pete would stay late and work on some of the electrical and apply the finishing coat of paint.

"Good day?" Pete asked.

"Really good. Thanks for asking me to help." He turned the screw on the outlet for the stove. "Can I ask you a question?"

Pete had his hand poked through the hole where the oven would go. "Shoot."

"How do you deal with regret? I've done some pretty stupid things in the past. They're tough to live down."

"Have you ever heard the verse, 'if the son sets you free, you are truly free?'"

"Not sure."

"Jesus said it. He was talking about being bogged down in sins of the past. The alternative is slavery."

Alfie nodded. "Sure can feel that way, anyway."

"So, here's my question outta that: Are you livin' like a free man, or like a man in chains? If you've been set free, you're free. No need to live any other way."

CHAPTER TWENTY-NINE

Celia

Leigh circulated through the room, smiling, squeezing hands and arms and necks and offering words of comfort while her daughter lay on the bed, barely a bump under her covers. Emily clung to Leigh's leg, gazing up in bewilderment at the host of people gathered around.

Leigh lit up the room. The sight of her gave no indication of the events unfolding in her orbit. The truth slipped out in the visitors' hushed voices, the nurses' deliberate disregard of the crowd in the room, the pallor of Michaela's cheeks, the sunken look of her eyes. They had moved her to a private room, and Leigh was attending to everyone in it like a cheerful hostess.

Two of the hushed voices behind Celia spoke. "Around three o'clock this morning, I think. Dave took the first flight out this morning with Emily."

"Poor thing. She wanted to be at home when this happened."

"Why was she here, anyway? Wasn't her last treatment yesterday?"

Pain stabbed in Celia's chest. She was here for them. For Caleb, and the hockey game.

"She's in God's hands now."

"She always was."

Celia shuddered, and moved closer to Leigh, who nodded solemnly, listening to a well-dressed woman. The woman held both of Leigh's hands in her own. Her husband stood beside her and listened intently, his arm around the woman's back.

Leigh's gaze landed on Celia. "Oh, Celia. Come here."

"'Scuse me, Doris. There's my friend Celia. She's here with her son Caleb." She looked around. "Where's he at, anyway? Oh, should've known--with Michaela."

She was right. Celia hadn't noticed him slip away. But there he stood, beside Michaela's bed. He held her hand and talked softly. Michaela's eyes opened to narrow slits and a smile broke on her dry lips.

Leigh engulfed Celia in her arms. Words caught her throat, and her eyes filled with tears, Leigh's sweater a blur of red.

"Oh, honey, it's okay. You know that right?" Leigh pushed Celia away and held her by her shoulders.

Celia shook her head.

"It's all right. She's going home to be with Jesus. She's gonna have everything she ever wanted."

She shook her head again, unable to take it in, her ears almost hurting at the sound of the words.

"She woke up real early this morning and told me this was the day she was going to meet Jesus, and she could hardly wait. She wanted to see everyone one last time." She motioned around the crowded room. "This is her sending off party."

"She's had this look in her eyes goin' on a week now. I thought sure you'd seen it first day you came back, the way you looked when you saw her--"

Her breath caught and she grinned and fanned with her hand at her face, dewy with tears. "She knows how wonderful it is in heaven. She's sad to leave us sure. But she's excited to get there and get her new body. One without cancer."

Leigh's voice dripped warmth like honey. Celia searched her face for some sign this wasn't as real to her as she made it sound.

"Come on, there's some people I want you to meet."

She held Celia's arm and turned her in the direction of the well-dressed woman. "This is my pastor's wife, Doris. And that's my pastor over there." She pointed across the room. "That man that's talking to the man with the beard. The man with the beard--that's my Dave."

Celia held out her hand to shake Doris's but instead she surrounded Celia in a hug, too. "Leigh's told me so much about you. It's been so encouraging for her to have you here."

Celia opened her mouth, but nothing came out. *She* had been an encouragement to *Leigh*?

Doris beamed at her. "Seems your son's got a natural bedside manner."

"He's quite a sensitive little guy," Leigh said. "Michaela's really attached herself to him. She felt so badly we were here, being that she made Caleb promise he'd be healthy for the game, and all."

She looked at her watch, "Oh Celia! He's missing the game now."

"It's okay, Leigh. He wanted to be here." Across the room, Caleb was actually making Michaela laugh. Her little body shook and a smile stretched across her face. She coughed a little into her sleeve and returned her hand to Caleb's.

Leigh and Doris excused themselves. "Make sure you introduce yourself to Dave," Leigh said.

Celia walked over to the bed and touched Michaela's hand.

"Hi, Mrs. Bennett."

"Hi, yourself." She struggled for words. "Are you in pain?"

"Naw. Too many drugs."

"You should be sleeping. We should leave you alone."

"I've had enough sleeping, Mrs. Bennett. I want to be awake when it happens."

"When what happens?" Caleb said. "You mean when you die?" A chill ran up Celia's spine. She glanced around the room, hoping no one had heard him.

"When I meet Jesus, silly." Leigh was right. Michaela did have a look in her eyes--a faraway look--as though she were somewhere beyond the realm of daydreams. Somewhere real and tangible.

"I wonder what he looks like. I know his eyes will be beautiful. You ever wonder what he looks like, Caleb?"

"Sometimes."

Celia glanced at Caleb, stunned by his response.

Bending down, she gave Michaela a kiss on her forehead, stroked her sallow little cheek, and left her and Caleb whispering at the bed together. Caleb knew how to comfort Michaela. That's probably all his comment had meant. Since he was doing such a good job of it, she'd leave them alone.

Remarkably, she found a chair, and sat down, encased in a bubble. A bubble of peace. Not the bottomless cavern of numbness that had threatened to suck her in all week, but peace like an extra presence in the room, real as any person standing there.

A strange assortment of people had arrived at Michaela's "sending-off party." The occasion was surreal, even offensive, but at the same time, not unhappy. Michaela, irreconcilably, did seem excited, her family genuinely happy for her. Doris and the pastor seemed normal enough, and Leigh--well--Leigh was her friend.

"Mama?" Michaela called urgently. Leigh was at her bedside in an instant. She smoothed the sweaty wisps of hair away from her daughter's forehead. The two murmured together for a moment. Caleb stepped away and came to stand beside Celia.

"Michaela would like to be with just her family for a little while, please." Leigh said. The crowd herded out of the room and filled the hallway. Caleb found a seat along the wall, and Celia sat down beside him.

A group of people huddled around Doris and the pastor, from Leigh's church, probably. A couple of the men bore some resemblance to her husband, with a similar stocky frame, pot belly, and salt and pepper hair. Another woman had Leigh's errant, blond hair and the soft folds that invited hugs. Amazing how many traveled from far away to see this little girl. Celia began to feel out of place as she took stock of the visitors, Caleb and her the only Ronald McDonald House friends.

She leaned down next to his ear and whispered, "We could try and catch some of the game, if you want. Or go back to Ronald McDonald House and see if it's on TV."

"No." His legs dangled, his feet just brushing the floor with the bottoms of his sneakers.

"What's that?" She motioned to something he held in his hands.

"This?" He turned it over so she could see the label. It was a chocolate pudding cup. "Michaela gave it to me. It was on her tray table."

"Oh my goodness, Caleb. You didn't have any supper! We need to get you something to eat."

"I'm okay. I'm not real hungry." He peeled back the thin tinfoil lid. "This looked good, though."

He dipped in a finger and licked it off.

"Sweetheart, let me at least find you a spoon. I'm sure one of the nurses--"

The door to Michaela's room swung open, and once more the group of people quieted, all eyes on Leigh.

"Caleb, Michaela would like to you to come in for a bit, if you'd like."

Caleb looked at Celia. "Go ahead, if you want to." She secretly hoped he wouldn't. Was it because she didn't want him to be with her if things should take a turn for the worse? Or because his absence would leave her alone and uncomfortable, sitting in a hospital hallway with strangers?

"Okay," he said, shoving the open pudding cup into her hand.

The door closed behind him. Now she was alone and uncomfortable, holding a pudding cup.

Doris slid next to her, filling the empty space Caleb had left. "How old is he?"

Celia stared at the door. "Nine. He just turned nine."

"Mine are all grown up now. But I had two boys. They're wonderful at that age."

She knew Doris meant well, simply trying to distract her from whatever transpired beyond that door. Doris was dear to Leigh, and for that reason alone, she should keep her mouth shut. But the pain was too real, too close to the surface. She was desperately afraid of what Caleb might be witnessing--afraid he would know the same thing would happen to him one day. One day in the next six months, if the doctors were right.

"I wouldn't know. He hasn't had a chance to be wonderful. We've mostly been here."

She wanted Doris to go away--to leave her alone so she could concentrate on worrying. So she could think up something to say to Caleb when he came out of that room, tears streaming down his face, traumatized, afraid, alone.

But she didn't. She folded her into her arms again. She smelled of lilacs and summertime. "Of course you have," she said, and she rocked Celia and held her while she cried. Cried for Caleb and lost innocence. Cried for Michaela and her beautiful life lived too briefly. Cried for Leigh and the friendship she would lose when Michaela met Jesus. Cried because she hoped Leigh was right, but she was sure she wasn't.

She was certain she made quite the spectacle--embracing this stranger, holding a pudding cup and sobbing uncontrollably--but she didn't care.

An alarm sounded, and footsteps came running down the hall.

Doris unlocked her from her embrace, and she followed her gaze down the long corridor as two nurses ran toward Doris and her and burst into Michaela's room. The door swung wide to reveal the cluster of people inside. Michaela was unhooked from most of the machines, only the IV trailing out of a limp arm. Her father held her, adjusting her in his arms, and her eyes fluttered open, then closed, then open again. Her gaze traveled beyond Celia, the softest hint of a smile on her face. Caleb pressed into Leigh's side, her arm tight around his shoulder.

Amid the beeping machinery and the flurry of the nurses and doctor, clear and loud, Leigh began to sing. The tune was *Amazing Grace* but not the familiar words Celia had heard before. For some reason, though the machines beeped insistently, warring for her attention, the song held her. The song and the little smile on Michaela's face.

Leigh's husband lay Michaela down again on the bed, and his voice joined Leigh's. Even Emily hummed along. Leigh's mesmerizing voice rose above all the other sounds. She sang out the last words, "as long as life endures," and the nurses and doctor stepped back, defeat in the movements of their arms and shoulders, written in their eyes. Her voice faded away, the sound of the heart monitor the only one left, long and flat and unwavering.

Celia searched each face desperately, from Leigh to her husband, Emily and Caleb. Dave bent down and picked up Emily, and she leaned out and reached for Michaela's still form. "'Kayla sleep now," she said.

Leigh bowed over her, brushed the sticky hair back from her forehead one last time, and kissed her. Celia hesitated, just inside the door. She didn't want to intrude, but she needed Caleb's attention. He shouldn't be here. What had she been thinking to let him go in?

Leigh waved her over. "Come on in, Celia."

Celia stumbled toward them, pressure building in her as she did. She didn't want to be there. She shouldn't be there.

She nodded at Michaela. "She looks so peaceful, don't she?"

Celia nodded, tried to smile, wiped tears from her cheeks.

"Oh don't cry, honey," she said, holding out her arms. "She's happy now. She's with Jesus." Celia accepted her embrace, but she wanted to scream, *How can you know that?* She took Caleb's hand and squeezed it hard. He squeezed back.

"We should go, sweetie," she whispered, tugging at his hand a little.

The medical staff had all left the room, and family and friends filed back in. Leigh took a deep breath and started her refrain once again with more words Celia didn't know. "When we've been there ten thousand years..." The rest of the group joined her, voice by voice.

Caleb didn't move. Emotion filled the room and crashed down on her, like a cloud unleashing pent-up rain. She needed to leave. "Come on, sweetheart. Let's let them be alone with her."

He nodded slowly, and they wove their way through the mass of bodies and made their way out.

That night, in the cold, quiet dark of their room, Celia listened to the rhythm of Caleb's ventilator and wished she hadn't left.

CHAPTER THIRTY
Alfie

Alfie stood on the step and fought the urge to drive the four hours back to Port Sandford. His heart thumped wildly in his throat and sweat forged halting pathways over the stubble on his cheeks. He swiped it away with a shirt sleeve and knocked on the door. Blue jays screeched, crows mocked and behind their noise persisted the rush of the river, but no sounds of movement emanated from inside the house.

He'd come to the back door because no one outside of town actually used their front doors, but the door facing the road would have a doorbell. He hesitated, knocked one more time, and walked around the house to the front door and rang the bell. Still nothing.

He turned toward the truck. The anxiety had drained from him, replaced by an aching heaviness in the pit of his stomach. All this way, only to turn around and go home.

Just then, gravel crunched as a car crawled along the curving, tree-lined drive and into the yard. He'd miscalculated. Celia must be returning from driving Caleb to school. He drank her image in, framed by the window of her four-by-four. Her features hardened, her lovely brown eyes clouded over with hatred when she saw his face, like watching a caterpillar seal itself inside its chrysalis without the promise of a better future.

Hershey bounded from the car first, but if she were looking for support or protection from the dog, she had been betrayed. He ran straight to Alfie and jumped up, his whole body wagging and trembling.

"Easy boy." Alfie chuckled. "Down."

Celia stared at him as if he were some foreign object--a meteor that mysteriously landed in her yard--and walked toward the door. Her gaze never wavered, but she said nothing.

Alfie's moment was slipping away. If she walked in the house and closed the door, what would he do? Bang it down?

He took a step toward her. "Wait, Celia. Please."

"I'll call 911."

"I just want to talk. Nothing more."

"Where's Mom?"

"She's doing inventory at the shop."

She sniffed. "So she doesn't know you're here. Maybe I should call her instead."

"I don't deserve even a moment of your time." He took a step toward her.

For a moment, the hard shell seemed to crack. "You're right about that. Come on, Hershey, inside."

"I found this at the cottage." He rushed forward and handed her a photograph, small and shiny with white borders--the Kodak Instamatic variety. The faded photo was from Hallowe'en, the year she turned five. She'd had a passion for Raggedy Ann that year, but when she tried on the costume in the hall mirror, her lips turned down, despite the lipstick smile painted on her face.

"What's wrong, sweetheart?" Adele had stayed up the night before to sew the little apron and fashion a small wig from red-orange yarn.

"Raggedy Ann is never by herself. She's always with Raggedy Andy."

Adele crouched down and smiled at the image in the mirror. "I've got a little yarn left. I could make myself a little wig and go with you."

Celia shook her head and the Raggedy Ann yarn-hair shook back and forth. "Raggedy Andy is a boy. I want Daddy."

So he donned overalls and the red-orange wig and went trick-or-treating with his daughter. Young, then, and muscular, he had a hard time pulling off the rag doll appearance. Adele laughed about it for days, and again when they developed the photo. Celia took to showing the picture off at show-and-tell and social occasions and at some point, Alfie quietly hid the snapshot before it made it into the family photo album. Recently, while sorting through a pile of his things Adele had boxed up and stored away, he picked up a worn book of floor plans and the photo

206

fluttered out.

The hard shell melted into a sad smile. "I remember this."

Alfie drew a breath.

"But I'm not this little girl anymore, and you're not this man, either." She handed it back to him.

"Keep it."

"I don't want it." She rattled the keys in her hand. Hershey cocked his head, and took an eager step toward the car.

"What are you trying to prove, anyway? Coming back here after all these years, waltzing back into Mom's life and trying to pick up where you left off, after almost thirty years--"

"I know." He wanted to say he had nothing to prove. But was that really true? All he had done since he came back was try to prove himself. With little success.

"Did you honestly think I would welcome you with open arms?"

"No." He shook his head, stared at the gravel and the ants crawling over and under the stones. "No, of course not."

"Then what do you want?"

"I want--" He wanted to ask her to sit on the porch swing or the back stoop, to sit and talk, to take just one unhurried moment with him. He longed for her to relax, to remove the wall she'd thrown up between them--or was he the one responsible for that?

"I've changed, Celia. Or I'm trying to. I don't expect you to believe me, or even see that it's true."

She adjusted her stance, threw the weight onto one hip.

"I know what I've missed. I've wasted a lot of years I can't get back. I would give anything to change the past so I could be here to watch you grow up--"

She sighed and shifted position again.

"But you don't want to hear any of that. I came to tell you I believe there is an answer for Caleb, and I want more than anything for you to know."

She narrowed her eyes. "We've tried alternative medicine. Mom must have told you that."

"I'm not talking about alternative medicine."

"We've already started chemo and radiation." A noisy flock of crows flew across the river and settled in the bare branches of trees, drowning

207

out the sound of her voice.

Alfie kicked the gravel. He knew what he wanted to say, but she'd think he was crazy--that he was the last candidate to have the answer, at least the kind of answer he was offering.

"I believe Caleb can be healed." He didn't look up. His voice was low.

"This Jesus stuff again? You've got to be kidding me. You know how this sounds, right?"

He nodded.

Celia laughed, a laugh void of warmth--dry and brittle and cacophonous, like the crows now circling the tamarack trees along the river. "This is rich. You of all people. I know why you left Mom--who and what you left her for. And now you ride back in on your high horse and you have answers from God?"

"I believe--"

"Fine. Keep it to yourself. I told you before to stay away from my son. Let me make things clearer. Stay away from my family--from me, from Caleb, from Jeff. Get it?"

She turned and marched to the house. "Stay away from the dog, too."

She yelled at Hershey, who still stood by his side, looking up expectantly. At the sound of her voice, the dog galloped toward the door, tail between his legs, repentant for an unknown crime.

* * *

The drive back to Port Sandford had felt longer than the jittery, caffeine-infused trip early that morning. He'd said what he meant to say, more or less, but left without satisfaction. He bought a coffee on the way out of town, although not because he felt like drinking it. He was too numb to taste anything. He had hoped that swallowing mouthfuls of the strongest cup he could buy would massage away the knot in his throat.

He pulled into town in the early afternoon. He fantasized that if he went home, ate some food from the fridge and cleaned up around the house, Adele might think he'd stayed home all day. But he was pretty certain Celia had already told her mom what he'd been up to. There would be no getting around this one. He'd have to own up to his mistakes--again.

He turned off the route he usually took home, the one leading past Every Bloomin' Thing, the little flower shop Adele owned with the studio in back where she taught art classes. He turned the truck toward the beach.

The lake was an icy color close to the shore, bluer and bluer until the horizon, where it seemed to run on forever. Lake Ontario was funny like that--more like an ocean, vast and bottomless. Dry leaves clung to the base of the trees lining the lake. The scene seemed more like fall than spring.

He hadn't traveled this way in a long time. Since he came back, he'd been busy with the sunroom and work. Some of the old cottages still stood, but new sprawling ones had sprung up--all considerably more elaborate than the older ones--obscuring the view of the lake.

He was about to turn around and head back. The knot in his throat had lessened, and he thought he might be able to eat the lunch Adele had left him back at home. He slowed down, figuring where to turn around when he saw a large building that seemed to rise up out of nowhere. The sign in front read "The Lighthouse, Sunday Service 10:30 a.m." This was Pete's church. He pulled up in front. A single vehicle sat in the parking lot.

A horn sounded behind him, so he swerved off the road and into the church drive, and parked beside the other vehicle. What was he doing here? He didn't make a move to leave, just sat there staring out the window as a lone tear fell down his weathered cheek. And another and another. He leaned forward over the steering wheel and gave in to regret. The weight of almost thirty years washed over and over him.

Beside him a car door slammed and a face appeared in the window. "You okay, buddy?"

Alfie nodded and waved, smudged the tears off with the shoulder of his jacket and started to turn the key in the ignition.

"Alfie? That you?"

Alfie squinted and studied the face staring in the window. It was Doug Atkinson.

Alfie slid out of the truck and shoved his hands in his pockets. "Sorry. I don't even know why I'm here."

Doug put an arm around his shoulder and walked with him toward the door of the church. "How about a cup of coffee?"

"Alright, sure."

Doug led him inside the building, past reception to an office at the back. "Not too many folks here on a Saturday afternoon, but I happen to

209

have a pot already brewed. Forgot my thermal mug here in the car. Guess that's a good thing, 'cause I saw you when I went to find it."

He motioned toward an office door. "Go ahead and take a seat in my office. Make yourself comfortable. I'll go pour the coffee. Cream and sugar?"

"Black is fine." Stepping into the office, Alfie read the name on the door. "Doug Atkinson, Senior Pastor."

"Okay, so two coffees, one black, one with lots of cream and sugar. Here you go." Doug strolled into the office carrying two mugs. "Have a seat here on the sofa."

Alfie accepted the warm mug and settled into the soft leather. "Thanks." He glanced around the comfortable office. Framed prints hung on the walls and a globe stood on the credenza next to a dozen family photos.

"Beautiful family." Alfie nodded in the direction of a picture in which three teenaged girls, two with braces, grinned broadly, leaning on Doug.

"Thanks. I'm blessed."

Alfie studied his coffee. "Sorry about that out there in the parking lot."

"Not a problem. Like I said, glad I happened to see you."

"I noticed the sign on the door. You're the pastor?"

Doug grinned. "So they tell me."

"I--I had no idea--"

"Did you need to?" Doug sat in an armchair at right angles to the sofa. He took a sip of his coffee and set it on the table in front of him.

"I'm sorry?"

"I find as soon as people get wind of the title, they stop talking naturally. Sometimes I like to be incognito. I'm not hiding anything. I just think sometimes it's nice to be known as Doug."

"I guess I should explain myself." Alfie hadn't taken a drink from his coffee yet. He held it in his lap and stared at it--something else to look at instead of the open, honest face of the pastor.

"No need, unless you want to."

He took stock again of the line of family photos. How much could this man relate to his problems? "I saw my daughter today. It didn't go well."

Doug said nothing, but nodded.

"I've messed up so bad, I don't know if I'll ever see her again--or my grandson. And then there's my marriage--" Alfie drew a deep breath, lay

210

back into the sofa and watched the big wall clock behind Doug's desk count away the seconds. "I can't seem to get it right."

Doug leaned forward. "I don't meant to sound like a bumper sticker, but have you tried prayer?"

Alfie chuckled. "A bumper sticker, eh?"

"Sometimes, instead of charging in and trying to do what we think will fix the situation, we need to admit that we don't know what we're doing. Then it's time to step back and let God have a hand in things. He's pretty handy at fixing."

"Let God handle it?" Alfie sighed. "How do I do that?"

Doug laughed and sat back into the armchair. "That's the hardest work of all. It's called trust."

Alfie faced Doug squarely. "Can't hurt to try. What I've been doing definitely hasn't been working."

"The hard part is not jumping back in to tinker with things on your own."

"Pretty much what I did this morning. Didn't go well."

Doug picked up the smiling-faced picture from the credenza. "You were looking at this picture earlier, right?"

Alfie nodded.

Doug smiled down at the images. "This was four years ago. This one is more recent." He snatched up another picture and set it down in front of Alfie.

"This is my youngest daughter, Rachel. And the little baby she's holding is my grandson. Rachel had him last year. She's seventeen. The daddy took off the day he was born."

"Oh. I--I'm sorry."

"Let me tell you, I wanted to get into that situation and meddle. Hardest thing I ever did, but I let her make her decisions, told her I would be there for her, and did a lot of praying." He raised an eyebrow and smiled at Alfie. "A lot of trusting."

Alfie nodded. Doug set the pictures back in their places on the credenza. "She's straightened her life out now; she's going back to finish high school, and she's making good decisions. And I'm so glad I didn't mess it up."

Alfie laughed. "Well, I did."

"It may not be too late. Remember: prayer and trust."

"Prayer and trust." He rose and clasped Doug's hand. "Thanks."

"Anytime. You know how to find me now." He gripped Alfie's shoulder.

In the doorway of the office, Alfie turned and looked back at Doug. "I wouldn't be too concerned about that 'pastor' label. I think you do the title justice, all right."

CHAPTER THIRTY-ONE

Celia

The front tire of Celia's bike hit the soft shoulder and she wobbled to a stop in front of Sarah. What had she been thinking inviting Sarah on this bike ride? In the four months since they had spent any real time together, she had missed her best friend's company. She figured an afternoon of cycling on the old railway path by the river would be just the kind of thing she wouldn't be able to refuse.

"You *are* out of shape." Sarah stood beside her bike, its frame as trim as her physique, and shaded her eyes from the bright May sunshine.

Celia forced a laugh. She was undeniably physically unfit. For months, her only exercise had been the walk from the hospital to Ronald McDonald House. But this afternoon, she had promised herself an escape from thinking about anything to do with the last few months. Sarah seemed to duck discussion of anything medical lately, so Celia decided she would enjoy her company and avoid the mention of hospitals, chemotherapy and radiation. She could use the break from all of it too.

"I guess you'll have to whip me into shape then, as usual."

Caleb and Justin were at school. Caleb had even gone a few full days the last couple of weeks. He felt better than he had in months, with fewer episodes of nausea. The tumor seemed to be responding to treatment--at least during treatment weeks. Doctors detected some regrowth during their weeks at home, but during those weeks Celia had been able to cherish her son and their time together. She still didn't completely agree with him being at school, but she couldn't deny it fueled him--more therapeutic, in a way, than the treatments. And school had become one of the few places he was able to be with friends. With Michaela gone, and soccer no longer an option, he had been lonely, and Justin had been as scarce at their house as Sarah.

"Your bike's in about as bad shape as you are." Her comment stung. The bike had been a gift from her the year Celia turned thirty-five. Nothing like Sarah's--fitted out with special handlebars and wheel rims for triathlons--it was still better than anything Celia would have bought for herself. As bad as the bike looked, she'd already wiped off the dust and cobwebs.

She didn't care what Sarah thought of the bike, but had her friend forgotten the reason why the bike and her body had suffered neglect? She fought to swallow the bitter taste in her throat. It might challenge her spirit and break her body, but she would enjoy this afternoon. She needed her friend.

"Let's do this." Celia threw her leg over the top tube. The river flowed beside them, fast and strong, higher than normal for this time of the year.

For a long time, neither of them spoke. Celia let the sun warm her skin, the wind fill her ears and reveled in springtime in the Valley. The orioles, finches and warblers were in full song, rising over the rush of the river. Pink and white trilliums dotted the grass beside the path and the ever-present odor of pine pervaded the air with the promise of warmer days. What a welcome contrast to the sterile halls of the hospital, nurse's uniforms and medical machinery.

The river began to widen, and they came to an area where the water was still and quiet. Sarah stopped and pointed. "Look! A beaver."

Celia squeezed her brakes and stuttered to a stop. "Where?"

"There, see? Along the bank." Her voice was hushed, and she leaned close, wisps of her hair tickling the skin on Celia's cheek.

She nodded. "I see it."

They watched in frozen silence as the animal glided through the water. Rivulets chased in the wake of its body.

She turned and stared at Sarah. "I've missed you."

Sarah's gaze followed the beaver up and around a bend in the river. "I know." Her voice, sad and distant, pulled at Celia's heart.

"I hoped you would come and visit us in Toronto again." Tears stung at the corners of her eyes. She swallowed against the lump forming in her throat.

"I know."

"I guess it's been a lot to take--everything going on with us." Celia stared out at the river. The beaver had vanished.

Sarah faced her. Her eyebrows pinched together, a hurt expression on her face. "Don't be silly. You're the one going through it all."

Clouds had moved in across the river. Patterns of light and shadow covered the patchwork farms that lay in the valleys between the Laurentians and the river on the Ontario side. People living in those farmhouses would be cool in the gloom of the cloud, the sunlight just out of reach.

"It's Dan."

"Dan? What do you mean?"

"If you think I've been avoiding you, Celia, you're right." Sarah wheeled her bike off the path, laid it in the grass. She sat down and rested on her elbows, staring up at the clouds that crept over the river on their way to the Ontario side. Celia lingered a moment on the path, gripping and ungripping the handbrakes, her bike a feeble shield between Sarah and her. Finally, she leaned it against a tree and sat cross-legged in the grass.

"After we visited you the last time, Justin came home and told Dan all about what happened to Caleb--the CN Tower, the hospital--everything. He wasn't trying to sensationalize anything, you understand, but let's face it, the whole thing was pretty traumatizing."

"I'm sorry. I felt for him--"

"This is not your fault." Sarah touched her arm. "It's no one's fault."

She glanced up at the sky. "Those clouds are moving in fast. Looks like rain. We should be heading back, I suppose." Neither of them moved.

She sighed. "Dan just thinks that Justin is too young to deal with all of this. He doesn't want him hanging around Caleb. He's afraid what will happen when he--if he--" She blinked hard and tears squeezed out and splashed on her cheeks. "Oh, Celia, I'm so sorry."

"It's okay," Celia said quietly. But it wasn't okay. In Celia's estimation, Dan hadn't been much of a father. And yet he'd chosen this moment to step up and be protective of his son.

She should have reached out to hug Sarah--to convince her it was okay. But she didn't. Stretched too tight bearing her own emotions, she couldn't handle Sarah's too.

A cool drop hit her thigh, then her nose. Droplets sunk into the water, disturbing its placid surface, one or two at first, next dotting everywhere, like a much-freckled face. She stood to her feet, breathed deep the aroma of fresh rain. "We'd better go," she said.

On the ride back, they pedaled hard, giggling hysterically as the rain pelted so furiously their clothes stuck to their skin and they couldn't see the path at times. The harder the rain fell, the harder they laughed, until they reached Celia's driveway, where they said goodbye. It wasn't a long farewell. There were no tears. But it was the last time Celia would see Sarah before the night that finally changed everything.

* * *

Celia hung up the phone. Jeff stood behind her again. He'd been popping out of his office all morning, hanging around while she talked on the phone. He acted as though he had something to say, but she had been making a series of phone calls she'd needed to make. Each time she put the phone down, she found several more messages--among them Caleb's teacher, who said she wanted to talk about some kind of cancer fundraiser. She ignored the messages and began to dial the number of a hotel near Children's Hospital in Toronto. Caleb had an MRI and a PET scan booked in a week.

Jeff laid a hand on her arm. "We need to talk," he said, his face pressed into a scowl.

"What is it?" she asked, and caught the impatience in her own voice.

They shared the house all day long. Why, then, did she feel so disconnected from her husband? The feeling of detachment crept in during their moments together--over dinner, or coffee in the morning, or as they settled into bed--like an uninvited guest at a dinner party, taking up space, consuming all the normal pleasantries and leaving them with only awkwardness and silence.

"I've been on the phone this morning with Bruce DuCharme."

"Who?" Celia glanced at her daybook and the scribbled messages.

"You remember--I did some work for him before."

"In Ottawa?"

"No. Toronto."

She did remember. Jeff had taken a two-week business trip to consult on-site with their staff, and wrote most of their policy and technical manuals--a lucrative contract. "Okay, right."

"He's got some more work for me."

"Great." She reached for her daybook and the phone.

Jeff laid his hand on her arm again. "In Toronto."

"Okay, even better. We can all stay together at the hotel when Caleb goes in for treatment."

"Hotel? What hotel--wait." He shook his head. "First let me finish telling you what I came to tell you."

"Okay."

"DuCharme wants me there this week to go over some details with one of his techies who's going on vacation next week."

"But that won't work. Caleb's here this week, and in Toronto next week."

"Celia, it's not like I can afford to turn down this business."

"Of course you can. This is our son we're talking about."

"No I can't." He lay a paper down on the counter in front of her, and thumped on it with his finger. It was a form from their medical insurance company listing several of the claims they'd made for Caleb's drugs and medical treatments. What wasn't covered by government health insurance had been handled through the policy Jeff had purchased for the self-employed. So far, things had worked out quite well.

This form, though, bore a large REFUSED stamped in capital letters.

"What's this?"

"They're saying some of the drugs Caleb is on are experimental, and they won't cover them."

She picked up the form and studied closer. "These are old claims. From January."

"Right. The claim went through a review by an adjuster and they've come back and decided it won't be allowed after all. Which means we owe for everything dating back as far as January." He grabbed the notice from her hand. "I've been on the phone in the office with them half the morning."

He sighed. "Celia, I need to keep working. I can't afford to turn DuCharme down."

He looked her in the eyes and waved the paper. "With this figured in, we're about as tight as we've been since I started out freelance."

She stared past him at the second hand on her desktop clock, filtered out everything but the lonely sound of its ticking.

"You mentioned a hotel," he said quietly.

"Yes. For next week during Caleb's treatments."

"Ronald McDonald House is full?"

"I didn't check."

He leaned with his hip against the counter and folded his arms, still clutching the insurance papers in his hand, the red REFUSED stamp staring her in the face.

"You don't understand. You haven't been staying there." She couldn't explain the too-tight-knit atmosphere at The House, how easily one could be sucked into the suffering of all those children. Caleb watched Michaela die, surely that was more than enough. Why couldn't Jeff see that?

"We can't afford a hotel. Have you already made the reservation?"

"No, I was about to."

"Great, then I saved you a phone call."

She yearned suddenly for the disconnected feeling--a cushion, a safe zone, something to buffer her from the rawness of everything.

He held her gaze while she searched for something to say.

"I'm going to go pack," he said. "There's a flight out of Ottawa early in the morning."

* * *

Celia fell asleep listening to Jeff read Caleb a bedtime story. Just before he did, he explained that he would be away for a few days. She pulled the covers tight and buried her head in the pillow and tried not to hear the sounds of Caleb's whimpering.

"Only for a few days, Champ," said Jeff, his voice thick. "We'll be together again before you know it."

Caleb's voice was small, inaudible, but she could fill in the lines. Caleb seemed to have adopted the philosophy that boys don't cry, though they never taught him anything like that. He rarely cried, even as a very young child. He'd take a tumble, pop back up and say with a grin, "I'm okay, Mom," as if he feared she would crumble if he were hurt. But the drugs made him moody, and the long absences from Jeff had worn on him.

"If they need me to stay past the weekend, I'll definitely come and be with you guys."

Caleb said something else, and the deeper tones of Jeff's voice took over as he picked up *Charlotte's Web* and began at the place where Wilbur tries to escape from the pen.

In the morning, Celia woke to the sounds of the crows chattering in the trees along the riverbank. She stretched her arm across the bed, forgetting, at first, that Jeff was already on his way to Toronto. She propped herself up on her elbow and drank from the glass on the nightstand. A pain like a thousand tiny knives cut its way down her throat. Her head pounded.

She glanced at the clock. Caleb needed to be out of the door for school in less than an hour. She lay back down and closed her eyes. With Jeff away, what difference would it make if Caleb didn't go to school today? The warmth of the bed seduced her. Her head thick with fog and her body aching, she needed to rest just a little longer.

"Mom, it's late. How come you didn't wake me up?" Caleb called from his room. Drawers opened and slammed shut.

She sat up and the room reeled. "Coming, sweetheart." Her voice scratched out only a whisper and her head kept a steady, forceful rhythm.

"Mom," Caleb said, bursting into her room. "Didn't you hear me?"

Her eyes met his and panic grabbed like fingers around her throat. She was contagious. Caleb could catch it. The smallest infection could--

"Caleb, don't come near me. I'm sick. I need to get to the doctor, but I don't want you catching whatever I have." She grabbed the closest article of clothing, held it over her mouth, and wrestled her housecoat around her, one-handed.

"You start getting ready. I'll make your breakfast and try to call the doctor's office," she said into the fabric of a T-shirt.

She ran to the bathroom first and pulled out a facial mask from a box they'd purchased at the suggestion of one of the nurses at Children's Hospital. She made her way to the kitchen and gargled with salt water at the kitchen sink, gagging at the pungent taste and the sting in her throat. When they'd first come home from the hospital, she'd bought a bottle of hand sanitizer for every room in the house. She squeezed a generous amount on both hands and rubbed thoroughly before she picked up the phone and speed-dialed the doctor's office.

No one answered--only the recorded message saying office hours began at nine o'clock.

219

What should she do? She decided on getting Caleb to school as soon as possible and just showing up at the doctor's office. She glanced at the clock again. Maybe she still had time to reach Jeff before he boarded his plane.

The voice mail on Jeff's cell phone sounded annoyingly chipper under the circumstances. She cleared her throat and swallowed, wincing at the pain, and tried to make her voice loud enough to be heard. "Jeff, if you get this message, call me on my cell."

Caleb came thundering down the stairs. "I'm ready."

"You're not wearing a hat," she said, and ran past him to her room. She grabbed her hairbrush, pulled it through her disorderly curls, dressed and ran back down the stairs. Each step rang agonizingly in her head, but she pushed through the pain.

"I'll get you a juice box and granola bar for the car. Let's go."

* * *

Dr. Chapman sat back in the wooden swivel chair. Except when he absolutely had to stand--when he examined stomachs and had to poke them, for example--he rode that chair deftly around his office. He would lean back to reach for a tongue depressor or lean forward to peer inside throats, listen to heartbeats and tap knees for reflexes, his backside never once leaving the chair. The last vestige of small town practice, he had been Celia's doctor since childhood. He'd delivered her, in fact. The chair creaked as he reclined, his legs spread wide. He thrust his chin forward, pressed his lips together and sighed.

"It's not good, Celia. It's strep throat."

She'd been afraid of that.

He wheeled behind his desk and reached for a pen and pad. "I'll write you up a prescription right now. You can get this filled within the hour, I'm sure. And not to worry. In no time, you'll be fine, but you're going to have to stay clear of Caleb for at least twenty-four hours. That streptococcus bacteria is dangerous stuff, especially with an immune system as compromised as his is right now. It'd be best to err on the side of caution."

She'd driven Caleb to school earlier. He was disappointed to arrive earlier than any of his friends. But she raced to the doctor's office where the receptionist, whom she had known almost as long as the doctor, ushered her in right away.

"What should I do?"

The chair creaked as he leaned back again. "Best thing would be to send him away. You've got full blown inflammation now. You were likely exposed up to five days ago."

"Oh no."

He glanced up from his notes and attempted a smile. "Oh, well now, I wouldn't worry. I think we've likely caught it in time. Just have Jeff stay with him. You stay somewhere else for a couple of days."

"Jeff's out of town."

He tipped his head forward and peered over his bifocals. "Can Sarah take him?"

"Uh--I don't--well, I'll figure something out." Small town or no small town, she'd managed to keep her little rift with Sarah quiet until now. She wasn't about to unburden herself in the doctor's office.

But what would she do? Who could take Caleb? A hollow feeling crept into the pit of her stomach as she realized the only solution. She would have to call her mother.

CHAPTER THIRTY-TWO
Alfie

Alfie parked the truck and strode down the hill toward the lake. A chill laced the air and had turned the depths of the lake green. He hoped the hint of remaining daylight and the twisted square glow from the windows of the sunroom provided enough light for him to chop wood for the fire.

He propped a smaller log on top of an old stump and lifted the axe high.

"What are you doing?"

The axe swung down, but without purpose, and the log toppled off in the grass.

"Adele. You startled me." He bent to kiss her, but she didn't lean toward him, just stood staring at him, her arms crossed.

"I figured we needed wood for the fire."

She shivered and pulled her sweater tighter around her. "Caleb's already in bed."

"Well, that's good." He picked the log up, propped it again, wedged the axe in a little, and raised it high.

"Good. It's not good. He's been here three days already, and he's barely seen you."

Alfie grunted in reply. Wood flew off in splinters and the axe wedged itself deep in the stump.

Adele stepped back. He knew she was watching him, trying to guess his thoughts. How could he tell her the truth? She sighed and pulled her sweater even tighter, and without a word stepped into the house.

The truth was, he'd asked for the overtime. Every day this week. Sure, he wanted to be with Caleb. Each night when he came home from work, he stood long moments in the doorway of the room where Caleb slept. He watched his chest rise and fall, listened to the reassuring sound of the ventilator, and inhaled the sweaty boy smell of the room.

But the memory of Celia's face twisted in anger, and the harshness of her words had sunk deep in his soul. He wanted to show her his love, and if he had to stay away from his grandson to honor her, he'd do it. No matter how much it ripped him in two.

Inside the house he built a fire and stacked a pile of wood on the hearth. He worked slowly and deliberately, making a pyramid of the pieces. He was aware of Adele watching him again as she cleared the supper dishes still on the table, ran water in the sink and wiped down the countertop.

Finally, she came to the hearth and sat down by the fire.

"I know what you're doing." She didn't wait for him to respond. "You think this is the right thing to do, staying away from him, but it's not."

"It's not?" He spoke the words like a question, but he didn't want her to answer. He knew he was right. She tried to understand, but she couldn't. She hadn't felt Celia's hatred as he had.

"Tonight at supper he asked me didn't you love him," she said.

He dropped a log on the top of the pile, and the whole pile tumbled down. "Of course I love him."

"He's just a child, Alfie. He doesn't understand this whole thing between you and Celia. All he sees is you're not there. Jeff's dad died when Caleb was a baby. He's never had a grandpa, and he was so excited to come and be with you."

He opened his mouth to speak, but she touched his arm and continued. "Celia feels the way she feels. If you spend time with him, she's likely to be offended, somehow. But if you stay away, that'll give fuel to her fire, too. She'll say you haven't changed. Can't you see?"

He thought of what Doug had said. Determined to do this differently, he'd already messed up too many times by plunging in and doing the first thing that occurred to him. He'd been praying. Every day. Prayer had given him the strength to stay away when everything in him wanted to talk to his grandson, teach him things, hold him.

He bent to begin reconstructing his pyramid.

She grabbed his arm. "Think about it?"

He nodded and kissed her. "I'll think about it."

That night, he dreamt Celia called and asked Adele to meet Caleb at a train station. For reasons he didn't understand, she planned to send him away. Why Adele couldn't go to pick him up, he didn't understand, either. Somehow the responsibility fell to him. But on the way to the train station, he abruptly seemed to be driving down a city street jammed with traffic. Horns honked everywhere and he searched the road ahead, but no sirens or flashing lights signaled the source of the problem. People shook their fists at him. One angry man leapt from his car and banged on his window, cursing. Alfie glanced at the clock. He was going to miss Caleb. The boy would be standing at the station with no one to meet him. Fear gripped him. Caleb would be alone. He would think Alfie had abandoned him. In the distance a sound grew louder. What was it? A car horn? A locomotive? No, a child, crying. Caleb.

He sat up. The sheets stuck to his body, covered in clammy sweat. Caleb called from the other room. He stumbled in the dark in the direction of the child's voice.

"Caleb? It's Grandpa. Are you okay?"

"Mommy!" He thrashed in the bed, panic in his voice.

Alfie sat on the edge of the bed and put his hand on the boy's chest. "Caleb? Caleb, it's me, son. It's Grandpa. You're at Grandma and Grandpa's house. Remember?"

Caleb moaned and opened his eyes. "Grandpa?"

"Right here."

"I think I was having a nightmare." He rubbed his eyes.

"I know what that's like. Don't worry, there's nothing to be afraid of. Are you okay now? Can I get you a glass of water?"

He yawned. "No, thank you."

Alfie tucked the covers around his grandson. "If you're okay, then I'm going to go back to bed."

"Grandpa?"

"Yes?"

"Will you sleep with me?" Caleb shifted in the narrow twin bed, made a space beside him.

"Grandpa?"

"Yes, of course. Of course I'll sleep with you."

Alfie lay in the bed, every muscle tense. Certainly this wasn't what

224

Celia had in mind. In the once silent house, the refrigerator hummed in the kitchen, the furnace roared to life in the basement, the clock ticked in the living room. Another sound rose up--words, as though not from his mind, but from the very core of him, came up. *This is what you prayed for. Show him love. Show him that perfect love drives out fear.* A peace like he hadn't felt in months rolled over him as though the air around him were heavy with it. *It will be okay.* He rolled over and held his grandson.

* * *

Before he opened his eyes in the morning to the smell of bacon and coffee, he could tell it was late. Caleb's side of the bed was rumpled and deflated.

He stumbled to the kitchen.

"What time is it?"

"I called Pete and told him you had a rough night. He said he'd manage without you for the day." Adele smiled and handed him a cup of coffee. "You're just in time. We made pancakes."

"With real maple syrup." Caleb's eyes were big. He wore a kid-sized apron and chef's hat. Good thing, too--as much batter had found its way onto him as into the pancakes. He delivered a plate, stacked with five pancakes, a fried egg and three strips of bacon and set it on the table in front of Alfie.

"Here's your syrup, and here's your orange juice," he said, arranging the items around Alfie's plate. "I set the table."

"Grandma, sit beside Grandpa." He took a seat on the other side of Alfie and dug a knife and fork into his own stack of pancakes. "What are we going to do today?"

What would they do? Since he'd come back, he'd been busy with one thing or another. He hadn't stopped to think what he would do on a day off--much less a day off with a kid. If he were on his own, he would probably find something to do in the workshop he had started to organize in the basement.

"Do you like to build things?"

"I don't get to do it much. Dad's not really into that kinda thing."

"Don't knock your dad. People like him go far in this world." He held out his worn, calloused hands. "I've never had your dad's kind of smarts. I do things with my hands."

"Can you show me?"

"I've got an idea or two. You finish up your plate and we'll head down to the workshop and see what we can dig up."

Caleb stared down at his plate and pushed a crispy piece of bacon across it.

"What's wrong, sweetheart?" Adele said.

"I'm just not all that hungry."

She and Alfie exchanged a look. "Do you feel sick to your tummy?"

"No, I'm just not hungry."

"Okay, well, eat what you can and join your Grandpa. Don't worry about cleaning up. I'll take care of it," Adele said, her voice high and tight.

In the workshop, Caleb marveled over each tool and half-finished project in the disorganized mess the place had become. The tools he had left behind all those years ago had been thrown in a rusty old toolbox. Newer tools he'd brought with him, and some he'd bought in the fall while he worked on the sunroom lay on the workbench--few stored as they should be. He'd only recently begun to make racks and slots so everything could be put away properly. Caleb didn't care.

"What's this one for, Grandpa?"

Alfie looked up from the bin of plans and woodworking magazines he rifled through.

"That's a miter saw. See here--this part that looks like a ruler? Suppose I wanted to make the frame to go around the door like this one." He pointed to the top of the workshop door. "I'd need a way to cut that angle right there perfectly straight so it would fit with the piece that runs down this side here. I can use a miter saw to do that."

"Cool." He crouched on the floor and peered into Alfie's box. "What are you looking for?"

"I have a plan here somewhere for a nice little birdhouse. Yep, here we are."

Alfie cleared a space on the workbench and spread the plans out.

"This is a special birdhouse for a bird called the Eastern Bluebird. There's a picture of it here in this bird book of your grandmother's." He opened the pages of Adele's field guide to the page he'd marked after breakfast.

"Wow. It's nice. I think I've seen those before."

"They're only in Canada in the summer. It's too cold here the rest of the year. But they'll start nesting any day now. They like areas in the woods with a meadow nearby where they can swoop down and eat the insects and berries they like. They especially like places close to rivers or creeks."

"Hey, like our house, right?" Caleb stood on his toes and surveyed the plans.

"Exactly. So you can take this home and get your dad to help you hang it up on a tree or a post near your house and you can watch them."

"Can we start now?"

"Yes. Safety first, though. Let's find you some safety goggles."

Making the goggles fit took some time. Since Caleb had lost so much hair, his head was small and narrow, and the goggles had nothing to grab onto. In a moment of inspiration, he found an old bucket hat with the fishing things. He planted the hat on Caleb's bare head, and strapped the goggles on top of it.

"How do I look?"

Alfie stood back, assessing. "Very handyman-like. Very manly indeed."

Caleb's smile stretched wide. "Okay, let's build a birdhouse."

They worked the rest of the morning. Alfie showed Caleb all the tools, gave him safety tips, and let him make his first cuts with the saw. Caleb bounced up and down on his toes when they bored the hole for the entrance to the house. "I did it! I did it!"

Adele came down when she heard his loud yells and pronounced it fine workmanship. "You missed your calling, honey. You should have been a teacher."

The two of them set to work sanding some of the rougher edges.

"Grandpa?"

"Hmmm."

"You know how you told me that Bible story?" Caleb glanced over at Alfie and matched the rhythm of his sandpapering to his grandfather's.

"Yes, I remember." A knot crept into his throat. "I'm not sure your mother appreciated that very much."

Caleb's brow furrowed, but understanding settled in his coffee-colored eyes. He continued sanding in silence for a moment, and finally stopped and looked Alfie in the eye. "I've been reading the Bible at night in my room. I hope it's okay, but I took the one from Ronald McDonald house."

227

Alfie stifled a laugh. "I think those copies are meant to be taken, actually."

"Really? I just figured Mom wouldn't buy one for me, and I wanted one."

Alfie swallowed. This conversation was getting difficult. Where was the peace from the night before? What were those words? *It will be okay. Show him love.* He picked up a screw from a small container. "I think we're ready for these pieces to go together. We'll use these here. They're called hinge screws. We're going to use a drill to drive them in. How about that?"

Caleb grinned. "Can I?"

"Of course," Alfie said, and handed him a hammer. "Set it in place first like this."

When Caleb had driven in six of the twelve screws, Alfie figured the boy had forgotten the subject of their earlier conversation. He was wrong.

"So I've found more stories about kids getting healed. And I noticed something. Every time someone came to Jesus and asked him for healing, he did it."

Alfie nodded slowly. "I never noticed that before, but thinking about it, I'd guess you're right."

"And whenever a whole crowd of people came to him, it says he healed them all." Caleb squinted and tucked his tongue in the corner of his mouth as he drove another screw in.

"That one went in a little crooked. Next time, when you set the screw with the hammer, watch the angle, and keep the drill perpendicular--straight out from the wood--when you drill it in."

Caleb sighed and released the tension in his shoulders.

"You want me to do the next one?"

"No, I'm okay." He set to work on the next screw. "So, do you think it really truly means that, Grandpa? Every one?"

"What's that?"

"Do you think the Bible really means that Jesus healed every single person?"

Alfie marveled at his grandson--this wonder of a person he hadn't even met two months ago. How different things had become in the last year since he'd decided his life needed turning around. Not easier--no, he couldn't say that--but better.

"If that's what it really says, I figure that's what it really means." He held up the birdhouse and turned it over, examining it at all angles.

"Are we done?" Caleb said.

Alfie handed the project to him. "You have yourself one Eastern Bluebird birdhouse."

"Wow. So cool." He tore up the stairs. "Grandma. Look at this."

* * *

That evening at bedtime, Adele encouraged him to tuck Caleb in. The boy had worn the bucket hat all day. While it had served a purpose in the workshop, it was intended for an adult--with hair. It came down low over his eyes and obscured half his face from view.

"Can I keep it?" he said as Alfie tucked the covers around him.

"Sure you can keep it, but you're not going to wear it to bed, are you?"

"Mmm-hmm."

Alfie didn't argue with him.

"I never finished asking you my questions today." Not much was visible of him save his lips.

"What questions were those?" Alfie picked up from the nightstand the book Adele had said she'd been reading at bedtime. "About healing."

Oh. Those questions.

"I found this other verse too. It talked about healing like it's already happened."

"What do you mean?"

"I'm not sure I get it." Caleb rested a hand on Alfie's leg. "But I think maybe, like you're already healed, but you might not know it yet."

Alfie was quiet. He had longed to talk to Caleb about this. But now that these ideas were coming from the lips of this bare-headed boy, he wavered. And he knew Celia would do a good deal more than waver if the talk ever reached her ears. He searched for the page in the book where Adele had left off.

"It could work like that, right? Like when you were still far away, I found your letters and saw a picture of you--"

Alfie closed the book. "You mean the letters I wrote to your mom? Does she know you found them?"

"I don't think so."

"When did this happen?"

"Last year. Before I got cancer. I was playing hide and seek with Justin and I found them in her closet." He yawned. "I knew you were my Grandpa. And at first I was kinda mad too, that you went away.

"But I opened this one letter and read it, and I felt like I knew you, and I could see how much you loved Mom, even though you went away. And I forgave you. Only you didn't know it yet."

Tears pricked at Alfie's eyes.

"Couldn't it be kinda like that? If you could be already forgiven and not know it yet, couldn't you be already healed and not know it?"

"I think that's a very good possibility. And a good explanation. You've got a good brain in that head of yours, Caleb."

As soon as the words were out of his mouth, he wished he could pull them back.

"I mean--"

"It's okay. I know what you meant. My brain is good. It's the cancer that's bad."

"You're right about that," Alfie said. He kissed the lips and turned off the light.

CHAPTER THIRTY-THREE
Celia

Celia's heels sunk deep into the sand as she trudged up the path to the cottage. Lilacs and lily of the valley, wood fires, and the wonderful damp smell wafting up from the lake mingled in the air, leaving it heavy with the fragrance of her childhood. Her mother had planted a rock garden since she was here last, though weeds sprang up as plentiful as the flowers.

As she reached for the doorknob, the door swung open. "Celia! You're just in time. I just pulled quiche out of the oven." Her mother held out open arms.

They hugged and Celia surveyed the room. "Where's Caleb?" A few things had been rearranged. A shiny metal Route 66 sign hung on one of the vertical beams at the edge of the room they'd always called the fireplace room. But for the most part, everything remained as it had always been. The overstuffed chairs faced the fireplace, a basket of fruit overflowed on the long oak harvest table in the kitchen, and the aroma of home cooking hung in the air. And yet, the place was different. There had been a shift in the atmosphere.

"Up at the point."

"By himself?"

"No dear," she said quietly, "with your father."

"He's been good today? Caleb, I mean?"

"As gold. Come. I've been waiting to show you something."

She followed her mother to the door off the kitchen that used to lead outside, but now emptied into a spacious sun-filled room.

"This is gorgeous. When did you have this done?"

"This was all your father. He did most of it himself while I stayed with you in Toronto, and surprised me when I came home."

Celia knew her mother wanted her to say something--to tell her wasn't that sweet, to let her heart soften toward this familiar stranger who'd walked back into her life.

"You moved your easel out here. Have you been painting lately?"

"Yes." She spoke with hesitation as she approached the easel.

"What is this?" Adele painted mostly watercolors, sometimes combined with ink. Occasionally she used acrylics or oils. The painting on the easel was a simple scene in watercolor--gently rolling hills fading off into the distance, a stand of evergreen trees. A river ran through the valley, splitting off in two directions. This painting was different from the ones her mother usually painted. She searched for a way to quantify it. The touch was still the same, the strokes familiar, like old friends. But it was as if the picture were lit from within. As though the image were more and deeper than the mere elements used in its creation. It reached out to some deep place in her.

Her mother had been watching her and smiling. "Do you like it?"

"It's--it's beautiful." She reached out to hold it. "May I?"

"Of course. I painted it for you."

"You did?"

She didn't know why she turned it over--what she thought she might find--but on the back, there was an inscription: *The Choice*, and what Celia recognized as a Bible reference, Deuteronomy 30:19.

"What's this?"

Her mother grew even more hesitant. "A Bible verse."

"I thought so. But why?"

Adele gently lifted the painting by its edges and turned it over again, regarding the image like a mother would her child. "You know, I don't know what I was thinking, doing this," she said.

"What do you mean?"

"I mean it seemed so real at the time. But this was probably a stupid idea." She set the painting back on the easel. "I don't want to offend you. You clearly told your father--"

"Okay, fine. But you did it, and now I'm curious. Tell me--"

A clatter from the back door of the cottage interrupted them. The

232

rusty spring hinge on the old wooden screen door protested loudly when opened. It was nearly impossible to walk through without making a noise, as Celia had discovered late at night in her teen years. Her mother never wanted to replace it, probably for the same reason Celia loved the noise made by the old screen door at her own house--the sound of coming home.

Caleb laughed, his voice full of the beach and the wind, and she heard with it the bass voice of her father.

"Adele?"

"In the sunroom."

Caleb rounded the corner. "Oh, hi mom."

"'Oh, hi mom?'" His face was pink and his eyes alive. He looked better than he had in weeks, maybe months. "You've been gone a week and that's all I get?"

She bent down and opened her arms wide and he ran to her for a hug. "You look good. Have you been getting lots of rest?"

The three of them exchanged glances and barely suppressed giggles. "Hardly," Adele said. "He's been a going concern."

She must have caught unease in Celia's expression. "Oh, don't you worry. He's been getting the proper amount of rest. But the fresh air's done him as much good, I'm sure."

"What's this?" Celia asked, tugging at the ridiculous oversized bucket hat he wore.

"It's grandpa's."

"It's a little big, don't you think?"

Adele's forehead creased. She held a finger to her lips.

Her father hovered in the entrance to the sunroom, staring, as though he wanted to say something, but changed his mind. "Adele, I'm going to go out and put some things away in the woodshed."

"Okay, honey. Wait--I almost forgot. Lunch is ready. Quiche."

"That's okay. I like mine better cold, anyway." The screen door banged shut behind him.

* * *

"Did you see this?" Over lunch, Caleb fairly burst with news of his week. He showed Celia a birdhouse he had made and told how he had fished with his grandfather and spent an afternoon at his grandmother's shop. Her mother had even dug through the small attic and pulled out Celia's dusty collection of Hardy Boys and Nancy Drew books. He'd lain in the sun on Adele's old chaise lounge and read. For Caleb, lying out in the sun meant long sleeves, two layers, dark sunglasses, and a hat. Chemo drugs made him more susceptible to damage from the sun, and the head that used to be protected by a thick mane of hair was now smooth and bare. But he sounded as though he'd enjoyed himself, nonetheless.

"Did I see what, sweetheart?"

"Grandma's painting."

"Yes I did."

"I mean the one she painted for me. Come see."

The room he stayed in when they visited was the one Celia had slept in as a child. She and Sarah spent many nights whispering in the built-in bunk beds as children. Caleb and Justin had done the same thing since they'd been big enough to sleep in a bed and not fall out. The room was only large enough for the beds, a small chair and the large chest of drawers. A blue and red airplane mobile hung from the ceiling over the chair, and blue curtains replaced the lavender flowered ones that had covered the windows when the room had been hers. Other than those small revisions, her mom hadn't changed a thing since she spent summers here almost twenty years ago. The small room overflowed with memories.

Caleb ran straight to his suitcase, already packed and sitting by the chair, pulled it up onto the lower bunk and found the picture. His painting depicted a brilliant sunrise lighting up the sky, reflected below on a shimmering lake, and above against overhanging clouds. The clouds became darker and gray further away from the sun, but those close to the sun burst with splashes of radiant color--yellow, orange, pink and pale purple. It was spectacular. Like the painting on the easel, it stirred something inside her.

"Look." He handed the picture to Celia and turned it over. Again, a small penciled inscription, *Rising Sun*, and another Bible reference: Isaiah 58:8. He looked up at her eagerly. "Do you know what that is?"

"I think so. Do you?"

"Yeah. It says, 'Then the light of my blessing will shine on you like the rising sun. I will heal you quickly. I will march out ahead of you. And my glory will follow behind you and guard you.'"

Celia sat down on the lower bunk, ducking to avoid hitting her head, and stared up at him., unsure how to respond. Finally, she said, "Who taught you that?"

"Grandma. When she gave me the picture."

"And what do those words mean, exactly? Do you know?"

"Well--" Caleb looked down at the picture. "I think it means that God will protect me and he'll make me better--he'll heal me."

She held the picture, drawn by its haunting beauty, yet frustrated that her mother had apparently joined forces with her father to push this message at Caleb. She'd had no choice but to leave Caleb with them this week, but she trusted them not to pollute his mind with these ideas. Caleb didn't deserve to be caught in conflict between her and her parents.

She sighed. "Beautiful, isn't it?"

"Yeah."

"I hope you thanked Grandma. It was very nice of her to paint this for you. Here." She handed it back to him. "You'd better pack it up. Why don't you check around under the bed and at the beach--make sure you have all your things. We're leaving soon."

She left the little bedroom, crossed through the fireplace room and into the kitchen where her mom stood at the sink cleaning up after lunch. She'd insisted on tidying up while Celia spent time with Caleb. Her mom stood with her back to Celia, scouring the pie plate at the sink while her father warmed up a piece of quiche in the toaster oven.

"We're going to leave now," Celia said.

Her mother spun around. "Really? We--I hoped you'd stay a little while."

"I want to get back before it's late. I don't want to wear Caleb out."

"Well, whatever you think is best, sweetheart." She dried her hands on her apron. "It is a long drive. You're welcome to stay overnight."

"I think we should go." She worked to keep her voice even, unemotional.

"Listen, about the paintings, I'd like to explain."

Celia shook her head. "That's not necessary. They're lovely. Thank you."

Her father pulled his plate from the toaster oven and disappeared into the fireplace room.

Her mom took her hand. "Those pictures are something new for me.

235

The first time, I didn't know what to make of things. But the one I painted for Caleb is my fourth one like it. Yours is the fifth."

"The fourth and fifth--like what?"

"Well, they're different from what I used to paint. I can't explain it exactly, but I get an image in my mind while I'm reading the Bible. I don't know how else to describe it except that it *belongs* to that passage. When I paint, the strokes come much more easily than anything I ever painted before. Like my hand knows the rhythm ahead of time--as though I'm following a pattern already laid out for me."

"You've always been a good artist, mom. This is probably just you hitting your prime or something." Celia took a deep breath. "I won't deny the paintings are beautiful. And they are different from what you used to paint. But I'm not happy you used them to give that kind of message to Caleb."

Her mom squeezed her hand and her eyes searched Celia's. "Just like those images belong to the verses, the verses and the images belong to people. The painting I painted for Caleb is his, just like the one I painted for you is yours."

The temperature rose in Celia's neck. "You can't actually believe that--"

"I do. I want you to look up that verse when you get home."

The back door slammed again as Caleb ran in from the lake.

"It's getting late. We really should go."

Her mother just stared at her, expectantly.

"How do you want me to respond? I don't even have a Bible."

"I'm just telling you what I feel." She smiled. "And I'm sure Caleb will let you use his Bible."

* * *

Soon after they left the cottage, Caleb made a pillow of his hoodie against the window of the car and promptly fell asleep. From time to time Celia glanced in the rearview mirror at his reflection, but she couldn't see his eyes. They were hidden beneath the rim of that ridiculous hat. For the most part, however, she was lost in the scenery that grew more rugged as they drove north, and in the maze of her own thoughts.

They were minutes away from home when Caleb sat up, spluttering and choking. Celia nearly drove into a logging truck as she stared desperately in the rearview mirror. "Caleb! Are you okay? Say something!"

She caught only one brief glance of Caleb's eyes under the rim of the hat. Eyes filled with terror, fingers fumbling at his trach.

She speed-dialed Jeff's cell phone and stepped on the accelerator. She had to get to the hospital. Now.

* * *

In the emergency room, doctors hooked Caleb up to a ventilator immediately, but the choking continued.

"Have you noticed any foul odor at the stoma site?"

"I don't know." Surely her mother would have told her. She'd shown her how to care for his trach, how to use hydrogen peroxide and saline to cleanse all the parts.

"Any discoloration on his dressing?"

"I'm not sure. He's been at his grandmother's."

"Fever?"

"I don't think so. No."

They removed the inner cannula from the trach tube, dropped it into a tray and plunged a suction tube into the stoma site. A horrifying sucking sound followed and the awful tension in Caleb's muscles finally relaxed. Celia glanced back and forth between Caleb's chest and his eyes. Was he still breathing?

The doctor removed the suction. "A mucus plug," he said. "He must have become congested. We'll put him on a decongestant, and when you get home, you can hook him up to a cough assist machine. Did the ventilator company give you one?"

She nodded and swallowed hard, her gaze never leaving Caleb, who smiled weakly at her and closed his eyes.

The doctor touched her arm. "He's okay. He's going to be okay. We'll get him checked into the hospital and keep him overnight, but these things usually clear up in 24 hours or so."

Her stomach fluttered--a familiar, sick feeling.

Jeff's voice filtered in from outside the curtain pulled around the cubicle. "We're in here," she called out, probably disturbing whoever was in the cubicle next to them.

Jeff pushed the curtain aside and stepped into the small space, panic evident in the muscles of his face and shoulders.

"I'll send a nurse with the decongestant and we'll get Caleb checked in to the hospital and hooked up to the ventilator overnight." The doctor smiled at Jeff. "Make yourselves comfortable."

* * *

A nurse stood by Caleb, checked his vitals and set to work readying the ventilator. Caleb shared the room with another patient, a young boy a little older than him.

"Where can I stay for the night?" Celia asked.

Jeff motioned to her. "Can I talk to you in the hall?"

She held up a finger, waiting on the nurse's response.

"Honey, can I talk to you now?"

She stared Jeff in the eye, trying to read his expression, and followed him into the hall.

"What is it? I was trying to find out--"

"Caleb told me he'd rather we didn't stay."

"What?"

"Have a look in the room."

Caleb was engaged in an animated conversation with the boy in the other bed.

"That's Emile Brosseau," Jeff whispered

She shrugged.

"He's the star player off the Jolliet soccer team. He's twelve. I think there's a fair amount of hero worship going on here."

"And?"

"Oh, come on, Celia. Emile's mother isn't staying overnight. You don't see how the delicate nine-year-old ego will suffer if you insist on staying?"

"A few hours ago--"

"He had a mucus plug. He's on the meds, the doctor says this will blow over in 24 hours, and he has a little more time before he's going back on the ventilator. We can give him that, can't we?"

She sighed in disgust, mostly because she knew he was right.

"What if he needs us?"

"We're 20 minutes and a phone call away. He'll be fine. The doctor said so. We'll go home, get a good night's sleep and we can be back here first thing."

She said nothing in response, but walked into the room. "Are you going to be okay, swee--um, Caleb?"

"Yeah, Mom. I'll be fine." He glanced nervously at Emile, and sat up a little. "I'll see you in the morning."

"Okay. See you in the morning." She walked out the door and Jeff smiled and took her hand in his. He started toward the elevator.

"Aren't you going in to say goodbye?"

"No way. He's had enough parental embarrassment for the day." He grinned and tugged playfully at her hand.

A half hour later, she walked into the house and set her purse down. She pushed away the thought that she might need to know where things were in the middle of the night, but set it deliberately on the bench by the door nonetheless. The quiet house seemed too empty of Caleb, and too full of her and Jeff. She needed to find something to do--something that would take her mind off the situation.

Jeff rummaged around in the kitchen. Jars rattled as he opened and closed the fridge door. She climbed the stairs, and at the top resisted the urge to go into Caleb's room and stare at the empty bed. Instead she crossed their bedroom and headed for the closet shelf where she kept all the photographs she'd had printed, but hadn't put into scrapbooks yet. Before Caleb's diagnosis, she'd worked on her scrapbooks religiously every weekend, but while preparing for the soccer fundraiser, she had fallen behind, and now months had passed since she touched them.

She reached up and pulled down the organizer she used to arrange photos chronologically. A shoebox tumbled down, the lid popped off and envelopes scattered all over the floor. She recognized them immediately. The postmarks were from locations all over Canada and the United States with a few from Mexico sprinkled in. A few were postcards--a man in a cowboy hat winking from Montana, fruit ripe for the picking on a Florida orange tree, a train blowing steam from Chattanooga, Tennessee. The blue skies in all of them had long ago faded yellow-white. She'd never opened any of the envelopes, though the edges of a few of the postcards were bent. She slumped on the floor beside the scattered mess and cried without understanding why.

She'd thrown these stupid things out more than once. The first time, her mother recovered them; another time, Jeff had come to their rescue. Ironic now, to think of the words he had used to hold her back: "One day, you may want to tell your son about his grandfather." If that was the only reason she'd held on to them, it seemed pretty clear now what their fate should be. She scooped them up and tossed them in the shoebox, preparing to throw them in the recycling, but one envelope caught her attention. It had been opened.

She set the shoebox down on the bed and slid the letter from its envelope. The postmark read Calgary, Alberta. From what she remembered of those days so long ago, it would have been the first stop her father made when he left them. She swallowed as she scanned the first lines, but the lump in her throat remained.

I made a mistake, Princess. I should never have left. Some thick-headed folks have to learn by making their own mistakes. I guess I'm just one of those thick-headed folks. I messed things up pretty bad. I don't know if your mama will forgive me, or if I can even forgive myself. But it would mean so much to me if you would forgive me. I know you saw me leave. I know you're disappointed in me. I should have turned around right then and come back, but I guess I was just determined to learn my lesson the hard way. Don't ever be like that, okay? Keep your tender heart. And if you can forgive me, would you write me at this address and let me know? Then maybe, just maybe, if your mom can forgive me too, I'll come home. I miss you, Princess.

"Thought you might be hungry. I made you a plate."

Celia jumped and clutched the letter to her chest.

"Sorry, honey, didn't mean to startle you. What are you--" Jeff stared at the crumpled paper in her hand. "Your dad's letters?"

"They fell. I was getting ready to throw them in the garbage." She wadded the letter into a ball and shoved it into the shoebox.

Jeff shook his head and sighed. "Don't you think it's time you finally forgave?"

"What do you know about it?" Her voice carried more anger than she intended, but she didn't know how to back down. And it was true. Jeff's family had been completely functional, and his parents died old and happy. He had no way to relate to how she felt.

Jeff set the plates on the dresser. "He gave us the money for Mexico, you know."

"He what?"

"He wrote us a check after he sold his rig, and gave us the money you used to go to Mexico. He was hoping it would pay for the treatments. He convinced me to give the whole alternative medicine thing a chance. What was left over, I used toward those drug bills the insurance company refused."

"Is this some kind of joke? How could you accept his money? And why didn't you tell me?"

"He didn't want me to tell you. He was trying to help. He's only trying to show you he loves you." Jeff sat down beside her on the bed. She turned and faced him.

"So you're on his side?"

"I don't think there are sides. There are just people who made mistakes."

"People? You're including me in this?"

"Not when you were a kid, Celia, of course not. But now, yes. I think you're making a mistake not to let him back into your life. And to make it difficult for him to see Caleb."

"He just spent the whole week with him."

"You know what I mean."

"I can't believe this." She held up the envelope with the Calgary postmark. "I suppose you're the one who opened this? That's what makes you such an expert on my father and his intentions?"

"I've never opened any of those letters."

She stared down at the box. "You know he's filled Caleb's head with all kinds of religious nonsense--about being healed by God."

"Caleb's talked to me about it, yes."

"And you think this is all okay?"

"I think it's okay to have hope. Your dad may be a lot of things, but he doesn't strike me as flaky. He seems pretty level-headed, kind of salt of the earth. I don't think he's apt to chase some kind of fairy tale."

"So what? You think this religious stuff is real?"

"I think I reserve judgment. I think if Caleb has hope to keep him going, that's a good thing."

"So alternative medicine is flaky, but religion is okay with you." She shook her head. "This is unbelievable."

Jeff took her hand. "Listen, Celia, I love you and I love Caleb. I want what's best for this family. And I don't think you holding on to all this pain is good for our family."

She pulled her hand away, focused on the words that hit her like poisoned darts. "What are you saying?"

"I'm saying I think you should give your dad a chance."

She dropped the envelope into the box and walked out of the room. She had given him a chance. For that matter, she'd given God a chance.

Both of them had disappointed her.

* * *

Celia picked up the phone before Jeff did. He'd fallen asleep in front of the television. They hung up the phone after talking to a nurse from the hospital, and she came down from the bedroom to find him. He was turning off the TV--some noisy infomercial about an ab workout machine. There were lines on his face from the sofa cushion, and his hair stood up on one side.

"What did they say was wrong? I didn't understand." His voice was fuzzy with sleep.

"I'm not sure either. It sounded like they think he may be hallucinating. He's asking for us."

He grabbed the keys and his wallet from the coffee table. "Let's go."

At the hospital, a pool of bright light spilled from Caleb's room into the dim hallway. Emile's bed was empty, and attendants crowded around Caleb's bed--two nurses, a doctor and an orderly. One nurse spoke to Caleb. She cooed in a soothing, patronizing tone. But her words were indistinguishable above Caleb's excited chatter. "You don't believe me, but I saw him. There's my mom and dad. They'll believe me."

As they hurried into the room, the doctor stepped forward to intercept. "He's having some sort of episode--perhaps a reaction to some of the drugs he's been on. He doesn't seem to be able to distinguish between reality and fantasy. We think perhaps he's had some sort of nightmare, but he remains very excited."

"May we speak to him alone?" Celia asked.

"What are you giving him?" Jeff stepped toward the nurse, who stood extending a small paper cup with pills and a glass with a straw poking out of it. She looked at the doctor.

"It's a sedative. To calm him down," he said.

"Is that really necessary?" Was there no end to the interventions her son had had to endure?

"He's been excited. This will help him get some sleep."

"How long will the effects last?" Jeff said.

"Four hours. Maybe less." The nurse smiled. "But hopefully, he'll sleep through the night."

"He might be a little groggy when he wakes up in the morning," the doctor said.

Celia sighed, the fight drained out of her. Jeff nodded, and the nurse held the cup and the glass out to Caleb again. He took the pill, popped it in his mouth and took a polite sip from the straw. He probably hadn't needed to, though. He'd learned to swallow most of his meds without water.

"See you in the morning, Caleb," the doctor said, and the medical staff filed out of the room.

Celia and Jeff assumed perches on the bed, an all-too-familiar family portrait. She stroked Caleb's face, brushed the hair out of his eyes.

"What's going on, honey?"

"I saw him, Mom."

She sighed. "I don't understand, sweetheart. Who did you see?"

"Jesus, Mom."

"Pardon?"

"Mom, I saw Jesus. Michaela's right. His eyes are beautiful."

Celia flashed back to the scene in Michaela's room. Her heart ached from the sickly sweet memory of it. When Michaela had talked about seeing Jesus, she was close to death. Was Caleb dying? Was this how it would end?

"He came in the room, and he stood right there." He pointed toward the end of the bed. "He was all dressed in white. He stood right there, and he told me he was going to heal me."

He was talking fast. The bed jiggled as he spoke and gestured. She understood now why the doctor had ordered a sedative.

"You know, sweetheart, there are a lot of doctors in this hospital you've never seen before, all walking around in white coats--"

"You don't believe me either?" His lip quivered.

Jeff's hand rested on her back. "It's not that we don't believe you, Champ. We're just trying to understand. What else did you see?"

"It was foggy in the room."

"Foggy?"

"Yeah, but not foggy exactly--you know, like on a really hot summer day."

"Hazy," she said. She didn't like where this was going, but couldn't resist jumping in. She needed to do something to help calm her son. His excitement was unnerving.

"Yeah, like that. But not normally hazy. Purple." His eyes widened. "It

243

was purple like Grandma's painting!"

"What painting?" Jeff said.

"The one you brought home from Grandma's?" she asked.

"No, not that one. The one she painted first. It had a picture of a big purple cloud over a farmer's field. She called it 'Glory.'"

A chill passed through Celia, as though some black fingers wrapped themselves around her heart. How could she allow her son to hold such wild hopes? And yet the alternative was worse: to be swallowed up in hopelessness--to give in to the yowling dogs that she'd kept at bay all these months.

Caleb yawned. "I'm getting sleepy. I'm going to close my eyes. You can still talk, though."

Jeff chuckled. "Okay." He leaned over and planted a kiss on his forehead.

Calm settled over Caleb. Another wait had begun.

CHAPTER THIRTY-FOUR

Alfie

Alfie stood outside the room and peered in. Adele had had another impression something was wrong, like the first time when Caleb had fallen. Like every time since when some sort of crisis had struck. These impressions of hers had become more accurate than weather forecasts. She had been up half the night, pacing the house, murmuring prayers under her breath. Alfie had slept through the first two hours, but when he rolled over and discovered her side of the bed cold and empty, he got up and joined the vigil.

At some point, she decided to call the hospital, "just in case." She accepted the confirmation of Caleb's admission without flinching. Within the hour they had packed a change of clothes and hopped in the truck, continuing to pray during the long silent ride from Port Sandford to Pontiac County Hospital.

As soon as they were on the hospital floor, Adele asked about Caleb's condition. The nurses had been pretty frank with her. Did Celia know the truth? If only he could spare her the pain she was going through now. If only he could fix this, like the leaky faucets at the cottage, the rusted hinges, the sunroom. But he had proven that his repairman skills did not extend to relationships. He held Adele's hand until she left him to be by Celia's side.

He assumed a post at the door and peered in at the drama in the room, his heart breaking. Everything he cared about in this world lay just beyond that door, but he didn't belong.

He prowled around the empty hallways, sat in waiting rooms watching meaningless television, and finally returned to the door to resume his post peering into Caleb's room. The sun was cresting the hills on the other side of the Ottawa River when Celia stirred. She sat in the chair beside the bed and bent forward, her arm around Caleb's thin, bald head. He longed to hold her and tell her it would be all right, as he had when she was small and band-aids and kisses fixed her world's biggest problems.

Adele joined him outside the door. "It could be a while," she said. "Why don't you go get us something to eat in the cafeteria?"

He nodded. He wasn't sure he should be here, anyway. On the drive up, he'd secretly hoped that under the circumstances, Celia would call a truce, allow him in. Now that they had arrived, so had reality. She probably hadn't even thought about him. Her thoughts were all of Caleb, as they should be. As his were.

A nurse excused herself and walked by them, into the room. Celia sat up and rubbed her cheek. A pattern of lines from the folds of the sheets marked her face.

The door opened wider, and this time Jeff stepped into the hall. He extended a hand to Alfie. "Good to see you."

Alfie nodded. At least someone thought so.

"I was just headed down to get some coffees."

"Care for some company?"

Jeff smiled sympathetically. At least he had an ally here.

"Let's take the elevator," Jeff said, pointing down a hallway turning left."

"What happened?"

"They're not sure. Sounds like a restriction to his airflow again, but they had him on oxygen and now it seems like things are okay. He's not on the respirator."

"But they wouldn't let him go home?" The elevator doors opened. The aroma of coffee and bacon met them.

"Observation." Jeff said. He stood outside the cafeteria and faced Alfie. "Something happened last night. I need to know. What exactly did you say to Caleb about Jesus?"

A sudden heat burned in Alfie's chest. "He was asking questions. I just answered them."

Jeff raised a hand. "This is not an accusation, Alfie. I wanted to know because last night Caleb was talking about seeing Jesus."

"Seeing him?" Heat rose in his face, now. "I definitely never mentioned anything like that."

Jeff resumed his slow pace as though the aroma of coffee were coaxing him onward. "The doctor thinks he was hallucinating."

"What do you think?" He didn't ask what Celia thought. He could only imagine.

"Hard to say. I mean, I know my son. It didn't seem to me like he was hallucinating, and yet--"

"Pretty big claim."

Jeff's brow wrinkled deeper. "Yeah, pretty big."

They filled four coffee cups and picked up packets of sugar and cream. Alfie shoved a bill at the cashier before Jeff could reach for his wallet.

When the elevator opened at their floor, Celia stood at the doors, finger poised over the buttons. "Something's wrong."

"What happened?" Jeff quickened his pace.

"Nothing. But that's what's weird. They came and gave him his tray of food and everything, and he didn't wake up. Do you think they gave him too much of the sedative?"

"Could be, but we don't know how long he was awake before we got here, either. He's probably just really tired. He had a pretty traumatic day.

"What time is it, anyway?" He glanced at his watch. "Maybe we should ask the doctor to come and have a look. Did they say when they'd check on him again?"

"A nurse came by. She said she'd be back later, but she didn't say when."

They had arrived at the door to Caleb's room. Jeff and Celia went in. Alfie hung back again. Jeff cast a commiserating glance over his shoulder. He was on the outside, again. Alfie stood by the half-open door, willing himself invisible, yet wishing against hope Celia would see him and invite him in.

"Go on in," he said to Adele who stood at the door looking torn.

The conversation continued in the room in hushed tones Alfie had to strain to hear. Celia tried to wake Caleb up. His chest rose and fell in a perfect, even rhythm with the ventilator, but he didn't stir.

"Sweetheart." Celia spoke a little louder and stroked his cheek. "Don't you want to eat? Caleb, wake up."

"Let's call the doctor," Jeff pushed the call button.

A nurse hustled in. "What's wrong?" she said. She held Caleb's wrist, seemed satisfied, and scooped up the chart at the bedside.

"He's not waking up."

A second nurse arrived. "Send for Dr. Covillaud."

When the doctor finally arrived, he put his stethoscope on Caleb's chest and shone a light into his eyes.

He studied the chart as well. "He had a bit of an episode last night, it seems. Is that right?"

Celia nodded.

"The doctor thought he was delirious. He saw, uh, something." Jeff said.

"And he was administered a benzodiazepine?" He raised his eyes and peered at the nurse.

"By the night duty nurse."

"Has he wakened since then?" He looked back at them again.

Celia shook her head. She pulled her sweater around her. "No." She took Caleb's hand and held it. "We were asleep for a little while, but I would have woken up if he did."

"And my wife has been awake since--"

"Since early this morning, when the nurse came in." She nodded in the direction of the nurse.

"Has he stirred since then?"

"No."

He put down the chart and picked up Caleb's limp hand. He took out a small instrument of some kind and poked Caleb's finger with it. A tiny droplet of blood formed on the end of his finger. Still no movement.

Celia covered her mouth. In his own chest, Alfie felt her panic.

"Excuse me." A well-dressed woman and a young boy approached Alfie. "Is this Caleb Bennett's room?"

He nodded.

"How is he? Emile wanted to say hello."

"He doesn't seem to be conscious," Alfie said to the woman. His eyes didn't waver from Caleb's limp form. "The doctor's examining him now."

The boy broke away from his mother and ran into the room. "Is Caleb okay?"

"No visitors," The nurse rushed toward him. "No visitors right now, please."

"I'm sorry," the woman said. She beckoned her son.

"Wait." Emile ducked under the nurse's arm and stepped further into the room. "How did he get it to do that in here last night?"

"Son--" The doctor took a step toward Emile, but Jeff raised his hand.

"What are you talking about, Emile?" he said.

The child took a first, nervous glance at Caleb, seemed uncertain for a moment, but looked again at Jeff and asked, "How did Caleb get the room to go all purple?"

CHAPTER THIRTY-FIVE
Celia

Commotion had erupted inside the room--the doctor, the nurses, Emile and his mother all crowded into the small room. Somewhere outside its doors, her father lurked. Celia needed air. She wanted out. But she wanted to hear what the doctor had to say. She needed to know Caleb was going to be okay. She stared in the faces of those assembled in the room. They all seemed frozen by what this child had said.

Finally, the doctor spoke, "Nurse, please deal with this."

The nurse broke from her trance, "I'm sorry, *madame*, but you'll have to leave." She ushered Emile and his mother from the room. Their low voices buzzed outside the room a moment and were gone.

She locked in on the doctor, all her hope resting on his next few words. "He appears to be in a coma. I'm sorry. We'll get him an intravenous solution, make him comfortable. I'm afraid there's nothing more we can do. He could have hours, or days--"

She grabbed her jacket and ran. The noise in her head swelled, making it easier to ignore the voices calling her as she ran down the hospital corridor in search of some way out.

Beside Pontiac County Hospital was a parkway with an expanse of mown grass, a bench and a sidewalk. Clusters of evergreen trees circled the area. The parkway stood at the edge of an escarpment with a wide sweeping view over a great swath of the Ottawa Valley. Celia ran there now, stood at the edge and clung to the railing. She gazed out over the trees and the hills rolling out in all directions until they became purple and hazy and hit the sky.

What was this all about? She couldn't reconcile what Caleb said the night before with the rest of the landscape--couldn't make it fit her normal life. Were those words his last? She shuddered. If she could entertain the possibility that what he said was true--if there was some chance he genuinely had a supernatural encounter with Jesus--then what had He come to do? Collect her son?

She pictured the horrible beautiful scene in Michaela's room that last day and cried the tears she never cried for her. They came wrenching out of her in agonized sobs and echoed off the closest hills, and she crumpled to the dewy grass and wept, all the fight gone out of her.

She wanted nothing to do with the notion that these events were part of some divine plan. Yet she wanted the peace Leigh had, the confidence Michaela had, and--she realized--that Caleb had.

Her head pounded, heavy from the weight of all that had transpired in the last few hours. She started to shiver, stood and pulled on her jacket, grateful she remembered in the stupor of the night before to grab it from the closet on the way out the door. She rubbed her hands together and finally resorted to shoving them in her pockets. Her fingers touched a piece of paper and she pulled it out: a pink flyer, folded in half.

A dry laugh escaped as she read. "Looking for answers? You've found The Answer." Father Lafontaine's brochure from the morning of the soccer fundraiser. She flipped it over. The parish contact information was printed on the back. She stared at the phone number. She needed to talk to someone about all of this. No one close to her seemed right. She wanted most to talk to Caleb, but perhaps an impartial third party would be right. After all, wasn't a priest paid to listen? She pulled out her cell phone and dialed the number.

"*Madame* Bennett." He answered right away, as though he had been expecting her call. Another dry laugh escaped under her breath at the incongruence of a priest in a century-old cathedral with call display on his phone.

"Father Lafontaine I--"

"I was so sorry to hear about your son. How is he doing?"

A lump formed in her throat and tears stung her eyes. "He's in a coma. Could you come to the hospital?"

"*Mais oui, Madame.* I can be there in half an hour."

She arranged to meet him in the park. He seemed surprised. But as

251

much as she wanted to be at Caleb's side, she had run out of the energy that had propelled her all these months to keep believing, keep fighting. She couldn't stare at her son's lifeless form in that bed and make conversation with those around it. She needed to talk about what Caleb had said, but she didn't want to talk to Jeff or her mom, and certainly not her father.

Father Lafontaine must have sped, because in much less than half an hour, he pulled up and parked at the side of the road. He walked across the grass, slender and grim in his black priest's clothing. He carried two small black books, "Shall we go to the bedside?" he said.

Realization struck her. "I didn't call you here to do last rites."

"*Je voix*, I see. I am sorry for the presumption," he said. "Then how can I help you?"

Perhaps in her desperation she had made a mistake. But she needed to understand. She had no idea how to begin. Out of everything that had happened, which details should she select?

"Caleb has recently come to believe, from reading the Bible, that God will heal him."

"I see." Father Lafontaine seemed to be weighing this information-- perhaps combined with the information she had already given him--that Caleb now lay in a coma.

"Last night, he said he saw Jesus in his room."

"You don't believe him?"

"I--well, Father, even you would have to agree, this kind of thing doesn't happen every day."

He smiled a knowing smile. "You would be surprised, I think, the stories I have heard, *Madame*."

"But he's just a child."

"So much the more. Do you read the Bible?"

"No." For the first time, she wished she had.

"Jesus himself says we must have faith like a little child if we are to enter the kingdom of heaven."

Tears welled up in her eyes. How refreshing, how liberating that sounded. Faith like a child. But how, when the facts stared her coldly in the face?

"Do you think your son would make up such a thing?"

"No, I'm sure he wouldn't." Caleb was many things--mischievous,

252

certainly--every bit a nine-year-old boy. But not a liar. Certainly never about something like this.

"But the doctors think he was hallucinating."

Except that didn't account for Emile. Certainly a hallucination couldn't be shared by two children.

"What do you think?" the priest said.

"I--I'm afraid."

"Of what?"

"What if it's real?" Relief washed over her, as though she'd released air she'd held in for too long. Her lungs ached, grateful for a fresh breath.

The priest held her gaze. He said nothing. A mourning dove sang his sad song from a tree nearby. The sun shone higher in the sky now, warm on her face. One more question needed an answer.

"Do you have a Bible with you?"

"*Mais, oui.* This is my Bible." He held out one of the small black books.

"I don't know where anything is. Would you read me a verse?"

"But of course. Which one?"

"Deuteronomy 30:19."

He opened the leather-bound book, flipped the pages back and forth, found his place and began to read. "'This day I call heaven and earth as witnesses against you that I have set before you life and death, blessings and curses. Now choose life, so that you and your children may live.'"

Celia's breath caught. Could the Bible tell her how to make Caleb live?

The priest looked up from the pages into her eyes. "This means something to you?"

"It--it's supposed to. It was an inscription from my mother."

The priest furrowed his brow.

"You know, *Madame*, if you allow me to say so, perhaps this is only the shadow of death."

"What do you mean?"

"Surely you have heard the famous passage that begins with 'The Lord is my shepherd...' You often hear it read at--"

"At funerals." Where was he going with this?

"I intended to say at public events, but, *c'est vrai*. It is often read at funerals.

"There is a part that says, 'even though I walk through the valley of the shadow of death....' Most people assume this is talking about actual death, but it cannot be. The shadow of something is not the same thing as the actual thing, *n'est pas?*"

The shadow of death. Choose life. Could she trust these words from a God she had never known?

"Celia!" From across the road in the hospital parking lot, Jeff's voice rang out.

"Celia!" He jogged toward her, yelling. "Celia, it's Caleb."

She touched Father Lafontaine's arm. "I'm sorry." She ran.

"He woke up," Jeff said when she reached him. "He asked for you right away."

They raced down the hospital corridor. Guilt struck her in her stomach and she tasted bile. She should have been there.

"I'm sorry--I'm so sorry."

"Celia, it's okay. It's Caleb. He'll forgive you for not being with him for a few minutes."

"I just had to--"

"I'm telling you it's okay. You've been by his side every moment for months."

But how could she have missed the moment he woke?

They reached the room, and she rushed to Caleb. "Mommy's here, Caleb." Her heart pounded and the words came out between panting breaths.

"I want Grandpa in here too."

"Grandpa?"

"Yes. I have to tell you both something. He needs to be here too."

Her father stepped toward the bed and stood beside her. She hadn't even been aware of his presence in the room.

"Okay, we're here," he said.

Caleb looked at Celia. "You have to forgive Grandpa."

She opened her mouth, but found no words to say.

"Jesus told me he wants to heal me, but you have to forgive Grandpa."

"Okay, sweetie." She patted his hand.

"You have to, Mom." He tried to sit up, and fell back against the pillow.

"Caleb, you need to rest." She tucked the covers around him again.

"Mom!" He grabbed her hand. "I mean it. You have to forgive Grandpa. Now."

254

A hard knot formed in her throat. Tears streamed down her cheeks. He was asking the impossible. Forgive the abandonment, the hurts of the child she once was, the heartache of missing him all these years, and do it right here, right now, on command?

"Caleb, it's not that simple." Her throat ached.

"Yes it is, Mom. You don't have to do it alone. Choose life."

She searched his eyes. Did he know what he was saying? Or more likely her mother had read that verse to him.

Caleb's eyes closed again. "Caleb?"

He didn't respond.

"Caleb, sweetie? Look at me."

She held his face. "Sweetheart?"

A hand touched her shoulder. Her father's. His face was red, his eyes wet with tears. "Celia, honey. I'm so sorry. I know those words don't seem like enough for all the years I wasn't there. I was wrong. I was a sorry, no-good loser. Please forgive me."

She looked back at Caleb. Jeff stood beside him now. The knot in her throat grew bigger and bigger.

She shook her head. "I can't believe you actually want me to talk to you about this now. Caleb is--"

"Caleb wants me to talk to you about this now. You can't do anything else for him now, but this you can do."

The knot broke. Years of tears spilled down her face. "You were my hero, and you left me. You walked away without even saying 'goodbye.' How could anyone do that to a child?"

"You're right. I was wrong. I am so sorry." The earnest expression on his tear-streaked face made her chest hurt.

She sobbed and sobbed. She crumpled into the chair beside Caleb's bed and held his limp hand between hers. Her father knelt beside her.

"I can never make it up to you--all those years. But I promise to do my best from now on. I'm not leaving now."

She looked into his face--his face that was the same as it was when she was a child, yet different--weathered and broken.

"I forgive you, Daddy."

He hugged her now, his embrace so firm and strong it melted her right to her heart. Her mom and Jeff stepped up beside them. Jeff put an arm around her, his face red and wet too.

A piercing sound screamed beside Caleb. The heart monitor.

The room sprang to life--nurses, orderlies and doctors appeared from nowhere shouting orders.

"Stand back!" someone yelled.

Celia's dad pulled her back, his arms still around her.

A nurse wheeled in a cart and a doctor pulled out the defibrillator. She held her breath.

"Clear!" the doctor commanded. He applied the paddles and Caleb's body lurched. Celia dug her fingernails into her father's arms.

"Clear!" he ordered again.

Twice.

"Clear!"

Three times.

Caleb's body lay still. No movement disturbed his peaceful rest. Despite the ventilator's steady rhythm, the line on the heart monitor continued flat and unwavering.

The doctors and nurses looked at each other, each mouth set in a grim line. The doctor shook his head. "Time of death--"

"No!" She pulled away from her dad and Jeff, pushed through the nurses and threw herself on Caleb. "Baby. Wake up."

"Wait." Alfie walked around the bed. He laid his hand gently on Caleb's chest. "God, we've done our part. Now you do yours."

Silence sat heavy in the room. The doctors and nurses exchanged nervous, knowing glances.

But Caleb's fingers twitched. Life came into his features. His eyes fluttered, and opened.

EPILOGUE

Celia stared out the kitchen window into the bush. Snow filled in the line in the snow where just this morning the tree had dragged its path, sweeping the snow aside until grass showed through. Once the massive spruce stood inside the house, its top branch brushed the ceiling. Jeff would find it a challenge to get the star on top.

She had looked out this same window earlier in the day with Caleb and lamented the spoiled snow in the backyard in the wake of the quest for the tree. It ruined the picture she wanted to take.

"That's okay," Caleb had said. "It's going to snow later today. After the snow falls, you can never see the mess from before. Everything's perfect again. Even better. Because there's more snow."

She picked up the tray of cookies on the counter, carried them to the coffee table and knelt down beside Caleb and Adele. The house smelled of mulled cider and popcorn, and underneath, the aroma of the tall spruce tree. "Hope you didn't start without me."

Adele smiled and shook her head. "But he's about to burst, I think."

"Can I open it now, Mom?"

"Go ahead."

He popped open the lid of the cardboard box and dug inside.

"No digging. You'll break them. Just take them out from the top."

Jeff approached from behind them. "I'm recording this on video. Say something different. You say that every year."

The phone rang. "Let the machine get it," she said. "It's probably Sarah. She said she would call to find out what time to bring Justin later. I'll call her back."

Alfie crouched down between Celia and Adele. "How did this tradition

257

get started, anyway, Princess?"

"Caleb's idea, I think. I don't really remember."

Caleb continued to dig in the box. He shoved up the sleeves of the turtleneck he wore. He wore mostly turtlenecks these days to hide the scar from the tracheostomy, despite the fact it had healed up unusually well.

"What are you looking for, anyway, sweetie?"

"My favorite one. The soldier." Crumpled tissue paper littered the floor.

Celia pulled out a tray of ornaments, then some smaller boxes. "It's in one of these, I think."

She reached back into the box and pulled out a small blue case. "Oh, here it is."

"The soldier?"

"No," she said, quietly. "The little ornament I bought the year you were born. It's broken. We discovered it last year. See? It used to say, 'Baby's First Christmas.'"

She looked at her mom. Adele grinned.

"What?" she said.

"I have a pre-Christmas present." She pulled out a small wrapped box. "Open it."

Caleb snatched it, pulled off the ribbon and ripped the paper. He opened the box and pulled out a beautiful glass ornament painted two shades of purple. The colors swirled together for a cloudy effect. It was stunning.

She leaned in and gently took it from Caleb's hands. "It's a kugel. Remember I told you about them last year?"

"The eBay ones?"

Adele ruffled his hair. "Yes, the eBay ones. Only I made this one. My most recent artistic endeavor."

"You made this? Mom, it's beautiful." Jeff leaned in from behind Celia, trying to get a better look.

"They also call kugels 'friendship balls' because each one is different, and they reflect light--just like love brings light into our lives." She held the ball up and turned it around in her fingers.

"It's purple," Caleb said. "My favorite."

Something shimmered in the light. "What's that on the side?"

She turned it around and held it up so they could all see the words written neatly in gold. "That's my special touch. Read it, Caleb."

"It says, 'Caleb's first Christmas, cancer-free.'"

Cancer-free. The words sent electricity through her--at once terrifying and thrilling.

She smiled and shook away the image of Dr. Oster as she frowned at the reports. "Quite remarkable. See here? This area shows signal change where the tumor used to be. The area is definitely smaller than the tumor, though. I don't understand it. All I can say is, we'll have to wait and see, maybe retest in a few months."

But Celia had begun to believe. She was beginning to hope.

Acknowledgements

C. S. Lewis said "for a Christian, there are, strictly speaking no chances." He referred to a "secret master of ceremonies" at work behind the scenes, orchestrating events. I feel that way about writing this novel. While it has definitely taken a generous portion of my own labor, I have benefitted from the influence of many whom God has brought across my path at just the right time. When I was discouraged, someone came along to encourage. When I needed instruction, God brought someone my way to teach me. For that reason, my "secret master of ceremonies" is the first I wish to acknowledge, followed by many who played a role in shaping me as a writer, and in making *After the Snow Falls* the novel you hold in your hands.

I wish to thank: Bonnie Hearn Hill, who gave me some of my first encouragement as a writer, and who guided this book in its infant state; Cec Murphey, for his generous investment and mentorship; Joyce Magnin and Randy Ingermanson, for their influence and encouragement; Lanita Boyd, Belinda, Jodi, Crystal, and my sisters and father, for reading and re-reading and still being excited about what they read; Daniel Wolens and Mary Beth Geise, for their advice on medical matters; members of the Toronto Moosemeat Writer's Group and others for seeing what needed improving and being faithful enough as friends to tell me.

I owe a debt to Brian Fisch and Angela Burgess of Webber Printing, Brandon, Manitoba for their generous assistance with refinements on the cover design for the print book and to Lorne Chapman of Chapman Photography, Markham, Ontario for his help with my photo for the back cover.

Most of all, I wish to thank my family who have each made some sort of sacrifice so I could find the time to write: my parents for providing me with a writer's retreat and encouragement along the way; my children for doing without me on my "writing mornings;" and their father, my dear husband, who followed a mentor's advice by encouraging me to pursue the things I love to do on the theory that it would ultimately make me a better wife. I hope you feel your investment has paid off.

Made in the USA
Charleston, SC
03 January 2013